Praise for S.S. Tu… novels:

Secrets of a River Swimmer

"S.S. Turner has written a profound story that is about all our lives. He has found the connection that makes us all the same, while remaining unique. His words will resonate with every reader as they see themselves, find themselves embedded in them. You will not escape, you will not want to escape from the depth of your own world he reminds you is yours to be lived, to survive and thrive. I am honoured to have read an advance copy of *Secrets of a River Swimmer* and cannot recommend it highly enough."
— Heather Morris, #1 *New York Times* bestselling author of *The Tattooist of Auschwitz*

"This is a beautifully written, almost lyrical, account of one man and how the river saved his life – quite literally . . .. It's magical at times, tragic at times, laugh out loud funny at times. It not only entertained me, it uplifted me."
– *Long and Short Reviews*

The Connection Game

"*The Connection Game* by SS Turner is a rare book. The complexities of humans, the intricacies of relationships, and the truth of this world are explored in a beautiful manner. Turner shows us that nothing is ever how it appears. It's all about the mind. Once you read the story of the Basilworths, you will forever see the world through a different lens. I highly recommend this book to people who are interested in the human mind. People who like reading psychological thrillers would love this book."
— *The Chrysalis Brew Project*

"A one-of-a-kind tale . . . a surprising and entertaining piece of work."
— Bill Fitzhugh, author of *A Perfect Harvest*

"If you enjoy psychological thrillers with slightly different views of human nature--this is a must-read."
— *Book Corner News and Reviews*

Golden

SS TURNER

THE STORY PLANT

This is a work of fiction. Names, characters, places, and incidents either are the product of the author's imagination or are used fictitiously. Any resemblance to actual events, locales, organizations, or persons living or dead, is en- tirely coincidental and beyond the intent of either the author or the publisher.

The Story Plant
1270 Caroline Street
Suite D120-381
Atlanta, GA 30307

The Library of Congress Cataloguing-in-Publication Data is available upon request.

Story Plant paperback ISBN-13: 978-1-61188-390-9
Story Plant E-book ISBN-13: 978-1-61188-417-3

Visit our website at www.The Story Plant.com

First Story Plant Printing: August 2024
Printed in the United States of America

0 9 8 7 6 5 4 3 2 1

(Dedication to come)

"I wish I could show you when you are lonely or in darkness the astonishing light of your own being."
— Hafiz

The Bull Shark Attraction

They promised me sunshine with all the trimmings. That's why I came—in search of home.

When I walked outside at Brisbane Airport, I breathed in the earthy-flavored air like warm, smooth honey which soothed my almost-deceased taste buds back to life. I'd spent far too long being cold and damp in Yorkshire's paltry excuse for a climate. It was time to make up for it in a warmer hemisphere where life was free and easy—the golden ticket. I was a Brit who'd watched too many reruns of *Wanted Down Under*, and now I was Down Under, ready to collect what I wanted from the promised land where conceiving and believing automatically led to achieving your dreams. It was all so simple.

"You look like the cat that got the cream," said an elderly lady walking past who observed me gazing at the sky in wonder.

"I feel like the cat that got far more than it deserves," I answered. "Can you believe this weather? I can't remember ever seeing a sky as blue as that."

"It's too humid for my liking," the elderly lady said.

"Really? I hadn't noticed," I replied.

"You will, once you take off those rose-colored sunglasses," she stated as she scuttled off toward the nearest taxi rank.

I followed her to the long taxi queue. My British genes provided me with a preordained ability to queue anytime, anywhere with the utmost respect, so I settled in to await my turn. However, within minutes it became clear the rules of the game had been turned upside down along with the hemisphere. Rather than the orderly and respectful queueing technique I knew and loved, the people around me were standing in disorganized clusters which made it unclear who was in front of whom. Oh well, I surmised, when in Rome . . . or in this case Brisbane. I made a mental note of who had arrived before me and who had arrived after me as I relaxed into this strange new world way of doing things. However, by the time I made it to the front of the queue, the groups had all but merged and a number of punters who'd arrived after me had somehow shimmied past without respecting basic queuing etiquette. Maybe the jet lag was kicking in. Maybe I enjoyed respecting others too much for my own good. Or maybe I was plain confused. But I thought it worthy of mention as yet another large, tanned man wearing a singlet and thongs migrated past me when he thought my back was turned. But my back was anything but turned. I'd witnessed him in his inglorious ineptitude and I didn't like the cut of his jib. "Excuse me, old chap?" I said.

This latest queuing etiquette ignoramus didn't seem to have heard me, so I spoke up. "I say, excuse me."

"What's up, mate?" he finally responded without turning around.

"It's just you overtook me in the queue. Do you mind ever so much remedying the situation?" I asked.

"Remedying the situation? Nah sorry, mate, I'm too busy catching a taxi for that," he stated as he stepped forward to take possession of the arriving taxi.

He waved at me with a lonely middle finger and a victorious smile as the taxi drove off, but I was too tired to reciprocate.

By the time I was finally being whisked off in a taxi toward the city center, I felt like the cat that couldn't smell the cream anymore and had lost its hunger anyway. I was exhausted. Travelling for thirty hours has a way of systematically dismantling the parts that allow you to function as a human. Unfortunately, my taxi driver didn't understand that I was beyond coherent conversation.

"How long are you staying in Brissie for?" he asked with a sharp, nasally voice which pierced through the exhaustion-induced grogginess I was existing within.

I tried to catch a glimpse of the driver's face but all I could see was his red baseball cap and the brown tuft of an unkempt goatee protruding from his chin.

"Just ten days," I responded.

"Then back to the motherland for you?" the driver asked.

"No. I'm waiting to collect my golden retriever from airport quarantine in ten days, then we're moving into rental accommodation in Maleny near the Sunshine Coast," I managed to respond.

"Why aren't you staying in Brissie? Are you suggesting there's something wrong with Brissie?" he asked with inexplicable aggression.

I took a deep breath. "Not at all, I love it here," I said as I gazed out the window at a gigantic recycled car yard we were passing. The old multi-colored vehicles were stacked on top of one another like discarded matchbox cars which had been packed away in a bottom draw within a room no one ever visited.

"I'm just saying it's an awesome city," the driver continued. "Most people arrive here to piss off somewhere else—like Maleny for example. But they're missing out if you ask me."

"I'm sure they are, the poor buggers," I said. "At least I've got a wonderful ten days ahead to get to know the city."

"Geez, you'll need more than ten days, mate. I've lived here all my life and I'm still getting to know the place. For example, did you know there are bull sharks living in Brissie River? Bull sharks, how good is that!" he exclaimed, full of pride.

"Are they dangerous?" I asked, without interest.

"Only if they've got their teeth in your ass," the driver explained as he made a hand gesture of a shark biting down on something, presumably a British ass. "Apart from that, they're just interesting. You know, *really* interesting."

I fell silent and wished myself asleep at the hotel. The driver diverted his attention to what was being said on the radio, which was playing at a low volume in the background. It was a news story being read by a young female newsreader: "Ten people have been hospitalized as the mystery gastrointestinal disease sweeps across Brisbane. The medical authorities are investigating all the possible causes but remain in the dark as to where it originated from. The authorities advise city residents to remain at home if they feel sick."

The driver shook his head before he muttered, "Give me strength, what an overreaction! Do the media in India make a bloody hoo-ha every time someone suffers a bout of Delhi belly?" He then turned the radio down and stared at me in his rear-view mirror, as if I may be the mystery gastrointestinal disease come to life in human form, there to spread destruction in my wake.

"Why are you travelling all by yourself?" he asked, as though a law may have been inadvertently broken on his watch.

"My friends all stayed at home when they heard the locals here may have cannibalistic tendencies," I said with a yawn, in a lighthearted attempt to get him off my case.

"Are you stupid?" the driver asked with growing agitation. "You've arrived in a globally significant city full of culture and character, and you're suggesting the locals eat people. Haven't you heard about Expo '88? Have some respect, *mate*."

"Sorry. It was just a joke from a sleepy traveller at the end of a long journey," I replied.

"I'll tell ya, mate, I thought you Brits had a half-decent sense of humor before I met you," he stated as a frown colonized his forehead. "But you shat on that parade from a great height, didn't ya?"

Overwhelmed by exhaustion and confusion, I fell silent, wishing the conversation to end. Thankfully, the driver got the message and stopped talking. By the time we arrived at the hotel, my head was involuntarily drooping forward and rolling from side to side as it used to when I was fighting sleep in the back seat of the car as a child.

"We're here!" shrieked the driver as he slammed the brakes with more force than was necessary, causing me to lunge forward like a crash test dummy. "Your hotel has views of Brissie River. Bonzer choice."

Once I regained my bearings, I got out of the taxi and gathered my belongings from the boot.

"Thanks for the lift," I said to the driver, willing him to leave.

However, he hovered like a blood-hungry mosquito with a passion for buzzing around the ears of foreigners needing sleep. He wound down his car window to continue his buzzing. "Make sure you sharpen your act, mate, and enjoy the world's best city while you're at it! Tell everyone what a bloody special place it is so they can experience it for themselves. As tourists, mind you. We prefer our visitors to bugger off to where they came from at the end of their stays."

"Yes, boss," I murmured through heavy-lidded eyes within my internal fog of discombobulation.

The driver then sped off without another word. Relieved to part ways with him, I rolled my tightly-packed bag toward the hotel reception like a robotic homing pigeon on the last leg of its homeward journey. After I'd checked in and located my hotel room, I promptly collapsed onto the bed. I had a day and a half's sleep to catch up on, which couldn't be ignored any longer.

Reconnected

The next morning, I was awakened by the pangs of hunger after a long slumber. At first, I couldn't recall where I was, but the foreign warmth of the air soon reminded me I was far away from the dank darkness from whence I came. An involuntary smile planted itself on my face and stayed there regardless of what I did. I'd long dreamt of living a better life in the promised land. The universe had delivered on cue when I'd won a ticket to attend the Make Australia Green Again Music Festival in Maleny, Queensland, along with a few days' accommodation during the event. I'd never won anything in my life, so it was a miracle to win a prize which presented a door I wanted to open at the very moment I needed an escape route from my life.

Winning that pub raffle had happened at a time in my life when things weren't going so well for Will

Watson. Understatement of the year. My girlfriend of seven years, Heidi, had ended our relationship in the most brutal of ways only a week earlier. And I'd just been fired from my job as a park ranger in the Yorkshire Dales for refusing to cull the park's deer population—insubordination they called it. The reality was I was fired just before Heidi dumped me. I'm no genius but I did the maths at the time. Heidi had insisted my newfound unemployment status wasn't the real reason she wanted to end things, but I knew better. She always fidgeted when she was lying. While Heidi fielded my questions that day, she fidgeted with her bracelet, her hair, and everything within reach like the world fidgeting champion during the gold medal event. As she searched around for something bigger to fidget with, she confessed she needed to be with someone "who knows which direction their life is heading." Translation: in full-time employment. Ouch. But she was just getting started. Heidi then confessed she'd already found a suitable Will Watson replacement who ticked the full-time employment box and then some. He was an accountant by the name of Hugo she'd met while waiting to cross the road at some traffic light. Who meets at traffic lights? The conversation turned uglier when I asked her what Hugo had that I didn't.

"Hugo has his shit together in every way you don't," Heidi replied as she stopped fidgeting in order to focus on systematically destroying me. "He has a well-thought-out life plan which he takes action toward every day. Do you know how attractive that is in a man, Will? You're just a frivolous, flaky man-child who couldn't organize a piss up in a brewery. You need to grow up."

I could almost hear my heart being ripped into miniscule pieces of irrelevance. If only I'd had the good sense to back away without another word. It was obvious we were over as a couple, so what was the point of prolonging the pain? But like a fool who believed his words mattered, I tried to defend myself in the face of an enemy I thought was once on my side. "That's so unfair!" I exclaimed. "I'm just an optimist, Heidi. I admit I'm not the world's most organized person, but my gut instinct has always served me well. I'm a functioning man, if I ever met one. And I dream big. I lost my job protecting deer for god's sake. Does bloody Hugo dream of making a difference?" It was the wrong question at the wrong moment.

"Hugo doesn't need to dream about it because he's already making a difference in the real world," she replied. "He coaches underprivileged boys who are growing up without a male role model in their lives. It's beyond sexy. Have you ever been *anyone's* role model, Will?"

The question hung heavy in the air, shouting out for a well-delivered one-liner to put Heidi in her place. However, I strongly suspected my list of hero-worshippers was a lot shorter than Hugo's, so I remained silent. My nonresponse seemed to grant Heidi victory in whatever battle she was so determined to win. She breathed in her success and sat a little taller as she prepared to deliver the knockout blow. "That's why I've been seeing Hugo behind your back for a whole year. I didn't think you'd be able to handle the truth, so I've been waiting all this time to find the right moment to break up with you. But I'm done waiting. I don't want to ever see you again, Will."

When it rains, it pours. I can't remember anything else Heidi said in her verbal assault on me that day. All I know was there was more abuse, a lot more. Each and every word was aimed at belittling me as a man and a human. In hindsight, that had been Heidi's modus operandi throughout our relationship. I was nothing but a punching bag she used to vent her long list of grievances about me—from her hatred of my dad jokes to her disdain for my love of the natural world. She once even chastised me for spending too much time watching David Attenborough documentaries. It's no surprise Heidi left me broken and in need of an escape route from my life. So up until the magic moment my name had been pulled out of that hat as the raffle prize winner, it had been pouring bad news in Will Watson's world. It's lucky for me, all downpours have to end one day.

Within hours of winning the pub raffle, I started googling about Maleny, the music festival, and everything in between. While there wasn't much information available about the music festival, Maleny presented online as my picture of heaven. The rolling green hills were as idyllic as any I'd encountered in Yorkshire, and they were accompanied by something I'd long wanted more of in my life: sunshine. As I read about Maleny on a damp, dark Yorkshire day, the decision to move had been a no-brainer. That's why I invested all my savings into moving Mia and myself to the promised land I believed it to be. The raffle prize had only included a small budget to cover my accommodation during the three-day music festival, but I was confident Maleny was the right place for us to call home longer term. If it was the home of a music festival celebrating making Australia green again, it surely had to be the right place for the follow-up event: the Make Will Watson Great Again Festival. I don't know why I believed that beyond the fact I trusted the universe to push forward the right door I needed to open. As Heidi so enjoyed criticizing me for, that's how I rolled in those days.

So there I was—in Australia, ready to start a shiny, new chapter of my life. I rolled out of bed and walked over to the window to peruse the scene outside. Brisbane River wound its muddy pathway through the city below in a surprisingly similar way to every other river city I'd ever visited—bull sharks or no bull sharks.

As I contemplated the blank page that lay before me, my gut instinct was to text someone, anyone, to let them know I'd arrived safely in Brisbane. Something along the lines of: *I'm in one piece in Brisbane where the sun is doing something I'm unfamiliar with. Thinking of you.* But who should I contact? Heidi certainly wasn't my person anymore. Then there was my foster father, Emmanuel. Until a few months ago, he could be found selling stuffed, dead frogs with tacky names to unsuspecting tourists in York, where he'd worked as a frog taxidermist his entire career. But Emmanuel was missing in action. He'd recently discovered he had a heart condition which had taken years off his life expectancy. To his shock, the doctors told him he only had five years left if he was lucky. After digesting that news for all of twenty-four hours, Emmanuel advertised his frog taxidermy business for sale so he could focus on his other passion, searching for the Loch Ness Monster. That meant disappearing from the face of the planet for months on end while he stared at the famous loch's mysterious waters, willing the monster to come to life. All the while, I was alive and well—and alone. I wondered if Emmanuel had even noticed I'd left the UK for Australia. In my heart of hearts, I knew the answer. The reality was no one was expecting or wanting a text update from Will Watson. I put my phone away.

After shaking myself out of my unfocused daze, I got dressed in a white t-shirt and beige shorts for a day of exploring Brisbane. However, first I needed to eat as I hadn't consumed anything of substance for more than twenty-four hours. With a forced spring in my step, I headed downstairs to the hotel's reception to ask for advice.

"Morning!" I beamed at the attractive young girl behind the desk. "Can you please point me in the direction of the best breakfast feast near here?"

"Morning," she said without looking up from what she was doing. "Sure, if you like a good eggs Benny, there's a place around the corner."

"Who's Benny, and what's he been doing with the eggs?" I asked with a smile.

"Eggs Benny. It's short for eggs Benedict," she replied without a smile.

"Aha. Yes, please point me in the direction of the local eggs, Benny," I responded.

"Look, turn left out the front door, and it's a stone's throw away on this side of the street," she said with slight annoyance.

“Thanks, although I must warn you, I can throw a stone a long way,” I continued.

“Have a great day, mate,” she said as she rolled her eyes.

When I walked outside the hotel onto the street, I was stopped in my tracks. The hot sun kissed my skin with more enthusiasm than I was expecting, causing time to pause on a busy Brisbane street while I warmed up a few degrees on the inside. I closed my eyes and held my arms up in the air so the vitamin D could work its magic on my pasty Northern Hemisphere skin. The passers-by on the footpath didn’t stop passing me by as I had my moment in the sun. When I reopened my eyes, I discovered they were giving me a wide berth and minimal attention. Who could blame them? I was just another pesky tourist blocking their pathway to wherever they wanted to go.

Once I regathered myself, I walked around the corner and found the breakfast café the hotel receptionist had recommended. I sat down at a seat near the window and waited to order. The café was quiet, but no one arrived to take my order. I got up and walked over to the serving counter. “Is it possible to order some breakfast, please?” I asked the thin, twenty-something-year-old man behind the counter. “I’m sitting beside the window.”

"What do you want?" he asked without moving from the spot.

"I've heard great things about your eggs Benny. I'll go for one of those, please," I said.

"Do you want avo, mushies, or sangers with that?" he asked.

"Sure, why not?" I said without a clue what he was talking about.

"Just one is included. It's three bucks for each extra," he explained.

"Give me the lot, please, I'm famished," I said.

As I awaited my mysterious breakfast, I made a mental note to learn the local slang. I was fast discovering it basically involved cutting words in half and ending each word with a syllable which allowed you to finish the word on a high note, as though everything was a question. Maybe it was. Afternoon became arvo, breakfast became brekkie, and definitely became defo. I would defo be glad I'd eaten a big brekkie come the arvo. I was fluent already.

When the waiter served breakfast, I took the opportunity to ask him, "Is there anywhere you'd recommend checking out while I'm in Brisbane?"

"Sorry, I don't know. I'm from South Africa," he replied.

"A fellow immigrant. Did you find it easy to find work when you arrived in Australia?" I asked.

"No, but there are some cash-in-hand jobs around if you're on a working holiday visa and are prepared to work for a pittance," he stated.

"I'm on a working visa but I'd been led to believe the job market is flourishing here for immigrants," I said.

"Maybe it is... if you can make yourself look and sound like an Aussie," the waiter responded with a tinge of sadness before he walked away to earn his pittance.

As I digested the waiter's words, I recalled Heidi and me watching an episode of *Wanted Down Under* a few months ago, a TV program which sold Australia's attractions to the rest of the world. The presenters had made it sound so easy to set up home in a country where everyone was friendly, welcoming, and ready to "crack open a coldie" to connect with old friends and new. To reinforce the point, they'd interviewed a Sydney café owner who claimed he couldn't fill his advertised staff positions "for love, nor money." As he pointed at his bustling city café rammed full of customers, he insisted it was a job hunter's paradise for immigrants because the locals were "too bloody lazy to do the real work." Confused by the waiter's contradictory feedback, I stared at my new world breakfast I'd been so looking forward to. Two overcooked eggs and a dollop of brown avocado wobbled in a state of pert dissatisfaction atop a mass of burnt toast, sausage, and mushroom minus the advertised hollandaise sauce. I was hungry so I ate it, but it tasted like warm roadside gravel.

Over the next week and a half, I explored Brisbane like any diligent tourist in a new land. I caught the ferry. I visited Southbank, Howard Smith Wharves, and Roma Street Parkland. I wandered the well-swept city streets and discovered Brisbane is a functional modern city similar to most other functional modern cities. One day, I caught a taxi over to Mount Cootha, where I climbed the track to the summit for a view of the city's skyline from a distance. The view of the city did what it said on the tin—it showcased a cluster of generic, gray office buildings of varying heights and ages. However, I was more interested in the blue-tongued lizard who was sunbathing on a rock nearby, like a miniature dinosaur who didn't believe in comets. It was the first time I'd seen Australian wildlife in the wild. When I approached, the lizard stuck its long blue tongue out and held it there as it stared at me. I recalled learning that sticking your tongue out is regarded as a polite greeting in Tibet, so I returned the sentiment. As soon as the lizard noticed my outstretched tongue, it retracted its own and scuttled off behind a rock as though it was offended. Despite the moment being cut short, the intense blueness of that lizard's tongue was my most vivid memory of those ten days in Brisbane.

When it was time to pick up my dog, Mia, at the end of her quarantine, I was overjoyed. Early that morning, I collected a hire car from near the hotel and drove to the animal quarantine section beside Brisbane Airport. It was a modern, cube-shaped building which would have made a functional space station on the Moon. The sound of desperate barking echoed from within the building's belly as its canine inmates called out to be released from their high-security prison.

"I'm here to pick up my golden retriever, Mia," I said to the middle-aged man on reception who was spinning his pen on his thumb like a bored school student.

"Ah yes. Mia has been one of our favorite guests. She's ready to go. You just need to sign here," he said as he spun the pen from his thumb into his hand and passed it to me.

I signed on the dotted line.

"That's the paperwork done. By the way, how old is Mia?" he asked.

"She's eight. Why?" I replied.

"No reason. It's just we thought she was older than that," he explained.

"It's probably her light-colored fur which makes her look almost gray," I said.

"Mia's in a crate in the pickup room around the corner," he explained as he resumed his pen twirling with renewed enthusiasm.

"Thanks," I said, before I wandered into the pickup area where lines of wooden crates housed anxious dogs on the lookout for their long-lost owners. I recognized their plight as if it was my own.

At first, I couldn't find Mia, so I called out my nickname for her, "Mutt Dog!" Within milliseconds, I heard a familiar deep bark which could only mean "Get me out of here this instant!" I soon found Mia standing inside a nearby crate with a broad smile on her face and an excited wag in her tail. I fiddled with the crate's entrance gate for a moment, and she barked at me to hurry up. Finally, the gate opened, and Mia came bounding out, full of excitement. As Mia jumped on top of me, knocking me backward onto the ground where her golden fur was all I could see, everything made sense again.

The Most Welcoming Town

Once Mia and I were buckled up in the hire car, I drove north on the motorway out of Brisbane. For a relatively unpopulated country, I was somewhat shocked by how much traffic there was and how crazily people were driving. One pickup truck driver weaved his way through the traffic at about a hundred miles an hour, impervious to the drivers around him whom he almost crashed into on a second-by-second basis. It was as if he was so bored that he'd decided to test the line between life and death in an attempt to spice up his day.

After an hour and a half of driving, I pulled off the motorway onto a single lane road. It was like crossing a line from the city to the country, and the traffic slowed down from twenty miles an hour above the speed limit to twenty below it. In short order, the road ascended a steep incline toward the summit of the Great Dividing Range, a coastal mountain range extending along the eastern coast. As we climbed, the trees gradually transitioned from generic, gray bushland to deep-green sub-tropical rainforest.

Fifteen minutes after reaching the top of the range, we arrived at Maleny, the regional town we were staying in. The pictures online had presented it as the Australian capital of all things lush and green, a region which looked remarkably similar to the English countryside I'd left behind. As a Yorkshireman, lush and green were top priorities, and Maleny didn't disappoint in person. The grass was thick, the cows were plump, and there were statuesque trees everywhere I turned. We could have been arriving in the Yorkshire Dales on an unusually warm and sunny day as we drove toward our new abode.

I soon located the house we were renting just outside Maleny's town center on a street with the curious name of Bald Knob Road. Either the area's founders were unusually focused on personal care, or they had a perverse sense of humor. I pulled up at our new home's mailbox which had a sign hanging from it with the words "Big Fig" on it. It was no mystery why. A gigantic fig tree patrolled the street frontage, exuding a commanding presence over the smaller trees nearby. Before I could dwell on the tree's immense age and beauty, Mia let out a short, sharp bark which could only mean she was desperate to get out. As soon as I opened the car door, she launched herself into the air before she landed on the lush green grass and rolled in her joy. I heard someone laughing nearby.

"Your dog's already at home, mate!" exclaimed a tall dark-haired lady with a high-pitched accent who was standing on the front veranda.

"She's travelled a long way to be here so it's time to celebrate—for both of us. I'm Will, by the way," I said.

"Hi, Will, I'm Wilma. This is my place, so that would make me your landlord," she explained with a short, sharp chuckle.

"Pleasure to meet you, Wilma," I said.

"As luck would have it, I was just finishing up with cleaning the house ahead of your arrival. The last tenants only moved out yesterday. The bastards left the house in a right old mess," she explained.

"Well, thanks for cleaning the place up," I said.

"So what brings you to Booking.com's most welcoming town in Australia?" she asked while making air quotes with her hands to emphasize the phrase.

"The most welcoming town, is that right? I hadn't realized. Welcoming is exactly what I need, so we're at the right place. I won a ticket to attend the Make Australia Green Again Music Festival, which kicks off next week," I replied.

Wilma stared at me as though I was an endangered species only known to exist in the world's most remote places. "Well, the village association will be glad to know they've got at least one attendee this year," she said, while laughing with far more volume than the moment seemed to warrant.

"That they do," I replied, perplexed.

"But you're staying on after the festival, aren't you?" she continued. "I've got you down as renting this place for at least six months."

"That's right, we're staying. I was a park ranger back in the UK, so I'm keen to do something similar here," I explained.

"So you're a greenie?" she asked.

"I wouldn't go that far but I'm pro nature and animals," I explained.

"Just don't invite me to any of your kumbaya singalongs aimed at bringing the forest back from the dead," she continued

"Noted," I said. "Why would the forest need to be brought back from the dead?"

"Didn't you hear about the bushfires last year?" she asked.

"Yes, but I heard the local forest had remained unscathed," I said.

"You heard wrong," she continued. "We lost a lot of remnant vegetation in those bushfires. The local powers that be decided to keep it quiet because this part of the world is famous for its lush greenness. That's what keeps the tourists coming back. We don't mind sweeping an ugly truth or three under the carpet around here."

"I'm sorry to hear that," I replied.

Wilma eyed me up and down as though she was assessing my application to be considered a real human. "Listen, you've got Buckley's of getting a job as a park ranger here. Most of Queensland's park rangers have been unemployed since the bushfires because there's no work for them until the forest grows back. That's likely to take years, maybe even decades."

"Wow," was all I could say.

"Come to think of it, I'd say you're fucked, mate," Wilma continued like a doctor delivering a long-awaited prognosis of a life-threatening condition. "Depending on your visa situation and how much cash you've got saved up, I reckon you'll last a couple of months at most before you'll have to fly back home. Thanks a lot in advance. That means I'll have to find a new tenant again soon. And that means more bloody cleaning."

"I'll be aiming to prove you wrong on that front, Wilma," I said with a forced smile. "I want to make this place my home."

Wilma chuckled as though I was a living rerun of one of her favorite comedy shows. "Do you know who you remind me of?" she asked through her laughter.

I shook my head and braced for impact.

"Hugh Grant's character in *Four Weddings and a Funeral* when he oversleeps for the wedding because of his floppy hair and even floppier attitude," she continued. "What a dickhead."

I wasn't sure if Wilma was insulting me or Hugh Grant's character in the film, but my hair and attitude suddenly felt floppier than I'd have liked.

"As I said, welcome to Maleny! I'd best be getting on," she said as she threw me a set of house keys. One of the keys landed in my hand at a sharp angle, causing my palm to bleed.

"Thanks," I replied as I clenched my fist in pain.

The place I'd rented was a Queenslander, which meant it was a large, sprawling wooden house surrounded by generous verandas on all four sides. It was charming, but it was also old, rickety, and in need of some serious work. OK, so we had a lot in common. There were holes in most of the walls, which must have been access points for small creatures, or reptiles, or God knows what.

Within minutes of entering, I could understand why our new abode was the cheapest rental available in the region. I was already regretting my decision to rent it sight unseen. That's what distance does to a person. You think you're seeing things clearly from the other side of the world. You assume you have all the information you need to make sensible informed decisions. In reality, you're driving in the dark while someone on the other side of the darkness is opportunistically benefiting from your ignorance. So ignorance is indeed bliss if you're a landlord by the name of Wilma. I could just imagine her hysterical laughter when she told her husband: "You'll never believe how much I rented that shit-heap on Bald Knob Road for! This silly floppy-haired British guy made a monumentally stupid mistake and rented it sight unseen. Sight unseen, I tell you. Can you believe our luck? Crack open the champagne! Let's get naked and do the Bald Knob Dance!" While Wilma celebrated my stupidity in my imagination, I got on with unpacking.

To say Mia loved our new home would be an understatement. She adored it. Not only did she have the front and back gardens to acquaint herself with, we also lived beside a number of stunning walking tracks which connected us with a vast world of strange-looking animals and insects to meet and sniff. Whenever she was outside, Mia charged off in multiple directions at once as the exquisite joy of discovery was almost too much for her to bear.

We had no neighbors within sight, but we did encounter the occasional person when we were out exploring the nearby walking tracks. On the morning after our arrival, we came across an elderly lady with dreadlocked gray hair and a wizened face. She was walking her boisterous boxer dog along the same overgrown forest track as us.

"Lovely day, isn't it?" I said.

"It is indeed. Are you the new fellow at Big Fig?" she enquired.

"I am. I'm Will and this is Mia," I replied.

"I'm Jude. I live over the road from you—behind the hedge," she explained.

"That makes you our nearest neighbor, I believe. Aren't the walking tracks around here to die for?" I replied.

"You're not the first person to reach that conclusion," Jude stated as she looked over her shoulder. "It's a funny little community you find yourself in."

"Funny ha-ha, I hope?" I asked.

"Don't we all," Jude said without elaborating. "So is it just you and Mia at Big Fig?"

"It is," I replied. "I'm recently single and ready to mingle."

Jude laughed. "If only there were some single human women for you to mingle with around here."

"Single, female, and human are indeed my top three requirements," I added.

"You may not be so picky after a few months in Maleny," Jude warned.

I chuckled nervously.

"I'd best get moving," she stated. "Feel free to reach out if I can help with anything that's lost in translation."

"Thanks, I may well take you up on that," I replied before I turned to leave.

As Jude wandered off, I felt an overwhelming desire to talk with someone, anyone, who knew me. Call it homesickness arriving ahead of schedule. I calculated it would be around nine o'clock at night in the UK, so my foster father, Emmanuel, would probably be in bed reading at the hotel he was staying at in Inverness. He was the only person on planet Earth who may have been half expecting a call from me, so I called him on his mobile. All I got was a dead signal. How apt.

I wondered why I still wanted to talk with Emmanuel after he'd disappeared from the face of the planet without a thought for me. Maybe it was because he was a rare human I'd once been close to. Or maybe it was because he'd survived the challenging pathway he'd chosen in life without flinching or faltering. Emmanuel was tough if he was anything. Against the odds, he'd somehow fought to remain in business as a frog taxidermist for three decades by catering to the demands of tourists wanting unique local gifts. His stuffed frogs were certainly unique. He once gave me a tour of his shop and introduced me to a few of his favorite creations, including a muscular frog lifting a barbell called "Fit Frank," a bespectacled frog writing at a desk named "Winston the Writer," and a running frog carrying a rugby ball under its arm called "Try-scoring Tyrell." As he talked about those damned stuffed frogs, it was obvious he knew them better than the people in his life—myself included. With excitement in his voice, Emmanuel explained that it was the combination of his frog creations acting like humans, along with giving them humorous names, which ensured his products sold so well. "People are a sucker for anything which reflects themselves back at themselves like a mirror," he enthused. Back then I laughed, but his words had gathered interest in my mind ever since. I wondered what Emmanuel would have named me if I was one of his stuffed frog creations. Then again, maybe not knowing was better.

Unemployed Outsider

The next morning, I decided to explore one of the region's famous national parks to check it hadn't been impacted by the recent bushfires. I wanted to be informed by facts rather than hearsay when I contacted the National Parks Department about jobs. So with Mia by my side, I followed the signs to Mary Cairncross Scenic Reserve, a local rainforest famous for its ancient trees from a bygone era. I held my breath as I drove, praying the forest hadn't been burnt down.

It was still early morning when we arrived at the reserve's carpark so there was no one around. I attached Mia's lead and we headed off on foot toward the park entrance. I'd learned the hard way in Yorkshire that whenever Mia roamed free and leadless, she had a passion for chasing wild deer for hours on end. I didn't want to witness a repeat performance with the more fragile Australian wildlife as I'd read that kangaroos and wallabies had a design fault which meant they could die by just becoming stressed. As a result, I held Mia's lead tight as we entered the park. When I noticed the rainforest was unscathed by the bushfires, I breathed out a sigh of relief. It was just as stunning as I'd imagined.

The footpath meandered around the park like an unrushed river in search of a reason to speed up without ever finding it. Mia held her nose high as she breathed in the scents of the vast world of plants, animals, and insects we'd entered. I'd once read that a dog's sense of smell is up to one hundred thousand times more powerful than a human's, so our walk in the rainforest was the equivalent for Mia of speedreading thousands of books while remembering every single word. As we rounded a bend in the pathway, something moved amidst the entangled scrub. Mia charged after whatever it was without a moment's hesitation, dragging me into the forest as I held her lead tight. Within seconds, I could see what she was so excited about. A pademelon, a highly strung cross between a kangaroo and a rat, was hopping away behind a dead tree stump. I held Mia back as it disappeared into the safety of the green undergrowth.

"Let it be, Mutt Dog," I said. "The wildlife will appreciate the space to go about their daily lives without being chased by an overly friendly dog." Heidi's face drifted into my mind when I said that. Who knows why.

Mia and I continued walking around the rainforest loop before we circled back toward the car park. By the time we approached the end of the track next to a wooden hut, I was as relaxed as a puddle of water.

"Hey, you!" someone shouted in our direction.

A tall, bearded man emerged from the other side of the hut wearing orange worker's overalls and a light-blue cap.

"Hello!" I called out.

The man marched over carrying the weight of a scowl on his forehead. "Didn't you see the sign at the entrance?" he grunted.

"Which sign was that?" I asked.

"The very clear, very obvious 'No Dogs Allowed' sign," he seethed.

"No, I didn't. Sorry about that. I kept my dog on the lead so there weren't any incidents to report," I replied.

He stepped forward into my personal space. "You're an incident to report."

"Pardon?" I replied.

"If you break the rules around here, there will be consequences," he continued.

"Understood," I said. "Do you work for National Parks then?"

"What's your name?" he asked as he pulled out a notepad with numbers scribbled all over it.

"Will Watson at your service," I said with a forced smile.

"Where are you from?" he asked.

"Do you want my address?" I replied.

"No, listen to the question. I know you're not from around here. Where are you *from*?" he asked again.

"Oh right. I'm from sunny Yorkshire. I arrived the other day," I explained.

"For what reason?" he asked.

"Do you work closely with the Immigration Department?" I replied.

It was a miscalculation. He put his face right up to mine. "I asked you a question, *mate*."

"This is my reason," I said, as I pointed at the rainforest.

His immobile facial expression indicated my answer didn't compute.

"I want to help protect the environment in this beautiful part of the world," I explained.

He nodded and wrote the words "unemployed outsider" on his notepad before he underlined them with more lines than were necessary to reinforce his point. "We don't need your help with that, mate, and we certainly don't want your dog in our parks. Remember what I said about consequences. Believe me, they're coming your way if you insist on doing what you're doing. The best thing you can do is book your flight home," he instructed before he turned to walk away.

I had an overwhelming desire to call out "Thanks for the warm welcome!" at his back, but common sense prevailed. Mia's sad eyes seemed to understand the rainforest was forever out of bounds to her.

With the words "unemployed outsider" echoing around my head and my cash reserves dwindling, I started googling for job opportunities as soon as we returned home. I remembered the South African waiter's advice that there were local employers out there who were willing to hire foreigners prepared to work for a pittance—like me for example. I started by checking out the National Parks website for park ranger job opportunities. With my fingers crossed, I read the words at the top of the website's employment page: "No employment opportunities at present. We'll advertise if and when that changes. Don't contact us in the interim." Plan A was already out the window, and Wilma's harsh prognosis of my job prospects was proving to be eerily accurate. That sure didn't bode well for what was coming. I had no option but to open my mind to alternative job opportunities.

After a few hours of online job searching, I reached the painful conclusion that there were almost no jobs advertised in the entire Sunshine Coast region. With a heavy heart, I saved the one and only local job I could find. I'll never forget the job advertisement: "Trash Collector needed yesterday at Holy Crap Rubbish Removals. You'll need to be a hard worker with a driver's license, a good attitude, and a tolerable personality." It was as far away from my dream job as a job could be, but it was all that needed doing. Besides, I was qualified—I had a driver's license, a good attitude, and a tolerable personality. Well, I used to, before I was fired because of my personality. Details. There was no escaping the fact that this trash collector job was my best option. Correction: my only option. So I applied for the job.

As I sent in the application, an image emerged in my mind of one of Emmanuel's stuffed frogs. I don't know why. I imagined he was called Austin the Aussie. He was a rotund frog with spiky black hair and an angry face. He wore a dirty singlet, board shorts, and thongs, and he stood beside a blackboard on which he was brainstorming "Australia's Will Watson Deterrence Strategy" in red pen. His list already included two items:

1. Narrow the list of potential jobs for Watson so dramatically that he starts to believe he's unemployable.

2. Make life so difficult for Watson that he'll have no option but to return to the UK in the unlikely event he's able to afford the airfare.

Austin jumped up and down as he pointed at his ideas like a proud father watching his young children excel in a competitive sporting match. I shuddered until the fiend evacuated my mind.

That afternoon, Mia and I drove to one of the nearest beaches, called Mudjimba. The name sounded like a tropical condition whose symptoms included being unable to do anything apart from sunbathing at the beach, and choosing nakedness over clothing whenever possible. It was the stereotypical image of the laidback Australian lifestyle I'd been sold when I lived in the UK, so Mudjimba disease was something I very much wanted to catch. However, part of me was starting to wonder if it was all a marketing lie designed to attract gullible tourists who were desperate to throw another metaphoric shrimp on the mythical barbie.

When Mia first laid eyes on the beach at Mudjimba, it was like all her Christmases had arrived at once. She sprinted along the sandy pathway toward the beach and launched herself into a roll of epic proportions on the silky sand. I laughed out loud, which inspired even more enthusiastic rolling, followed by her running around in circles on the soft white sand while growling news of her ecstasy to the heavens above. I sat down and watched her play like that for at least an hour. By the time she returned to my side, she was panting with her tongue hanging out.

"Let me guess...you like the beach," I said to her with a smile.

As we drove home from Mudjimba, I turned on the radio which was playing a news update being read by an older man who sounded annoyed: "The mystery stomach bug continues to spread across Brisbane with hundreds of people spending the day in the bog. The medical authorities are advising anyone with a stomach problem to work from home, preferably close to a dunny at all times. They also advise those with the stomach bug to be careful laughing out loud after a few accidents were witnessed around the city in recent days."

Mia's apprehensive eyes and ominously still tail told me she'd had enough of the news. I concurred and turned the radio off.

The Price of Paradise

Mia and I had always been close. Back in Yorkshire, she had a way of understanding whatever I was thinking. I used to take her and Heidi's black Labrador, Misty, along with me whenever I went jogging in the Dales. It had been my main form of exercise for years. Misty would charge ahead like the excitable explorer she was, while Mia would run after her because the two of them were the best of friends. Just at the moment I wondered where they'd disappeared to, Mia would return to me with a concerned expression on her face which understood my thoughts. A few minutes later, Misty would reluctantly follow her back. Even then, I suspected Mia could read my mind, but that didn't make any sense at the time.

Before breakfast the next morning, Mia and I headed off for a walk along the narrow, unkempt pathway which connected the back garden with the

Serenity Trail, a paved, circular track which was lined with sandstone engravings of local poems. One of the engraved poems was memorable for not mincing its words:

Don't forget to make the most of today
Because it will end.
Don't forget to wonder at life's mysteries
Because they'll remain unsolved.
Don't forget to laugh at life's random ups and downs
Because it's the only way to enjoy this wild ride.
Don't forget you're alive
Because one day you'll die.

As Mia and I walked past the frank engraving, we encountered an enormous brown python curled up in the middle of the track. It must have eaten recently as there was a large, stationary lump protruding from its belly, warning all that nature can be cruel and twisted. I wondered what the lump had been when it was a living breathing creature. Mia stared at the python with a quizzical expression revealing she knew it wasn't chase-worthy and deserved her utmost respect.

"Big one, isn't it?" said a voice behind me.

I turned around to find Jude approaching with her bouncy boxer.

"It is, and it's well fed," I replied.

"Looks like a possum to me. My other half must have missed one again," Jude said.

I wondered why Jude was talking about her partner as possum-eating competition for the python, but I decided not to ask as I wasn't sure I was ready for the answer.

"We were just marvelling at the way snakes command respect from one and all," I replied.

"If only everyone thought like that," said Jude with concern quivering in her voice. "Respect is an endangered species these days."

"Has something happened?" I asked.

"Let's just say I preferred life as it used to be. The modern world and all the changes it brings are just smokescreens that allow the corrupt to make more money at everyone else's expense," Jude stated.

"You'd have thought there'd be a moratorium on corrupt behavior here on account of how beautiful this part of the world is. Surely human ugliness should find somewhere nastier to reveal itself," I responded.

"Tell that to the village association," Jude said.

"What's their story?" I asked.

"For starters, they arranged the flooding of Baroon Valley to turn it into the godawful dam it is—just to make some extra cash from supplying drinking water," Jude explained. "They certainly didn't do that out of the goodness of their hearts. Now we all have to live with the consequences."

"So Lake Baroon, down the road, only became a dam recently?" I asked.

"Fifteen years ago," Jude explained. "And the people who made that disastrous decision are still making disastrous decisions on a daily basis. All the time they're growing richer and morally poorer."

"Well, I'm counterbalancing their energies," I replied. "My ethics are thriving, but my bank account needs emotional support."

Jude laughed wholeheartedly. "You'll fit right in around here," she said as she turned to leave. "Just remember, when you live in paradise you've got to pay for it in other ways."

As I walked away, I wondered how much I could afford to pay for paradise, and whether credit would be accepted in this part of the world.

A few minutes later, my mobile rang from an unrecognized number.

"Hello?" I said.

"G'day. Is that Will?" asked a man's deep nasal voice.

"It is. Who's this?" I asked.

"Raymond Marchester. I'm the manager of Holy Crap Rubbish Removals. There's nothing we can't move," he said with a forced chuckle.

The name rang a bell. I remembered I'd applied for a job with this guy's company.

"Raymond, hi," I replied, aware my accent didn't sound remotely Australian. I contemplated attempting an Aussie twang, but I knew it would sound fake and inauthentic. I braced myself for Raymond being shocked by my foreignness ahead of asking questions about my less-than-ideal visa situation.

"I just rang to say you've got the job!" he stated as though I'd won a prize. "Congratulations."

"Don't you want to interview me first?" I asked.

"No need, mate," he answered. "We only employ trash dashers on casual contracts. If you're a good bloke, we'll keep you on. But if you're a dickhead, we'll let you go after a shift or two."

"Wow, that's a deceptively clever strategy," I responded. "What is a trash dasher, exactly?"

"That's what we call the company's front liners, the guys who remove the crap no one else wants to even think about," Raymond explained matter-of-factly.

"I see," I said as my heart sank.

"Your first shift is seven o'clock, Monday morning," Raymond continued. "So do you want the job, Will?"

"Count me in, Raymond," I replied without the enthusiasm he was geared up for.

"Bonzer," he said. "I'll text you the depot's address. Just wear some crappy clothes you don't mind throwing out. The smells you encounter as a trash dasher can be hard to get rid of—and sometimes hard to forget. See you Monday morning."

"See you then," I replied.

Mia and I continued walking as I digested the unexpected career turn I'd just committed to. The only words running through my mind were the name of my new employer...Holy Crap.

Up ahead, an older man was approaching us along the footpath. He had a long curly moustache and an untamed beard, and he wore a khaki uniform with the words "Platypus Whisperer" emblazoned on the front of his shirt. He reminded me of an eccentric Australian version of David Attenborough without a documentary crew when he needed one.

"Morning," I said.

"Beautiful day, isn't it?" he responded.

"Stunning. Are you searching for platypuses then?" I asked.

"No, I'm in search of people to introduce to platypuses so I can earn a crust," he stated. "Platypuses are beautifully simple. People are the tricky ones."

"I see," I replied.

"There's one now," he said, as he pointed at a nearby creek.

"A simple platypus or a tricky human?" I asked.

"She's a beauty," he said, ignoring my question. "You see that ripple in the water beside the log to the right?"

"I do," I replied.

"She's swimming just below that ripple. She should pop up for air in the next minute or two," he continued with gravity.

It was obvious platypuses were the main reason this fellow got out of bed in the morning. He fell silent as we waited for the platypus to reveal itself in all its glory. My inner Brit searched for small talk to fill the awkward silence, but the Whisperer was so focused on watching the ripple that I felt invisible. Mia pulled at her lead indicating she was ready to move on, but I stood firm as I was determined to meet an elusive platypus face-to-face. The ripple in the water suddenly changed direction which suggested the big reveal was imminent. However, it then disappeared behind a log, leaving us with an even longer, even more awkward silence which definitely needed filling.

"She's a busy one, isn't she?" asked the Whisperer.

"She is," I said, realizing the platypus wasn't going to show itself. "We best get moving. Nice to meet you."

"You, too," he responded as he stepped closer. "You've got a feel for what I do here. Please recommend my services to anyone searching for platypuses...or what they represent."

I walked away perplexed. What did platypuses represent?

The Festival

The next morning, I awoke early in anticipation of three days of the Make Australia Green Again Music Festival. As I got dressed, I realized I knew nothing about the festival, including the names of the musicians scheduled to perform. The website comprised a basic home page with the words "Let's sing together about making Australia green again" on it. When Mia realized I was leaving her at home during the festival, she gave me a look which could only translate into, "If I'm not welcome there, it's surely not worth going." For a moment I believed her and considered staying at home, but I reminded myself I wouldn't have been in Australia if I hadn't won a ticket to attend this event. Who was I to look a gift horse in the mouth?

"I don't think dogs are welcome at most music festivals, girl," I explained to Mia before I walked into Maleny alone.

When I arrived in town it was a normal day on the main street. Shoppers walked in and out of the shops while old folk wandered up and down the street without an apparent objective. My festival ticket listed the venue as "The Pandemonium Podium, Maleny," so I walked along the street in search of a podium homing a thriving music festival. After walking up and down the main street three times, I couldn't find anything resembling a podium or a music festival.

In the hope of asking for directions, I popped my head inside the local barber shop. As I did, a row of eight men seated along a waiting bench turned their heads in unison to stare at me. They all had the same cropped blonde hair which seemed counterintuitive to their queuing for haircuts. With their sixteen eyebrows concurrently raised to the maximum incline, I felt an overwhelming need to explain my intrusion in their world. "Excuse me," I said to a female barber who was in the middle of a haircut near the door.

"Yeah, mate," she replied without looking up from the almost bald male head in front of her.

"Can you please point me in the direction of the Pandemonium Podium for the Make Australia Green Again Music Festival?" I asked.

On cue, a loud symphony of hilarity erupted throughout the shop. The eight waiting men and the two men getting their hair cut all roared with laughter. I was perplexed, so I awaited an explanation. However, all that arrived was more laughter as those barber shop customers inspired collective hysteria out of one another. That is, apart from the female barber and her male counterpart. They were busy completing their haircuts, even though there was no hair left on the heads they were hard at work on. The female barber was so focused on the job at hand that she'd completely forgotten about my request for directions. A minute later, when the hysteria subsided and silence recolonized the small shop floor like an old friend, all that was left were blank stares from the waiting bench.

"Does *anyone* know where the Pandemonium Podium is?" I asked again, this time redirecting my question toward the row of eight waiting men.

As if an on switch had been pressed again, the men's faces instantly transitioned from blank stares back to uncontrollable laughter. It was perplexing. Those barber shop customers were acting like I was a stand-up comedian delivering the funniest one-liners the world had ever heard. When one of the waiting men tried to draw breath, he appeared to be in genuine pain from his exertions. To ensure my presence didn't lead to anyone's death from overlaughing, I turned to leave. "Thanks anyway," I said as I exited the shop.

Perplexed, I crossed the road and once again walked up and down the main street. This time, I vaguely heard what sounded like a guitar being strung in the distance. *Bingo!* Finally, I was getting closer to some festival action. I searched around for a "Make Australia Green Again Music Festival" sign, but none revealed itself along the streetscape. However, I did notice an alleyway running away from the main street toward where the guitar sounds were emanating from, so I walked over to investigate. The alleyway ran alongside a café, down some stairs, around a corner, and then down some more stairs which connected with a road across from a small park. As I approached, the guitar playing was getting louder and was accompanied by the soft murmur of a voice. It was a far cry from a pumping music festival, but I followed the sounds into the park just in case it was a warm-up act.

Other than a couple of benches underneath some gum trees toward the back, the park was empty. The guitar playing sounded like it was coming from the park bench area, so I walked onward through the unmown grass. As I approached, I noticed someone was standing on top of one of the park benches with a guitar in hand. It was a huge, tanned man wearing a blue cap, a cream beer-stained singlet which had once been white, ripped board-shorts, and half-broken thongs. Even from a few yards away, he smelt of stale beer. The man was strumming his guitar at random intervals, but the sound he created couldn't really be called music. It was more like the noise a beginner would make the first time they ever picked up a guitar. And how could I describe the sound coming out of his mouth? At a stretch, he sounded like he was imitating African tribal music in the most derogatory, condescending, and darkly comical of ways. Tribal folk across Africa must have been turning in their graves. "Um, ohhh, um, ohhh, um, ohhh, ummmmmmmmmm," he hummed as he strummed. "Oooooh, ah, ooooooooh, ah, oooooooooooooh, ah..."

As I tried to make sense of the bizarre scene, I noticed a sign beside the bench...an awful sign delivering an awful truth to all who would listen. In other words, me. It read: "Let's Make Australia Green Again – enjoy the show!"

I nearly fell over when the realization sank in that this was the music festival I was so excited to have won a ticket to attend from the other side of the world. After the initial shock, its close cousins, disappointment and dismay arrived, followed by a feeling which had been stirring in my soul ever since I'd landed in Australia...I felt like an idiot.

The guitar-playing hummer didn't care, or even notice my inner turmoil. In fact, he kept delivering his racket without acknowledging my presence in any way. "Ooooooh, ooooooooooooh, oooooooooooooooooh, ooooooooooooooooooooh," he half stated, half hummed as he stared blankly into the great empty yonder just past where I was standing.

After a few minutes of being frozen to the spot and praying it was all a terrible mistake, I retreated from the park, or rather, the scene of the crime. Desperate to escape, I crossed the road, walked back up the stairs, jogged along the alleyway back to the main street, and speed-walked home.

When I arrived home, Mia greeted me at the front door with sympathetic eyes which recognized my pain. They didn't have a hint of "I told you so" behind them as they could and should have. I sat down on the ground and accepted a sympathy rub from her as the truth sank in: that I'd travelled all the way around the world for a big fat lie which had been dressed up as the solution to all my problems. Rather than throwing another shrimp on the barbie, I *was* the shrimp on the barbie.

The Wrong-Footed Audience

After a long weekend of not attending any fake music festivals, I awoke early on the Monday morning and got dressed in my oldest, least fashionable outfit. It turned out to be a poor-fitting Hawaiian shirt with bright intermingled yellow and pink flowers and a ripped pair of khaki cargo shorts. Mia gazed at me with shock in her eyes before she sat down next to my wardrobe, willing me to make a more visually pleasing choice.

"I get it, Mutt Dog," I stated. "But remember, this isn't a fashion show. Are you coming?"

Mia galloped over to the car and jumped in. I joined her for the drive down the mountain to Maroochydore where the depot was located. Within half an hour, I'd located Holy Crap Rubbish Removals. The slogan "Give 'em heaps!" was written in large maroon letters beneath the picture of a smiling ant carrying an old piano about a hundred times its size on its back. “Poor bugger,” I said to both the ant and myself as I parked the car.

Mia and I walked over to a group of men standing in front of an ad hoc reception shed which had pieces of rusty corrugated iron dropping off its sides like bark. That it was still standing at all was a remarkable feat of happenstance. A confident middle-aged man with a booming voice was addressing the group with emphatic hand gestures which demanded they take notice. The men were dressed in the same orange overalls and blue caps, and they all had unkempt, fuzzy beards and slightly bemused expressions on their faces. If you’d been tasked with finding a group of cloned individuals, you’d have struggled to find other such similar-looking men.

“So remember, the client is always right,” the man in front explained like a teacher addressing a remedial class. “If I hear of anyone else telling a client where to shove their rubbish again, I won’t be so lenient. Who have we here?” he asked when he noticed me.

“Will Watson at your service, old chap,” I responded.

“Old chap” was something I’d often said to men I didn’t know but was trying to bond with. It was one of those remnant habits which uncontrollably popped up when I least expected or wanted it to. It was generally well received in the UK, but it was being met by doubt and confusion in Australia. A pregnant pause descended upon the group, followed by a few contagious smirks of condescension. I kicked myself on the inside.

"I'm not so old, Will," the man in charge answered. "We spoke on the phone. I'm Raymond. And may I say, I've never met someone with such experimental dress sense before."

"Thanks," I replied. "I've come prepared to get dirty."

One of the men in the group laughed harshly, as though he'd unexpectedly been tickled somewhere he thought was off limits.

"Will, these are the trash dashers you'll be working with," Raymond explained. "We all congregate here for group training before each shift begins, and we all report back each evening with our trucks empty and intact. Write those words down, please, Will: *empty and intact*. They are the two most important words in the vocabulary of a trash dasher."

I pulled out my notepad and wrote down the words "empty and intact." I also wrote the words "my career prospects are" before them to lighten the mood. At least it made me smile.

"Right, I want everyone to collect today's rubbish with a helpful spring in your step. Good luck, boys. Will, if you come with me, I'll get you set up with a truck for today's job," Raymond explained as he ushered me away.

I followed Raymond toward a long line of rickety, rusty trucks while Mia followed a few steps behind with unusual caution.

"Nice dog," Raymond said. "Will she be joining you in the truck?"

"She will. Is that alright?" I asked.

"It's OK, but always check with the client as to whether they're happy she gets out of the truck. Some people are funny about dogs and anything else they can complain about, you know?" Raymond explained.

"Oh, I know," I said.

"So here we have the trash dash truck fleet," Raymond explained as he pointed at a line of decrepit vehicles before us. "They've all seen their fair share of action, but they're still reliable and they get the job done."

"I can relate," I said with a smile.

"This is yours," Raymond explained, ignoring my attempted joke. "Truck number thirteen. I hope you aren't superstitious?"

"Not today, no," I replied.

"Now, there are only two things you need to understand about these trucks," he continued. "Firstly, you should only ever be in first or second gear whenever you're driving up or down the mountain. Trust me on that. And secondly, there's a control stick inside the glove box for the hydraulic lifter. You'll get used to it, but it's a little tricky to control. Just remember to wrap the straps all the way around any heavy items before lifting them."

"Got it," I responded. "And where do I take the trash once I've collected it?"

"Buggered if I know," Raymond said with a shrug of his shoulders.

"Pardon?" I asked.

"That's the creative part of the job," he stated. "You can take it wherever you want. Just don't bring it back here."

"Oh right. So are there some rubbish tips nearby?" I asked.

"There's one around the corner," Raymond explained. "But they charge people to dump their rubbish there."

"I assume that's a normal business cost for a trash collecting firm?" I asked.

"You assume wrong, mate. The best of my trash dashers arrive back at the depot with their trucks *empty and intact*. I don't ask them any questions. I just pat them on their backs when they get the job done. Otherwise, I don't tend to employ them again," Raymond explained. "We have a fit in or fuck off policy, you see."

"Oh right," I said, feeling sick all of a sudden.

"The only other information you'll need is the address for today's pickup," Raymond explained. "Where's that notepad of yours? I'll write it down for you."

I handed over my notepad, forgetting about my mood-lightening addition, which Raymond read out loud for my repeat benefit.

"You're a funny guy, Will," he said slowly. "*Real* funny."

"Thanks," I replied.

"Can I give you a piece of advice?" Raymond continued with growing seriousness.

"Of course, yes," I responded.

"You're acting as though you have an audience who cares about what you say and do. But you're really standing alone and lonely in the corner. Do you know the only way anyone attracts an audience when they're all by their lonesome like you?" he asked.

"Tell me," I replied with genuine interest.

"By sticking around, putting in the hours, and here's the important part...by being an audience member for others. You need to learn how to be a team player before you can get away with the kind of shit you're trying to pull off," Raymond said as he threw me the truck keys before he turned to leave.

Mia gave me a look which could only translate into "Ouch!" in dog language. Once Raymond walked away, she growled ever so softly at truck number thirteen as though it was a rival dog, there to test her boundaries. To her dismay, it remained resolutely unmoved by her warning.

"It's OK, girl," I explained as I held the front door open. "It's just for a short while. Who knows, it may even be fun."

Mia jumped into the truck without her normal enthusiasm.

Truck number thirteen was a unique vehicle. As we drove away from the depot in first gear, it hopped around like an angry kangaroo which didn't enjoy being told which gear to hop in. I moved it up to second gear in the hope it would be happier there, but the engine dropped out as soon as I did. We were surrounded by heavy traffic, so grinding to a halt wasn't ideal. I waved an apology at the cars around us, but they reacted with angry hand gestures ranging from shaking fists to the middle finger. Where were these mythical laidback Aussies *Crocodile Dundee* had showcased as a dime a dozen? If I could have demanded a retroactive movie ticket refund, I would have. Keen to avoid upsetting more drivers, I turned on the ignition and hopped forward again in first gear. It was ugly but at least we were moving. Mia gazed at me with her eyes full of worry.

"You watch, Mutt Dog, we'll laugh about this in the years to come," I said without conviction.

The truck's hopping habit calmed down once the engine warmed up. It was still less than roadworthy, but at least the truck moved forward rather than up and down when I accelerated. The address we were due at was on Maleny-Montville Road, only a couple of miles away from our new home. That meant driving up and down the mountain twice on the same day. As we approached the gradual incline at the base of the mountain, the truck gave out a loud gasp as it blasted its backlog of discontented chemicals into the atmosphere. In preparation for the climb, I moved the gear-stick down from fourth to third which resulted in a more abrupt deceleration than I'd expected. A driver behind us long-honked his horn like a furious trombone, so I pushed down on the truck's accelerator while praying for a more collaborative response. By then, gravity was working against us as the hill's incline steepened. When the truck made it clear third gear wouldn't cut it, I remembered Raymond's advice about only climbing mountains in first or second. However, when I moved from third to second gear, the truck slowed down to twenty miles an hour in a fifty zone, and the car honking from the expanding queue of cars behind us was becoming deafening.

"I'm sorry!" I shrieked out the window, but I wasn't appeasing the frustrated drivers.

I contemplated stopping by the side of the road to let the drivers behind pass, but I knew my chances of restarting the truck on the mountain's incline were nonexistent. So I pulled the truck over as far as I could to the left-hand side of the road and let the drivers behind overtake at their convenience. As they passed, most of them made their displeasure evident with a final emphatic hand gesture. "You're a dickhead!" shouted out a man in an accelerating black Range Rover.

"Thanks for the feedback," I said under my breath.

Mia gave me a sympathetic look.

An hour and a half later, we finally arrived at the top of the mountain after a tortuous journey. The pickup address was at the end of long driveway lined by yellow and pink flowers that were meticulously spaced out. The house was a modest white cottage surrounded by lush green fields dotted with relaxed cows who were lazily chewing on lush green grass which smelt like freshly brewed green tea. It was the first time in my life I'd been jealous of a herd of cows, but they were advertising their contentment for the whole world to see. I parked the truck in the front of the cottage, opened the door, and jumped down.

"Wait here a moment, girl," I said to Mia, who looked disappointed to be left behind.

A huge spiky-bearded man wearing a tea-stained singlet walked down the front steps of the cottage to greet me. He was six foot six and built like a tank. As he walked, he positioned each footstep with the razor-sharp focus of a robot following a meticulous list of instructions. "G'day," he said without enthusiasm.

"How are you, Mr. O'Hara?" I replied.

"You're late," he stated.

"Sorry. It took longer than expected to get this old lady up the hill," I explained as I pointed at the truck.

"I'm not interested in excuses, thanks, mate," he said.

"Sorry," I reiterated.

"The water tank is behind the house," he explained as he turned to walk in that direction.

"Do you mind if my dog joins us?" I asked.

"I'm easy, but I'll shoot her if she upsets my cows," he snarled.

"I'm sure she'll be fine in the truck," I added.

With his measured footsteps, he slowly led me behind the house toward a dark-green plastic water tank that had been split open on one side. It was lying in a half-broken heap like a casualty of a war over water resources. Leaves and dark black gunk congregated deep inside, and it emitted the pungent rotting smell typical of rain-drenched rubbish which has been left to fester.

"What happened here?" I asked.

"Termites," he stated without further explanation.

"I didn't realize they ate plastic," I responded.

"Of course they bloody don't. They ate the wooden base supporting the water tank, so it collapsed after the storms filled the tank with water the other week," he said, rolling his eyes skyward.

"What an unlucky chain of events," I said.

"Be fast," he stated. "When you back your truck up, make sure you don't upset my cows because that would upset me."

"I'll do my best," I responded, not wanting to imagine what he was like when he was upset if this was him relaxed.

O'Hara gave birth to a short. sharp, grunt-heavy laugh which implied my best would never be good enough. Then, without another word, he turned and slow-stepped back toward his house, leaving me to survey the inexplicable scene of destruction in his back garden. My initial prognosis was that I was going to need a lot of luck if I was to collect that water tank.

I returned to the truck where Mia was having a nap. "It's best you stay in the truck, Mutt Dog," I explained. "He's not a dog person."

Mia stared at me as if I'd just told her black was white.

After starting up the truck's engine, I hopped forward in first gear. I'd hoped we could skip the whole hopping through the gears rigmarole since the engine was already warm, but the truck insisted. The make-do dirt driveway was littered with deep holes and rocky bumps, so the combination of hopping forward and driving on an uneven surface made the journey feel like we were riding an unhappy bull in a rodeo. Mia sat up near the open window in case she needed to jump out to save herself.

O'Hara re-emerged on his veranda with a cup of coffee in time to witness truck number thirteen hopping past his house. I could see him half laughing, half grunting at my expense. However, I had more pressing issues to deal with as I parked the truck beside the broken water tank. Up close and personal, the tank appeared far too large and awkward to be moved by truck number thirteen. And if I was to attempt the pickup, I needed to turn the truck around which meant figuring out how to put it into reverse. After a few minutes of wrestling with the gearstick, it eventually clunked into what I assumed was reverse. A high-pitched beep announced to all that the truck was indeed reversing, or the world was ending, or both. The beeping was so loud it hurt my ears. Mia concurred. She flattened her ears backward like a distressed hare.

"Sorry, Mutt Dog!" I called out. "This won't take long."

A loud bang suddenly emanated from behind the truck so I slammed the brakes on. Thankfully, the reversing beep stopped, but when I checked the side mirror I could see I'd reversed into the water tank, rather than beside it. I heard some angry shouting coming from inside the house, so I got out of the truck to hear O'Hara's latest complaints.

"I told you not to upset my cows!" he roared. "That bloody beeping made one of them shit itself!"

I gazed over at the nearby cows who were engrossed in their delectable grazing activities, then I looked back at O'Hara, who by then was calling me a "half-witted Pom with learning challenges." I put a finger to my ear to indicate I couldn't hear him. He shot a few more double-barreled expletives in my direction before returning inside. I breathed a sigh of relief, then I walked over to the broken water tank to figure out how on earth I was going get it aboard the truck. It was hard to imagine a more awkward shape to shift.

Remembering Raymond's advice, I located the strap attached to the hydraulic lift and pulled it out. The good news was it was long enough to wrap all the way around the broken circumference of the water tank, which I did. But the bad news was the whole thing looked wrong from a physics perspective. The tank had ripped plastic hanging off it at awkward angles, so a swift and easy lift into the truck would be impossible. My only available options were blind hope or certain failure. I was in familiar territory. I located the hydraulic lift's control from within the glove box and readied myself for my inaugural trash lifting attempt. After taking a deep breath, I pressed the green button and hoped for the best.

The same cacophonous beeping as for reversing emerged from within the truck's belly, showcasing a distinct lack of imagination by its creators. After O'Hara's repeated warnings about upsetting his cows, I checked on how the beasts were doing. Thankfully, they'd wandered off to a more picturesque part of the paddock to shit in peace. The rope around the broken water tank slowly went taut as the hydraulic lift started living up to its name. It then elongated from taut to stretched and the water tank lifted slightly around its middle while the hydraulic lift made uncomfortable squeaking noises. However, despite the hydraulic lift's best efforts, the water tank's top and bottom sections remained stubbornly rooted to the ground. I pressed the red button to abort the mission, but neither the clunking noises nor the beeping stopped. If anything, the beeping only increased in volume, as though its warnings were becoming more urgent.

O'Hara returned to his back veranda to watch the show, so I braced myself for his next round of his abuse. However, after noting his precious cows were fine he just tossed his half-full cup of coffee in my direction before he walked back inside.

By then, the middle section of the water tank was around a foot in the air as the hydraulic lift continued to take the strain. The top and bottom sections were still refusing to budge, and the tank was splitting further open along the fault line which had cracked in the first place. The splitting plastic made a god-awful noise akin to fingernails being scraped across a blackboard. It was too much to bear, so I covered my ears. But there was more to come. The hydraulic engine transitioned from over-revving to functional at exactly the wrong moment. The water tank exuded a final screech of pain as it ripped apart in the middle. In response, the rope shot upward like a slingshot before the two halves of the tank collapsed in inelegant heaps alongside one another.

I contemplated driving straight back down the mountain and returning truck number thirteen to Raymond empty, intact, and unemployed, but I went to check on Mia first. She looked up at me with love in her eyes, a love that recognized her owner was at the end of his tether. That one glance from Mia was enough to bring me back within the confines of my tether.

Upon surveying the two halves of the water tank, I realized that splitting it had actually solved my problem since the two smaller sections were easier to move than the whole tank. So I stepped forward and lassoed one half of the tank before I called upon the hydraulic lift's services again. Strangely, I noticed there was some charcoal around the base of the tank where it had been attached to its wooden base. I filed it under weird in my mind and pressed the green button on the hydraulic lift. The beeps once again warned away. Then, the bottom half of the tank lifted straight up off the ground, and I was able to navigate it into the truck's belly with the control panel. Once I'd dumped it, I encircled the rope around the other half of the tank and deposited it inside the truck. I couldn't believe it. The water tank had been collected.

"And that's how it's done," I said to Mia as I did a little jig to celebrate.

With the enthusiasm of a marathon runner crossing the finish line, I called out to O'Hara, who'd by then returned to his veranda, "I've collected your water tank as requested, Mr. O'Hara!"

"About bloody time!" he replied with the disdain of an antimarathon demonstrator. "Next time don't upset my bloody cows, moron."

"You have a good day, sir," I replied with a smile.

As the truck hopped back along O'Hara's potholed driveway, I smiled at Mia and she returned the sentiment. It had been a successful outing. I let the truck hop itself back into a regular rhythm before we drove back down the mountain in second gear. When we reached the bottom, I remembered we still had to deposit the old water tank somewhere if we were to return the truck to the depot empty and intact. After weighing up the options, I decided to take it straight to the local tip so they could recycle the plastic.

Conveniently, the tip was located only half a mile away from the truck depot. It was a vast industrial building homing long lines of rectangular skips into which vehicle owners were throwing their discarded items with competitive passion. One man wearing a mud-stained singlet nearby called out "Goal!" every time he threw an item into a skip. I reversed the truck up to an empty skip, and with the hydraulic lift's help, I dropped the two halves of the water tank into it. Two loud satisfying crashes broadcast to the world a job well done.

"That felt good," I said to Mia as I drove the truck to the exit booth.

"That'll be eighty bucks, mate," said the rotund, red-faced man within the booth.

"Pardon?" I replied.

"Eighty bucks, please," he said.

"I think there may be a mistake," I responded. "I just dropped off a plastic water tank for recycling."

"No mistake. We don't recycle. We burn, and burning costs money," he stated.

"Wow," I said. "Do you know where I can recycle around here?"

"Nah, mate," he stated. "That's eighty bucks."

He reminded me of a parrot which only had one line to gift the world. I hoped for this fellow's sake that all his customers were charged eighty bucks so he wouldn't have to think on his feet.

"Do you accept credit cards?" I asked.

Without responding, he yanked my credit card out of my hand and pressed it to his payment machine. "See you next time."

With a sigh, I drove the truck out of the tip and we were soon back at the depot. It was four o'clock in the afternoon, but it felt like we'd spent a month on the road. Raymond waved at me from within his make-do reception shed before he walked over to greet us.

"Welcome back, Hawaiian Shirt," he stated.

"You mean me?" I asked.

"The boys gave you that nickname earlier," he stated with a proud smile. "They can explain it to you later."

I was pretty sure I could figure out where the nickname had come from.

"So how was your first day of trash dashing?" he asked. "Is the truck empty and intact?"

"Well, I survived," I responded. "And yes, the truck is empty and intact. I dropped the water tank off at the local tip."

"You're the last of the big spenders, aren't ya? Well done, Hawaiian Shirt. Here's your pay for the day. You can come back tomorrow," Raymond stated as he handed me an envelope.

"Thanks," I said as I stepped down from the truck.

Mia and I walked back to the hire car where I sat motionless for a few minutes to take it all in. I then opened the envelope to discover a fifty-, a twenty-, and a ten-dollar note. I'd made eighty dollars and I'd spent eighty dollars depositing the water tank at the tip. So it was a break-even day, apart from all the petrol I'd used travelling to and from the depot. I laughed out loud at the economics of trash dashing.

Butt of the Joke

By the time we arrived home, I was exhausted. I walked straight into the bathroom and turned on the rusty shower tap. As the lukewarm water washed over my body, the water tank's pungent smells and turgid memories washed down the drain in teeny tiny pieces. I scrubbed away at my skin with the remnant of a soap bar a previous tenant had left in the bathroom. It was almost impossible to create any soapy froth with it, but it was the equivalent of bathing in a five-star resort after the day I'd experienced.

"Sorry we didn't go for a dog walk today, Mutt Dog. The day got away from me," I said to Mia after I'd showered. "Are you happy with an evening play in the garden?"

Mia jumped up in the affirmative and charged outside. I retrieved a beer from the fridge and followed her into the garden where she was already rolling on the thick green grass. Being Mia looked like a far better way to live than pretending to be human, so I put down my beer and laid on the grass beside her. By then, she was rocking her body from side to side while grinning at the heavens above. I followed her lead and wiggled my bum on the grass like it was the eighties.

A few seconds later, I heard the sound of uninhibited laughter nearby. I sat up to discover Jude leaning over the fence, watching our rolling display. "I always knew the golden retriever owners were having all the fun!" she exclaimed.

"It's been one of those days," I confessed. "It was either this or running naked through the bush where the wallabies are easy to offend."

Jude roared with laughter. "So what happened?"

"Well, today was my first day working as a trash collector, which was the only job I could find," I explained. "Let's just say it was a fiasco."

"Oh dear," Jude responded.

"I experienced truck problems, rude people, and trash collection nightmares, and those definitely weren't on my 'to do' list when I arrived here," I explained.

"I did warn you about the locals," Jude replied.

"You did, but I wasn't expecting to encounter the world's meanest man who was more concerned about his cows' wellbeing than mine," I said.

"So you've been to O'Hara's place?" Jude asked.

"You know him?" I replied.

"He's infamous around here for loving his cows and hating people. A real charmer, you could say," Jude answered.

"Well, I'm glad he stands out as unusual. If he was normal in these parts, I'd be on the first plane out of here—if I could afford it," I stated.

"Did you pick up a broken water tank by any chance?" Jude asked.

"How on earth did you know that?" I replied.

"My other half worked as a rubbish collector for a while. He was once called out to O'Hara's place to collect a broken water tank. Something about termites eating its base," she explained.

"That's strange. He must have a monumental termite problem," I replied.

"Or a monumental problem with telling the truth," Jude said.

"That's a common theme I'm encountering," I added.

"How so?" Jude asked.

"Well, when I was in Yorkshire, I won a ticket in a pub raffle to attend the Make Australia Green Again Music Festival. It happened when my girlfriend Heidi had just broken up with me, so let's just say I was open to the prospect of a trip to anywhere but where I was," I explained. "However, the festival ended up being a sick joke. There was just one guy on a park bench making the worst noise I've ever heard, and I was the only one in the audience."

Jude appeared to be holding back more laughter.

"Not you too!" I exclaimed. "What's so funny about this festival?"

"It's a local joke the village association plays to make it look like the locals actually care about the environment. However, that couldn't be further from the truth," she explained. "Every year, it's the same. They ask Big Man, a gruff local without the slightest semblance of musical talent, to stand on that park bench and make the unpleasant noises you heard. Not a single local ever attends as everyone knows it's a joke, but there's usually at least one poor gullible tourist who falls for it. The village association makes sure of that by offering free tickets as raffle prizes to various unsuspecting pubs in the UK. Now I'm talking about it, it's cruel rather than funny, isn't it?"

There it was. In that moment, I met Will Watson for the first time...the gullible fool who'd fallen for the village association's unsophisticated joke against humanity. I'd been right to feel like I was the butt of the joke, because that's what I was. And that joke had played a starring role in bringing me all the way around the world to a place where I was now stuck in the economic mud. After spending all my money to get Mia and me to Maleny, I was unable to afford the return airfare to the UK. The village association had outdone themselves. Why did I believe life would be easier in this part of the world?

Brethren

The next morning, Mia came bounding into my bedroom at the crack of dawn to remind me to take her for a walk before we headed off to the depot. I rolled over and hid my head under the pillow. She growled her displeasure in my ear.

"You sure know how to make your wishes known, Mutt Dog," I said as I rolled out of bed.

After I got dressed, we walked over to the Serenity Trail. The sun was breaking through the wisps of mist rolling over the fields like a teacher addressing a class of distracted pupils. The more it asserted its didactic presence, the more the mist listened and allowed it to shine through. I breathed in the crisp, fresh air while Mia savored the surrounding scents like a smell connoisseur. And there was one smell to the right which particularly interested her. She lunged off the pathway, toward the creek.

"Easy, girl," I said as I held her lead tight. "What is it?"

Up ahead was a viewing platform which provided visitors with a glimpse of the platypuses in the rock pool below. It was the stuff of dreams for the Whisperer. Mia dragged me toward to the platform as she sniffed the air with enthusiastic curiosity. Once we reached it, she stared at the muddy water below as though everything within sight could be alive if only we were to open our eyes. However, the only action in the vicinity came from a kookaburra which was laughing on the branch of a nearby tree. Its high-pitched hysteria escalated through the musical notes until it hit a glass ceiling at C, which it fought to break through in recognition of my life being so hilarious. I forced an appreciative smile in its direction. As I did, the semblance of a ripple emerged in the water below, suggesting it had important news to impart. The ripple encircled the center of the pond as though its creator was trying to start a whirlpool but wasn't an expert in physics. It eventually stopped circling and raised its head above the water's surface to reveal itself as a busy little platypus, wagging its tail like a dog. I don't know why but I was sure she was female. The sun glistened off her oily fur, highlighting gray streaks of wisdom alongside her smooth dark-brown body. Mia gazed up at me as if to say, "I told you so," before she directed her friendliest smile toward the platypus.

"I know, girl," I responded. "What a remarkable creature she is."

The moment was cut short when the kookaburra laughed again. The easily offended platypus dove back underwater to escape to a peaceful and quiet place where no one else could mock her—a place without humans around. This time, there were no ripples on the surface to explain what was happening underneath the water.

"We'd best get moving," I said to Mia.

Mia and I walked most of the way around the circular track until we found a half-hidden pathway veering off to the right in the direction of home. We followed the shortcut, which connected with the road for the last half mile of the return journey. That route allowed us to pass by the houses of some of our neighbors we were yet to meet, though most of them had grown thick hedges along the street frontage which hid their houses from view.

As we followed the road homeward, a noise sounding like a gaggle of geese communicating with one another suddenly echoed around us. Mia didn't pull at her lead which implied she'd already decided the noisemakers weren't chase-worthy. A few seconds later, we heard a loud screech followed by a surprised squawk, before a black Range Rover came speeding around an upcoming bend in the road. I jumped out of its way and pulled Mia to the side just in time to avoid being run over. The words "Body Relaxation Experts" were advertised on the side of the car as the driver sped away with minimal relaxation in the accelerator region. Mia gave me a worried look.

We continued walking around the bend in the road where we discovered a group of birds were congregated around one of their brethren who was lying motionless in the middle of the road. My heart sank. They were guinea fowl, and one of them had just been run over by the speeding Range Rover. The driver hadn't even stopped to help. The injured guinea fowl was still alive and conscious, but there was blood everywhere and she was clearly in considerable pain. The other guinea fowl cleared a space for us to gain access to their friend. The injured guinea fowl looked up at us and the other guinea fowl with interest, but she was broken and couldn't stand up or move. She had kind eyes that wanted everything to be better for everyone else. Mia licked her broken and bloody wing while the other guinea fowl didn't protest. I bent down to pick her crushed body up off the road, and she allowed it with a gentle appreciation. The other guinea fowl contributed a range of squawking sounds which implied they were fine with us helping, while also reminding us that their friend's life mattered.

With the injured bird lying in my arms, I walked to the side of the road where a hedge blocked the entrance pathway to the nearest house, which I assumed was where the wounded guinea fowl's owners lived. The pathway was completely covered by the hedge so we couldn't enter. I called out, "Hello! Hello!" toward the house.

Within seconds, a response came from a wolfhound who charged at the hedge while barking with aggression. I instinctively held the injured bird above my head and stood in front of Mia. The wolfhound continued barking at us through the hedge for a few minutes before a lady's voice shouted out, "Who's there?"

"One of your guinea fowl has been run over," I explained to the green wall between us.

"Is she alive or dead?" she asked without the surprise I'd expected.

"She's *alive*!" I responded with more volume than was required.

Instantly, a nearby section of the hedge moved as if by dark magic. It was attached to an electric gate which opened to reveal a hidden but well-maintained driveway—like a prop used for an escape scene in a Bond film. A frantic middle-aged woman with brown hair strewn across her face stepped forward. "When did it happen?" she asked as she scooped the injured guinea fowl up from my arms.

"Just now," I explained. "A black Range Rover drove over her and then sped off without stopping."

"That *bastard*!" she seethed.

"Do you know the driver?" I asked.

"Unfortunately, yes. He peddles relaxation while he destroys everything in his pathway," she explained. "We started with seventeen guinea fowl. We're down to six thanks to *him*."

"Sorry to hear it, but what about this girl," I said, pointing at the guinea fowl who appeared to be listening to every word. "Shall I call a vet?"

"No need," the woman responded. "My husband will take care of it."

"I think she has a chance," I added. "She's conscious and is interested in what's going on around her. Maybe she just needs time to heal."

"Thanks for your help," the woman said as she turned to leave.

The injured guinea fowl held my gaze before she was carried off to wherever she was going next. I was glued to the spot as I was sure she was trying to communicate something important to me. But then she was gone, and the hedge-covered electric fence closed even faster than it had opened. It was as if the guinea fowl had never existed at all—as if the house behind the hedge wasn't really there.

Mia and I continued homeward with heavy hearts. I couldn't stop thinking about the injured guinea fowl. I'd only met her for a moment, which happened to be her darkest moment, and yet she was so graceful, forgiving, and accepting of her fate. How does anyone smile through pain like that?

The Old Bathtub

When Mia and I arrived at the depot for day two of rubbish collecting, the other trash dashers were congregated around the make-do reception shed, but Raymond was nowhere to be seen. Mia and I walked over to join them.

"Morning!" I said. "I haven't met you all properly. My name's Will."

"Hawaiian Shirt! You're back!" replied a man wearing a singlet with long greasy hair hanging out the back of his cap.

"We had money on you being a day one quitter," contributed a short tubby man with a spikey moustache.

"Sorry to disappoint you, but as I said to Raymond yesterday, 'I'll be back,'" I said with my best Arnold Schwarzenegger *Terminator* impression. Rather than being greeted with a few pity laughs, the trash dashers reacted as if I'd just sworn at them in an offensive foreign language. I was once again standing alone in the corner.

"So guys, I've got a question for you," I said in an awkward change of subject. "Where do you recycle all the trash you collect?"

"What are you, a greenie, Hawaiian Shirt?" asked the long-haired man.

"I'm just a trash dasher who wants to drop his truck back empty and intact at the end of the day," I explained.

The group roared with laughter as if I'd told them the funniest joke they'd ever heard. I was perplexed. In this strange southern land, every time I said something funny, people were offended. And whenever I stated a cold, hard fact which couldn't possibly be funny to anyone, the locals found it clever and hilarious. Everything was upside down.

"You're a classic, Hawaiian Shirt," stated the short tubby man.

"Thanks," I said. "So where do you drop off your rubbish?"

They continued to ignore my question.

A couple of minutes later, Raymond emerged from within the reception shed, carrying a pen and a large pad. "Morning, crew, and welcome back, Hawaiian Shirt," he said with a wink to the rest of the trash dashers, which implied he was either a happy winner or an amused loser in the bet about me returning for a second shift. “As usual, I’ve got an important training session lined up ahead of today’s jobs.”

Raymond knelt down and thumped his notepad onto the ground with dramatic flair. The trash dashers were clearly well versed in what this meant as they crouched around the pad with interest. I joined them, and Mia completed the circle with an uncertain half wag in her tail.

“Right,” Raymond began as he drew an uneven circle on a page of his notepad like an artist creating a drawing of consequence. “This circle represents us trash dashers.” He took a deep breath before he drew a larger uneven circle next to the first one. “And this circle represents the local community. Now I have a question for you...who makes the rubbish we collect?”

“That’d be the community?” half asked, half stated the short stocky man as he pointed at the large circle as though it was a living, breathing piece of trash.

“Well done, Beefy,” said Raymond as he drew a few piles of mess around the community circle like an artist in blissful flow.

“So if the community makes the rubbish and we service the community,” Raymond continued as he drew a final pile of rubbish larger than all the others, “what’s the best way for us to grow our business?”

The trash dashers were stumped so I put my hand up. “By becoming an active member of the community,” I contributed.

“Almost, Hawaiian Shirt, *almost*,” Raymond responded with a sympathetic shake of his head.

“By paying a larger bribe to the powers that be?” asked the long-haired man in all seriousness.

“Not quite, Murph, but good guess,” Raymond replied without the sarcastic edge I was expecting. “OK, I’ll tell you. We’ll generate more business by helping the community make more rubbish for us to clear up.”

“We’re doing them a favor,” Raymond continued, “but we’re really doing ourselves a favor. Do you understand what I’m sayin’?”

No one responded, and I didn’t have a clue what he was talking about. “Can you please explain that for me, Raymond?” I asked.

The rest of the group smirked as if I was the village idiot there to entertain them with my daftness.

“Oh bless,” said Raymond. “Hawaiian Shirt doesn’t understand. Anyone care to enlighten him?”

“Maybe Hawaiian Shirt should piss off back to England where he can drink tea and eat biscuits with the King,” added Murph with a harsh, high-pitched giggle which came from the dark depths of his soul.

"Maybe he'll even find himself a job he's qualified to do when he's there," added Beefy.

The trash dashers reacted with more forced chuckles customized to communicate that I was as unwelcome as Brisbane's stomach bug just after a bout of Delhi belly.

"That's today's lesson, boys. Here are today's job sheets," said Raymond without answering my question or addressing the trash dashers' insults as he handed each of us a sheet of paper.

Mia gazed up at me with a "What on earth was that all about?" expression. I couldn't answer the question behind her eyes.

The address I was due at that morning was a few miles toward home in a suburb called Palmwoods where I was scheduled to collect an old bathtub and a toilet. Truck number thirteen was parked where I'd left it the previous night. It smelt of decaying scunge after the last night's rainfall.

"Good luck figuring it all out, Hawaiian Shirt!" called out Murph as he sped past in his truck.

The pickup address was a small bungalow on a back street of Palmwoods. When we arrived there weren't any items ready for collection on the street, so I jumped down from the truck and knocked on the front door. A diminutive elderly lady with wiry white hair stepped forward with a smile which didn't quite reach her eyes. "Are you here to collect the bath and toilet?" she enquired with a soft voice.

"Guilty as charged, Mrs. Hurst," I replied.

"Hang on, are you *British*?" she asked with concern wavering in her voice.

"I am indeed, Mrs. Hurst, but I can say g'day and move bathtubs like an Aussie," I responded.

"We'll see about that," Mrs. Hurst replied with an enthusiasm deficit.

I signalled to Mia that I'd be back in a moment before I followed Mrs. Hurst inside. We walked along a thin dark corridor toward the back of her house.

"You see," Mrs. Hurst explained, "once a snake has run its scaly body over something as intimate as a bath, it just needs to go—no questions asked."

"Did you say a snake?" I asked.

"This way," she said as she led me into a bathroom which connected with the hallway. It was a generic, older bathroom with a cream bathtub enclosed within an unfashionable beige wooden frame beside a well-loved toilet. To say the bathroom stank would be an understatement. A putrid smell hung in the air like an unwelcome remnant of troubled ablutions from the past.

"So what are we looking at here?" I asked.

"It's a bathroom," Mrs. Hurst explained without elaborating.

"I mean, where are the items you'd like me to collect?" I asked.

"Right there, sonny," she answered. "One toilet, check. One bathtub, check. It's all there."

"Oh right. Mrs. Hurst, for your information, we only collect items which are ready to be moved. However, this toilet and this bathtub are still installed," I responded as calmly as possible.

"Nothing gets past you, does it?" Mrs. Hurst replied with more than a hint of sarcasm.

"I'd love to help you, Mrs. Hurst, but..." I started.

"Here's a question for you, sonny," Mrs. Hurst interrupted. "Are you going to remove these two little items like an Aussie man who gets shit done? Or are you going to cry to mommy like a British wimp who doesn't want to fit in here, leaving a little old lady with a big problem to sort out all by herself?"

I wondered if Mrs. Hurst was in cohorts with Heidi. She certainly shared her disdainful opinion of my merits as a real man. But fair play to her. She'd cornered and entrapped me with her words like a guilt-tripping expert.

"Nothing's too much trouble for our loyal customers, Mrs. Hurst. Have you got any tools I can use to uninstall the items to be removed?" I asked.

"Geez, I'd have thought you'd come with your own tools," Mrs. Hurst responded. "I've only got a jackhammer which I use in the garden. I suppose you can use that."

A picture popped into my mind of Mrs. Hurst using her jackhammer to attack the weeds in her garden. I imagined her explaining to the weeds that they were unwelcome in this part of the world and had to be exterminated as she turned the jackhammer onto its highest and loudest setting.

"I can work with that," I replied. "By the way, do you mind if my dog comes inside?"

"Whatever," Mrs. Hurst said. "I'll get the jackhammer."

I went outside to retrieve Mia from the truck. She was half-asleep and jumped to attention when she saw me.

"It's another challenging job, Mutt Dog," I explained.

Mia jumped down from the truck, ready for action.

By the time we arrived in the bathroom, Mrs. Hurst had returned with her rusty jackhammer, which must have been at least thirty years old. "Just don't break it," she stated as she handed it to me. "If you do, I'll want it replaced." Then she left me to it.

"Yes, I'm a miracle worker, Mrs. Worst," I said when she was out of earshot.

Mia smiled, then she lay down outside the bathroom door as if to say, "This could take a while."

I attached the jackhammer to the nearest charging point.

"I'm shutting the door to protect your ears, girl," I explained to Mia.

Despite never having used a jackhammer before, I pressed the green button just to see what happened. The jackhammer's vibrations jarred violently throughout my body, causing me to involuntarily jump up and down like an overenthusiastic raver without a sense of rhythm. Since I was on the dancefloor anyway, I decided to keep going. I aimed the jackhammer at the base of the bathtub and stepped closer until it connected with the plaster. Then I let it do its business. Plaster flew in all directions as the jackhammer made light work of detaching the front edge. Within seconds, it was following the line of plaster around the right-hand side of the bathtub like a railway track. Soon, that side was free, and the jackhammer was working through the plaster at the back of the bath. It then almost dragged me with it around the last bend as it pulverized the final section of plaster into dust. Against the odds, the bath was uninstalled and ready to be removed. In celebration, I took a selfie of myself giving a thumbs up with one hand on the jackhammer which stood victorious beside the detached bathtub.

With my newfound confidence, I turned the toilet's water tap off and let the jackhammer also make light work of detaching the toilet from the floor.

As soon as the jackhammer's engine fell silent, I heard Mia barking at the door. I opened the door and she charged into the bathroom with her eyes full of worry. She sniffed at the old bathtub like a sniffer dog searching for drugs inside.

"It's OK, Mutt Dog," I said. "It worked. We can now remove these items and get moving."

While Mia continued her search for whatever she was looking for, I picked up the toilet and poured the remaining water inside it down the nearby basin. Then, I carried it to the truck and threw it inside before returning to the bathroom.

"Moving this bad boy is going to take a little more nous," I said to Mia.

I bent down and put my hands under the bathtub's detached wooden base, then I lifted it up so I could drag it out of the bathroom on its side. Mia backed out of the bathroom ahead of me as though she was guiding me out. As I followed her, I suddenly noticed a strange pattern inside the bath's base which was moving like one of those mind-altering pictures. I bent down for a closer look, and the strange pattern lunged at me. It was a python! I screamed and jumped out of the way just in time to avoid being attacked by the enormous serpent which was upset that its home was being moved.

"So you found Monty then?" called out Mrs. Hurst, who was laughing from the other end of the corridor.

"Monty?" I asked.

"Monty the Python. He's certainly never heard a man scream like *that* before—at least not a real one," she said with more laughter at my expense.

"So you knew this python was living underneath the bath?" I asked.

"Why do you think I called you out? Where will you take him?" she replied.

"Where will *I* take him? Isn't this a snake catcher's job, Mrs. Hurst?" I asked.

"There's a general assumption that the trash collector should take away *everything* inside the items being collected," Mrs. Hurst explained with a smirk to acknowledge a successful entrapment maneuver had been executed.

"Why doesn't that surprise me?" I responded.

After taking a deep breath, I picked up the wooden structure and dragged it toward the truck. Monty the python hung on for the ride, but I didn't care anymore. Python or no python, I was going to finish the job. I used the hydraulic lift to load the bathtub onto the truck.

Before leaving, I called out to Mrs. Hurst who was watching me from her front veranda. "That's me, Mrs. Hurst. I've removed the bathtub and the toilet, python included. Nothing's too much for our treasured clients."

"Whoop-de-doo," she said. "I hope you aren't expecting a tip for doing what was expected of you in the first place."

As I drove away from Mrs. Hurst's home, I had an overwhelming desire to text Heidi the photo of me holding the jackhammer along with an explanation along the lines of: "Getting real man work done down under. Just removed a bathtub homing a massive python. No sweat, babe." That would have showed her I can get shit done like the best of them. But I reminded myself Heidi had moved on with Hugo, the patron saint of all things manly. And I was on a new page of my life—a page which didn't require me to impress her anymore. So why I was still thinking of her?

As I refocused on the winding road in front of me, I remembered I still had a load of rubbish to dump. Dropping it off at the tip guaranteed a loss-making day, and in good conscience I couldn't dump them by the side of the road as I suspected my colleagues did. Then an idea occurred to me. What if I was to store them inside the shed at the back of the house so I could recycle them into something of value? It may even be a way to earn some extra cash on the side. So I drove the truck home, backed it into the garden, and used the hydraulic lift to deposit the bathtub and toilet beside the shed. Monty the python remained asleep despite all the movement. Rather than waking him up and scaring the bejesus out of myself, I dragged the bathtub into the shed and left him inside it. His thick midsection suggested he'd eaten recently, so he was due a few months' nap while the creature he'd last strangled became one with his digestive system. Mia was less interested in what was happening than usual. She jumped down from the truck and climbed up the front steps to the veranda where she lay down.

"You joining for the return journey, girl?" I asked.

Mia remained motionless where she lay.

"That's fine, Mutt Dog. Back shortly," I said.

I drove the truck back to the depot where I left it empty and intact, and returned home an hour and a half later. Mia was still fast asleep where I'd left her on the veranda. I sat down next to her on the top step.

"Another day in paradise," I stated. "Are you tired, Mutt Dog? I can understand why you would be after the past few days."

Mia peered at me without her normal enthusiasm as the front gate opened and Jude walked through carrying a hessian bag.

"How are you, Jude?" I asked.

"I've been better," she said. "Can I come up?"

"Come grab a step," I replied.

Jude put the hessian bag down next to the front door, then she sat down beside me.

"They're grapefruit—the juiciest ones you're likely to come across. Between you and me, they're the secret to my aging so well," she explained.

"I was going to ask," I responded. "Thank you, I love juicy grapefruit."

"Are you alright?" I asked.

"I don't know," Jude answered. "I've lived here for over seventy years, and each year the locals seem to become a little meaner, a little less community minded, a little less human."

"Sorry to hear it, and I'm even sorrier that I'm not more surprised," I said. "Has something happened?"

"It's just a feeling in my bones," Jude replied, "a feeling that tells me bad things are happening around us."

"You need a beer, pronto," I said as I stood up. "Back in a jiffy."

When I returned, Jude was stroking Mia's tummy.

"You've made a friend for life," I said as I handed Jude the beer and sat back down.

"What's this?" Jude asked as she parted some of Mia's fur to gain a view of her skin beneath.

I felt the area on Mia's back Jude was focused upon, where I discovered a small lump. Mia sat up abruptly when I touched it.

"That's strange," I responded. "What do you think it is?"

"I don't know. How's she been?" Jude asked.

"She's been tired this afternoon. Beyond that, she's been her normal enthusiastic self," I replied.

"I'd get her checked out by the vet if I were you," Jude advised. "It could be nothing, but you never know."

"I will," I said. "Mutt Dog, did you hear that? It's time you met the local doggy doctor."

Mia put her head down on her paws, willing a change of subject.

"So how can we help recreate the community you once loved?" I asked.

"Build a time machine?" Jude suggested. "I'm running out of time in this life and most people aren't interested in changing for the better. As long as they're spending money on things that don't make them happy, they're happy to be unhappy."

"But look at where we live, Jude," I said as I pointed at the stunning sunset below. "Isn't this enough?"

"It's enough for you and me," she responded. "But we need to coexist with the other monkeys in the jungle, and most of them are playing by different rules. Oh, don't listen to me, Will. I just need a change of scene."

"Are you thinking of moving?" I asked.

"Wolf is from New Zealand originally," she responded. "If we can't find what we're looking for here, we may move there. Apparently, the scenery is stunning, the people are friendly, and the possum population is out of control."

"They're the exact reasons I moved here. Well, minus the possums. Like an idiot, I believed the grass would be greener in this part of the world," I explained. "Is Wolf your dog?"

"Ha! He *is* pretty furry," Jude said. "No, Wolf is my partner. He's a possum hunter. He's run out of work since he wiped out the possum population."

"Wolf kills possums?" I asked.

"Yes, they make a wonderful soup," Jude said. "You should pop over and try it the next time Wolf finds a possum to shoot—if that ever happens again."

"That sounds *interesting*," I said as I threw up a little in my mouth.

"In the meantime, don't trust anybody," Jude advised as she stood up to leave. "There's something afoot in this befuddled community."

"I believe you," I said.

After Jude left, I texted Raymond, "There's a family emergency at this end. I won't be in tomorrow, but I'll be back on Thursday."

"No skin off my nose either way, Hawaiian Shirt," Raymond texted back without a smiley face.

Club Vet Resort

When I awoke the next morning, I was aware I had urgent business to attend to in the form of a vet visit. After drinking a strong coffee, I looked up the details for the local vet which was due to open in an hour.

"Morning, girl," I said to Mia when she woke up. "The good news is we're going for a walk, and the bad news is we're visiting the doggie doctor this morning."

Mia diverted her gaze from mine in protest.

After breakfast, we headed off on foot toward Maleny. We encountered the confusion of guinea fowl at the same bend in the road where their friend had been run over. The term "confusion" as the collective term for guinea fowl made a lot of sense up close and personal. They were clucking out of tune with one another while they wandered in multiple directions at once. I searched for the injured sixth guinea fowl within their ranks but she wasn't there. Mia's eyes revealed her distress. All we could hope was that she was recovering and would reunite with the confusion soon. In the meantime, I was confused enough for all of us.

Suddenly, a loud blast of music caused me to jump. I turned around to discover a thin, elderly man with unkempt white hair was cycling toward us with an ancient stereo hanging off his front handlebar, playing dance music. Once my ears adjusted to the loud volume of the music, I recognized the song as "Wake Me Up." I waved at the old man, but he kept cycling straight at me with a cold hard stare which failed to recognize me as a fellow human being. It was clear he wasn't going to swerve to miss us, so I jumped off the road with Mia in tow to avoid a collision. The guinea fowl were perturbed by the loud music and scuttled off into a nearby field with unusual focus. As the old man cycled past, he half sang, half shouted, "So wake me up when it's all over, when I'm wiser and I'm older," as though he was the only person around.

"Maybe he didn't see us," I said to Mia as we continued on our way. She looked doubtful.

By the time we arrived in Maleny, it was nearly nine o'clock. The vet surgery was located on a side street lined with eucalyptus trees full of chatty flying foxes engaged in gossip. Mia held her nose high as she smelt the vast array of earthy, guano-rich smells encircling us. With the "Vet" sign looming up ahead, she tried to divert us off course by pulling me onto a footpath signposted as the Obi Obi Trail.

"Let's explore that track another day," I explained. "Today we need to get you checked out."

We entered the door to the vet's surgery to discover the waiting room was rammed full of people. However, there were no pets in sight.

"Hi," I said to the young, red-haired woman at reception. "I'd like to make an appointment for my dog to see the vet, please."

"You're in luck, we don't have anyone booked in this morning," she responded.

"Really?" I asked as I gazed at the many people seated in the waiting room. "What about them?"

"They are neither pet owners *nor* customers," the receptionist replied with a disdainful nose raise. "Please take a seat for a few minutes."

I sat down and waited on a chair while Mia stood next to me without her normal ease. There were eleven people seated around us, and they were all preoccupied with reading magazines and newspapers. A middle-aged man with silver hair was lying across three seats nearby with the air of a vacationer at a beachside resort. He was reading the front page of a newspaper with the headline "Brisbane's Mystery Gastro Disease Continues to Cause the Runs." The man's relaxed posture couldn't have been more at odds with the bad news he was reading about.

"Excuse me," I said to the man. "What are you all doing here if you don't have pets with you?"

"Waiting and chilling," he responded without going into more detail.

"Waiting for what?" I asked.

"For the library to open," he answered. "The village association recently changed the library's opening time from nine o'clock to ten o'clock. That affects people like us, you know. So we had to find ourselves somewhere to sit for that extra hour. The vet staff will no doubt complain to the village association soon. Once that happens, we'll get what we want—an earlier library opening time. That's the way things work around here. In the meantime, this is a lovely spot to hang out. I've always liked animals."

The man returned to reading his newspaper as though a waiter may appear shortly with cocktails by the pool. Before I could dwell on this less-than-normal situation, a toned, blonde-haired woman with an efficient walk marched over to me.

"Mr. Watson?" she asked. "I'm Michelle, one of the vets here. This way, please."

Mia refused to budge so I had to drag her by the lead into the consulting room.

"How can I help?" Michelle asked.

"This is Mia. She's got a lump on her back I'd like you to check out, please," I replied.

Mia rammed her body behind the chair I was sitting on so the vet couldn't reach her.

"It's OK, girl," I said. "This lady just wants to help."

"Can you show me where it is?" Michelle asked.

Mia refused to exit her hiding spot, so I located her lump through the gap between the chair and the wall, and showed the vet.

"Hmmm," Michelle said as she felt the lump. "That feels like a heat spot. Has Mia moved here from a cold climate recently?"

"She has indeed," I said, full of relief. "We've just moved here from Yorkshire."

"OK, then I'm 99 percent sure it's a heat spot," she stated. "Would you like me to arrange a biopsy to make sure?"

"Ninety-nine percent is the type of odds I like, but yes, please, let's double-check," I responded.

Michelle took a small sample from Mia's lump which made her jump out of her hiding spot like a child who mistakenly thought they were safe in a game of hide-and-seek.

"I'll call you with the results," she stated.

"Thanks," I said.

As we wandered out of the vet surgery, one of the older women sitting in the waiting room had fallen into a relaxed reverie and was snoring loudly. The silver-haired man I'd met gave her an angry look indicating her snoring was disturbing his peace and quiet. However, the woman remained oblivious and let out a loud pig-like snort indicating she was possibly enjoying a meal in her dream. Someone reacted by hurtling a magazine across the room at her. It just missed her head and knocked a lamp off the table, causing the waiting room to become dark and unhospitable.

Mia charged out onto the street as though she was escaping after a lifetime spent on death row. The sun shone all the brighter for the vet's favorable prognosis of her lump.

As I was breathing in the good news, I received a text from Raymond. "Hawaiian Shirt, if you're still in, I have a job for you in the morning. Bring along a disposable pair of gloves and a can-do attitude. This is an important client."

"Count me in, Raymond," I texted straight back, aware that my bank account was dropping like a stone.

As Mia and I walked back toward town, we passed a park bench with an old man wearing a holey green jumper sitting on it. He was typing on the latest Apple laptop, which he was charging at a nearby charging point along with a brand-new iPhone. "Excuse me," he called out to me. "Do you mind if I say hello to your dog?"

The old man's hair was straggly and overgrown like an untamed hedge, and he smelt of guano even from a few yards away—but Mia seemed fine with the idea.

"Sure," I said as we stepped closer.

"What a beauty she is," he replied as he scratched Mia behind her ear.

"Her name's Mia," I said.

"Hello, Mia," he responded. "My name's Mad Jack, but you can call me Jack."

"And I'm Will. Nice to meet you, Jack," I said. "What a clever idea charging your devices at the council's expense."

"Oh, they owe me, *believe* me," he replied without explaining himself.

"Really?" I asked.

"But I don't approve of political jokes," he continued.

"Why not?" I asked.

"I've seen too many of them get elected," he stated matter-of-factly.

As I laughed and Mad Jack sat a little taller, the infamous black Range Rover emerged out of nowhere and parked up beside us. In short order, its shiny front door was thrust open. A tall, rotund man with spiky black hair and gold-rimmed sunglasses emerged, thumping his boots onto the pavement and announcing his arrival to everyone present. Mad Jack shifted nervously in his seat, while Mia repositioned herself out of view underneath the table.

"Just when my day was going so well," Mad Jack stated with annoyance.

The Range Rover driver marched over to us with the air of a man who'd spent much of his life highly ranked in the military and not much time lowly ranked as a nice person. He halted in front of us by bringing one foot down next to the other with more force than was necessary, then he yanked his eighties-styled sunglasses from his face. "What have we here?" he asked as he stared at Mad Jack, who was living up to his nickname thanks to some wonky eye movements.

In the absence of a reply, the Range Rover driver diverted his questioning gaze toward me.

"Will Watson," I said as I stood up and presented my hand for shaking.

He stared at my hand as though it was infected while he left it hanging.

"*Mad* Jack," he stated as he ignored me, "how many times do I have to explain to you that the public charging points are for contributors. That means people who pay their taxes, people who are members of the community, people of worth. It doesn't mean cretins who reduce the area's property prices by their very presence."

Mad Jack responded by unplugging his devices and packing his stuff into his moldy backpack in silence.

"Do you know what happens to people who ignore council rules?" the Range Rover driver continued as he clenched his fist.

Mad Jack wasn't interested in hearing the answer. Once his possessions were packed away, he scuttled off without a word.

"Good riddance to bad rubbish!" called out the Range Rover driver to Mad Jack's retreating back.

Mia remained motionless underneath the table, trying not to breathe.

"Will Watson," he stated out loud as though my name was a complete sentence in itself.

"Guilty as charged," I stated.

"You live across the road from that old hag, don't you?" he continued. "I saw you talking with her the other day."

"If you mean the lovely Jude, then you'd be right," I replied. "I am indeed lucky enough to call her my neighbor."

"That tells me you enjoy spending time with reprobates," he stated. "You've already befriended the village's homeless person and the region's least with-it hippy. You're a real social anticlimber, aren't you?"

"I'm just doing my best to live and let live," I replied.

"And you're a *foreigner*," he continued as though that explained everything. "In that case, listen carefully, Watson. It's taken years to build Maleny into the special place it is. You should understand that I won't stand for anyone entering our world who lowers our standards."

"You can rest easy on that front. I want this place to become my home," I replied. "I want to contribute to this community."

He looked me up and down as though he was assessing my ability to contribute to anything. "You want this to be your *home*? No way, Watson. Eradicate that frivolous idea from your demented head. For starters, we don't need another homeless reprobate around here. And secondly, there's the issue of your working visa. You've got a maximum of six months to look forward to, then it's bye bye, regardless of your misguided ideas."

"Not if I qualify for a skilled migrant visa while I'm here," I stated.

"It's in the name, Watson...*skilled*," he said. "You're automatically disqualified because you don't have any skills."

"We'll see about that," I replied.

"Did I mention I'm the chairman of the village association? I'm going to let the association know all about you and your disgusting social challenges. You'll soon learn it doesn't pay to be an unskilled social anticlimber in this part of the world," he stated before he turned to leave.

After marching back to his vehicle, he sped off with far more acceleration than was needed, leaving us with the smell of burning rubber to remember him by. Mia peered out from under the table with a look of relief. We both breathed out.

Beneath the Ripples

That evening, my phone rang from a number I wasn't expecting to hear from. It was Emmanuel. "If it isn't the yeti of the south!" he exclaimed when I answered the phone.

"Hi, Emmanuel," I said. "How are you?"

"I'm alive and kicking," he responded. "I thought it was about time we caught up."

"It's been a while," I replied. "Are you still ignoring all sensible medical advice and searching for Nessie?"

"When was medical advice ever sensible?" he replied. "I'm having a jolly old time in Scotland and there's not a damned thing anyone can do about it."

"I'm worried about you," I stated without intending to sound like the parent, as I was in the habit of doing with Emmanuel.

"I'm worried about *you*," he replied. "Ever since you flew away like a lost homing pigeon, I've been dreaming about what you were like when I first met you all those years ago."

"What was I like?" I asked.

"You were content, happy even—despite all the challenges life threw at you," Emmanuel stated. "But you've changed."

"Have I?" I replied. "Or was I just a clueless teenager who was good at burying the less than beautiful parts of my life? You know, little things like the fact my parents were killed in a car crash when I was sixteen. Minor issues like the fact I was assigned to the care of a foster father who cared more about his stuffed frogs than his foster son. How *is* Fit Frank these days?"

There was a long pause as Emmanuel digested my unusually honest words. "It's not Fit Frank you should be worried about," he finally responded. "It's Terrence the Toll Collector."

"Pardon?" I replied.

"Terrence was one of my bestsellers throughout the eighties and nineties. Would you believe I sold thousands of versions of him?" Emmanuel continued. "He was always purchased by the same type of customer—men who were dealing with unresolved issues. Men like you, for example."

I felt uplifted when I realized Emmanuel appeared to be understanding my plight for the first time in forever. However, that was swiftly followed by frustration that we could only talk about real issues with the help of his damned stuffed frogs. I took a deep breath and made a decision to talk Emmanuel's language. "If I'm honest, I jumped at the opportunity to move to Australia to avoid talking with Terrence back in Yorkshire. However, it turns out there are even scarier versions of that annoying frog Down Under."

"An Australian version of Terrence the Toll Collector?" Emmanuel responded. "I imagine he walks around with a frown on his suntanned forehead and a bullwhip on his hip. If only I'd customized one when I was a taxidermist. I'm sure he'd have been my bestseller ever."

"So what are you're *really* doing in Scotland, Emmanuel? Are you facing up to your own Terrence?" I asked.

Emmanuel paused as he considered my question. "I suppose I am. When a man reaches my age and realizes time is running out, time starts to mean something again. Life starts to feel urgent, important even. With that shift, Terrence sensed his window of opportunity to collect his tolls from me may be shorter than he thought...so his toll requests have become more urgent."

"What sort of toll requests?" I asked.

"He wants proof that I believe my life will mean something one day. You know, confirmation of my faith. But the more I stare at the waters of Loch Ness, the more the little guy enjoys testing my faith in everything apart from Nessie's existence. If only she'd raise her beautiful head above the water's surface, that would get him off my case," Emmanuel said.

"I thought you'd mastered the art of having faith, thanks to the wisdom of all those stuffed frogs guiding you along the way," I replied.

"We all have our moments," Emmanuel responded with noteworthy sadness.

"Are you worried about your heart?" I asked.

"Not the one beating in my chest," he replied. "I just know I need to listen carefully right now."

"To whom, Emmanuel?" I asked.

"To whomever or whatever is causing the ripples around me—like Nessie for example," he replied.

"But what if those ripples are just being caused by the wind? Or a living creature who happens to reside underwater in a normal and most unsupernatural way—like a platypus for example?" I asked.

Emmanuel fell silent.

"And what if there's nothing beneath the surface at all?" I continued. "What if you're just searching for Nessie to avoid accepting the truths in your own life? What if we're all doing the same thing?"

"Now you've got me worried," Emmanuel replied. "Are you alright, Will?"

"I was going to ask you the same question," I responded.

"I must dash," he replied as he rushed to hang up in typical Emmanuel style. "Good luck finding whatever it is you're searching for."

"You too, Emmanuel," I replied. "*Please* take care of yourself."

When I hung up, I felt uneasy. Emmanuel thought I was the one who was chasing rainbows despite the fact he was searching for the Loch Ness Monster. Why did he think I was unsure what I was searching for? I lay on my bed awaiting clarity to arrive. However, all that arrived were images in my mind of Terrence the Toll Collector holding out his greedy hand to collect his precious toll. Terrence was scarier than most of Emmanuel's stuffed frog creations. His skin was green and scaly like the rest, but his face was ugly—and human. And not just any human. I recognized that angry face. There was no mistaking it. Terrence the Toll Collector had the black Range Rover driver's face...and he was just as furious with me for existing. But there was more to it than that. The ugly green beast seemed to think I owed him for unpaid debts of the past. As I pictured him growing impatient to collect whatever he wanted from me, I fell into a welcome sleep.

The Pissing Hierarchy

Early the next morning, Mia and I headed to the depot for another day of trash collecting. The trash dashers were once again congregated around Raymond for morning training, so Mia and I joined the circle.

"Hawaiian Shirt!" exclaimed the stocky man known as Beefy. "We thought you'd..."

"Quit. I know. You mentioned that last time in a similar situation, I believe," I stated.

"Can't ya laugh at yourself, Hawaiian Shirt? Is that what this is about?" an angry and tense Beefy asked.

"I laugh at myself on a daily basis," I replied. "But today I'm not in the mood to hear the same insults over and over. Let's change the mix, eh?"

Beefy appeared as shocked as if I'd told him he was a skinny vegetarian, while Raymond chuckled to himself.

"Welcome back, *Will*," Raymond said. "Today's training is about toilet etiquette."

"Pardon?" I asked.

"That means where to go when you need a piss or a dump on the job," Raymond explained for my benefit.

"Thanks, carry on," I said.

Raymond dropped his large notepad onto the ground with its infamous thump and we all gathered around. "Let's discuss the pissing hierarchy," he stated as he drew a triangle which he divided into a two-levelled hierarchy. "The question is: where's the ideal place to take a piss when you're working at a client's property?"

"In the dunny?" asked the long-haired man known as Murph.

"Not quite, mate. That's your second-best option," Raymond said as he wrote "Dunny" on level two of the hierarchy.

"In the sink?" asked Beefy, full of confidence and lived experience.

"Nah, mate," said Raymond with a shake of his head. "Anyone else?"

The group remained stumped and silent.

"The answer is...on a tree," explained Raymond as he sketched a tree at the top of the hierarchy. "However, here's the instructive point I want you to remember: only piss on a tree if there's one available which doesn't provide full visibility of your wedding tackle. That means positioning yourself behind the tree rather than in front of it." Raymond enacted the whole process for a deeper understanding before he continued. "You see the feedback we've received from clients is that they prefer it when you don't use their toilets on account of the mess you guys make. And some clients have highlighted that they prefer not seeing your joysticks hanging out when you're pissing on their trees. It's all valuable feedback."

"I get it," responded Beefy with greater clarity. "Does that mean the third best option is the sink?"

"Nah, mate," said Raymond. "The sink isn't in the pissing hierarchy at all. The only acceptable alternative to a tree is a client's toilet if, and only if, you've asked for permission first and you clean up after yourself afterwards."

Beefy nodded as the day's learnings sunk in.

"Ideally, there's only one reason you should be entering a client's house at all," Raymond continued.

"To check out their TV?" asked an enlightened Beefy.

"To collect the items to be removed from the premises," responded Raymond as he handed out the job sheets for the day. "Get in and get out as soon as you can, and keep your peckers out of sight at all times. That's it, boys. Have a good one."

When Mia and I walked away from the morning's training, she gave me a look which could only mean, "We dogs know a lot more than you humans." I nodded in the affirmative before I read my job sheet for the day. It revealed I was due at a house on our very own Bald Knob Road in Maleny, so we had another day of ascending and descending the mountain ahead of us.

As we drove away from the depot, Mia fell straight to sleep while I listened to a radio show debating whether climate change was real or imagined. The radio host claimed to have the latest global climate change data at the ready to discuss in depth. However, he got side-tracked and launched into a monologue about why Australia wasn't responsible for climate change. Then he ranted and raved about his love of four-wheel drive vehicles and how that was a dearer issue to him than climate change. I turned the radio off and thought cool thoughts.

Within an hour, we arrived at 87 Bald Knob Road, ready for the morning's collection. The entrance was a long driveway lined by the most perfectly maintained hedge I'd ever seen. At the end of the driveway was an architectural wonder of a house enclosed almost entirely by glass walls which showcased a Lego-like world of neat rooms and designer furniture. There was a five-car sandstone garage to the left of the house which homed a brand-new black Range Rover with the words "Body Relaxation Experts" advertised on it. Of course it did. I considered driving straight back out again, but there was no time for that. On cue, the front door of the house was thrust open, and the infamous black Range Rover driver marched out as if he was expecting me to arrive at that moment. "About time, Watson," he announced from the lofty heights of his front veranda. "Good news...I've got some *more* rubbish for you to acquaint yourself with."

"Where is it?" I asked, not being in the mood for any more of his abuse.

"At the back of the house in the fire pit," he answered. "We tried burning a few things but not everything burnt."

"I'll collect it now," I responded, desperate to be anywhere but where I stood.

I drove around to the back of the house, and sure enough there was a fire pit full of half-burnt items including old beds, a wardrobe, a chest of drawers, and some old farm machinery. The messy scene was in stark contrast to the flawless house only yards away. I noticed the nearby bushland was also charcoaled, suggesting the fire had migrated from the fire pit into the surrounding bush.

Without wasting a second, I filled the truck with all the items of rubbish. They were soggy and smelt of rotten cheesecake, but all I cared about was getting the job done as fast as possible.

Once I'd finished and was about to jump into the truck to speed away, the black Range Rover driver marched over. My heart sank. "One more thing, Watson," he said as he held an index finger in the air as though he was conducting an imaginary orchestra before he dropped his finger down to press dial on his mobile. "Is that Holy Crap Rubbish Removals? I'd like to speak with the manager, please." He winked at me as he waited on the phone.

"Did you say your name is Raymond?" he asked. "This is Ben Flinders. Yes, that's right. Thanks, we're proud of the work the village association do to make this part of the world shine brighter. Now, an important question for you: are you Will Watson's boss?"

"Great," he continued once he'd heard Raymond's response. "Well, I just wanted to let you know that Watson pissed all over our toilet seat while he was on the job today."

He fell silent for a few welcome seconds as Raymond responded.

"No, he didn't wipe up after himself," he continued. "He left his disgusting mess all over the toilet seat like a wild animal or something. I suspect he enjoyed the whole experience. My wife is devastated and has called a professional cleaner to come and mop up Watson's mess."

Watson's mess. Maybe he knew about the state of my life after all.

"It is indeed shocking," he concluded. "I know you'll deal with it promptly and professionally, sir."

When he hung up, he gave me a victorious grin before he turned to leave.

"How did you know about today's toilet training?" I asked his back as he walked away.

"How does anyone know anything?" I heard him ask the universe.

Relieved the conversation was over, I drove truck number thirteen back along the driveway en route to the depot. Raymond called me a few minutes later. I prepared myself for the worst.

"I know what this is about, Raymond," I said. "I believe his name is Ben Flinders."

"You're right, but not for the reason you think," Raymond replied.

"Go on," I said.

"I know you didn't really piss all over Ben Flinders's toilet seat," he explained.

"Oh good," I responded. "How did you know that?"

"Because you're, how you say, civilized," he explained. "I can't imagine you've ever left your piss on a toilet seat in your entire life."

"You've summarized my life rather accurately," I replied. "So what's this about then?"

"Ben Flinders is important to us as a business and you've gone and bothered him," Raymond explained. "Please be nice to Flinders from now on."

"Just so I'm clear, what does 'be nice to Flinders' mean to you?" I asked.

"It means listen to him," Raymond said with noteworthy annoyance. "If he recommends avoiding certain people, there's a good reason for it."

"What if he's just got an issue with me being a foreigner?" I asked.

"It's not that," Raymond responded. "The owner of our business was originally a refugee from Vietnam. He's now known as the Trash King and is worth upwards of thirty million dollars. Ben Flinders has been a huge supporter of his over the years and it's been helpful for our business. Do you understand what I'm saying?"

"I think so, yes," I replied.

"I'm hoping you can learn how to fit in here," Raymond concluded.

"You and me both," I said to the skies above.

The News

When I returned home that evening Mia fell asleep early, so I sat alone on the top step amidst the stillness of the evening which resembled an apparently innocent entry point into a deeper, darker void. I gazed up at the stars which shone bright across the clear night skies. It was impossible to make sense of the galaxy, never mind the entire universe. Then I noticed a cluster of stars of roughly similar brightness which had formed a perfect circle within their tiny corner of the galaxy. Each of them shone bright individually, but their combined shining power was far greater as a cluster. The night's dark powers withered in that miniscule corner of the sky. The glow of the star cluster created a cordon sanitaire around the illustrious power of their collective.

My mobile phone shattered the starry quietude. I'd forgotten it was in my pocket. "Hello," I answered.

"Is that Mr. Watson?" a lady asked.

"It is," I responded.

"Michelle from Maleny Vets here," she said. "I'm ringing with Mia's biopsy results."

"Oh yes. Hi, Michelle," I replied.

"I'm afraid I have bad news," she stated.

My heart raced. I tried to sit down but realized I was already sitting down.

"Oh?" I said.

"That lump on Mia's back is not a heat spot as I suspected," she stated.

"What is it then?" I asked.

"It's a rare and deadly form of cancer," she half whispered.

Time stopped. Her words computed but they didn't make any sense.

"*Cancer*? How? Why?" I asked.

"We don't know how or why," she said. "Sadly, two thirds of golden retrievers suffer some form of cancer during their lives. That's the case with so many dog breeds these days."

"So when you say rare and deadly, what does that mean?" I asked.

"It's hard to say. Some dogs can live for as long as a year with it, but some only have a couple of months left," she explained. "It really comes down to how healthy they were before the diagnosis, and how the cancer is treated."

I was speechless.

"Pop into the surgery to discuss Mia's treatment options when you're ready," she concluded.

"Will do," I said as I hung up.

The expression "the world comes crashing down" had always been an abstract concept to me up until then, but in that moment my world came crashing down in the most brutal of ways. The idea of Mia being sick and not having much time left couldn't possibly be right. It was like the universe was finally admitting to me that all the good in the world was nothing but a trick of the light.

I lay down beside Mia and put my arms around her. "Everything will be OK, Mutt Dog," I whispered. "We'll do whatever is needed to make you well again."

Mia opened one of her eyes in recognition of my words before she drifted back to sleep. I joined her. I slept in that position all night despite the intense pain the hard wooden surface caused my body. In fact, I welcomed it as I felt I somehow deserved it.

When I awoke, I couldn't move at first. I had pins and needles in both my legs as my body had become one with the veranda. After some effort, I was able to disentangle myself and reanimate my limbs. As I did, a kookaburra laughed loudly which inspired the rest of its riot to join in. Their hysterical laughter was normally a wonderfully tropical way to welcome in a new day, but that morning it was as inappropriate as a bad joke at a funeral. "Shut up!" I shouted at them, but that only encouraged them more.

I remembered I was due at work that day, so I texted Raymond. "The family emergency is Mia. She's really sick and needs looking after. Is it OK with you if I work for only a couple of days a week from now on?"

Raymond texted back a few minutes later. "That's OK, Will. She's a special dog. I'll put you down for Tuesday and Thursday shifts from now on."

"I appreciate it," I texted in response.

Everyone knows the last thing you should do amidst a medical emergency is to google about the disease. I ignored that advice like a fool. I consulted doctor google for hours about the type of cancer Mia had, the treatment options, the prognosis, and everything in between. Within minutes, I learnt it was regarded as a death sentence, and the best thing owners could do was to slow down the spread of the cancer and ensure their dogs were as comfortable as possible as the inevitable approached. An array of emotions congregated within me as I digested the awful facts google was sprouting. Shock and disappointment led the way, followed by anger and distress, which in turn led to an overwhelming feeling of sadness.

Once I ran out of tears, I drove Mia to her favorite beach at Mudjimba. I couldn't think of anything I wanted to do more than watch her enjoying herself at the beach as though she had all the time in the world. And she didn't disappoint. Mia charged along the entrance pathway before she slid onto the beach's silky sands on her side. She then jumped into the air and sprinted in ever decreasing circles while growling with excitement. It was as though she was preprogrammed for joy, no matter what was happening. I let myself become lost in her joy.

A few minutes later, Mia noticed me watching her. She stopped rolling, trotted over, and sat down beside me. The two of us then watched the ocean like explorers contemplating a new frontier. The whitewash of the water frothed along the tops of the waves like white horses charging toward a goal they'd long wanted but had somehow forgotten about. Mia leant her body into mine like she did whenever she was worried about me. Our bodies warmed each other in the cool breeze. We sat like that for hours.

Buying Time

Mia and I visited the vet again the next morning. In contrast to our first visit, the waiting room was vacant when we arrived.

"Where are the squatters?" I asked the girl behind reception.

"We complained to the village association about those lowlifes," she responded as she shook her head. "In response, they reopened the library for that first hour of the day as they wanted."

"So the squatters are the clever ones then," I said.

"You could say that," she answered. "But we also benefitted."

"How so?" I asked.

"A local dog breeder popped in to showcase her latest border collie puppy litter to them one morning," she replied. "Would you believe she sold the entire litter to those squatters, so they'll be our clients for many years to come. They started out as fake clients, but they ended up as real ones."

"That sounds like an inspiring business strategy," I said.

Michelle the vet walked over to me and gave me a warm hug. "I'm so sorry about Mia. What a nightmare."

"We're not giving up yet," I replied as I wiped a rogue tear away.

Michelle escorted us to her room, but Mia remained as reluctant as ever to follow. Once again, I had to drag her there. Before she could hide under a chair, Michelle jumped forward to peruse her lump.

"How can we fight this?" I asked.

"The cold hard truth is it comes down to economics," Michelle explained. "Have you got pet insurance?"

"No," I admitted, kicking myself on the inside.

"Right. Well, the most powerful treatment I can recommend is vitamin C therapy combined with some Chinese herbal remedies," she explained. "The combined results are better than from chemotherapy, and it's a regenerative strategy rather than one which weakens the dog's immune system."

"Sold," I said. "Count us in for that."

"The bad news is this treatment costs five hundred dollars and a vet visit each week," Michelle explained.

"Sold again," I said. "I'll figure the money out even if I have to sell a kidney. Just save Mia, please, Michelle."

"Will, there's something important you must understand," Michelle continued. "No one and no treatment can save Mia at this point. We're just trying to buy her some time along with a decent quality of life."

"Well, let's buy her a full life," I replied. "She's only eight years old, so I reckon she's due another seven good years."

"That's unrealistic, I'm afraid," she said.

Mia gazed up at Michelle with sad eyes which understood exactly what was happening.

"If only Mia could tell us what she wants and needs at this point," I added.

"I'd like to think we vets know more about how to improve dogs' wellbeing than any dog could," Michelle stated matter-of-factly.

Mia gave her a pointed look which suggested she didn't agree.

As we walked home, I contemplated Michelle's words. Did we know more than dogs about dogs? Or anything for that matter? Why did so many humans believe they knew so much about so many things? I was certain Mia knew more than most humans, including me, about her own life—probably mine as well.

When we returned home, I sat down at my laptop and googled "talking with dogs." There was a surprisingly long list of articles on the subject. Some people believed they could hear their dogs' thoughts when they meditated. Others believed their dogs could communicate with them in a range of languages when they were presented with alphabet buttons they could push with their paws. There was even a YouTube video of a woman asking her dog what he thought of space travel. He responded by spelling out the word "ESCAPISM" with his paws. I laughed out loud. However, I couldn't shake the nagging feeling that most of those people were blissfully delusional for the simple reason they wanted so desperately to hear their dogs talk. They were willing an illusion to become a truth despite the evidence to the contrary. Not that there was anything wrong with that—I'd done exactly the same thing throughout my seven-year relationship with Heidi. However, it was time I dug deeper, beyond the illusions.

As I continued to scroll, I came across a website called The Pet Communicator. The business description read: "I communicate with dead pets. I can always prove it to owners by providing answers from their pets that only their pets can provide. Money back guarantee." In the murky world of pet communicators, it was as confident a statement as

I'd come across. In addition, the long list of google reviews for The Pet Communicator's services were overwhelmingly positive. One lady had written: "Miranda Minsky is a force of nature. She has been speaking with my German shepherd Max for a few weeks now. Some people will consider me crazy for believing her, but I know it's true because Max communicated things to Miranda only he could know. For example, he told Miranda where he'd hidden one of my old slippers a few years ago. Sure enough, when I searched for it, there it was. He also confessed to Miranda that the reason he'd hidden the slipper was because he was so embarrassed when he'd realized he'd chewed it beyond the point of oblivion. He didn't want me to be upset with him when I found it. I cried when I heard that. Miranda is a pet communication genius." I kept scrolling and only found one negative review: "Miranda Minsky is a fraud and a con artist who convinces innocent people she can talk with their pets knowing full well how vulnerable they are. Don't trust her." I decided to ignore that one because it didn't include any details and sounded more like a personal vendetta.

My interest in The Pet Communicator was officially piqued. However, there was the not insignificant problem that she only conversed with dead pets. Regardless, I decided to email Miranda Minsky that afternoon to enquire about her services.

Dear Ms. Minsky,

I understand you specialize in talking with dead pets. What a unique profession.

I'm writing to request your help to communicate with my dog Mia who is still living. Mia has been diagnosed with a deadly form of cancer so I'm unsure how much time I have left with her. However, she has important things to tell me, now, while she's alive. I can feel it.

Could you by any chance adapt your services to include working with one living dog? Mia's got the most beautiful soul, so I'm sure you'll enjoy working with her.

I look forward to hearing from you.

Sincerely,
Will Watson

When I went to bed that night, I let Mia sleep next to me. Up until then, the bed had been out of bounds to her, but I happily changed the rules from then on. It was a comfort to have her lying beside me, although the one aspect I found challenging was sleeping through her erratic snoring. That night, her snoring escalated from slow and steady to scared and frenzied in the middle of the night, causing me to awaken. I comforted her until she settled back to sleep.

Since I was awake anyway, I walked into the kitchen for a glass of water. While I was drinking, I heard something or someone walking on the front veranda. Inexplicably, it sounded like a small child was prancing around on the timber floorboards wearing high heels. With my heart racing, I tiptoed over to the fly screen door and looked around outside. As I did, the sound stopped. Then it started again a minute later. This time, it was moving away from the screen door. I located a torch in the top kitchen drawer, took a deep breath, and marched out onto the veranda to investigate who was there.

By then, the high-heeled intruder was on the other side of the house, so I tiptoed around the veranda like a graceless Bond actor in need of training. As I rounded the corner, I let go of the tiptoeing charade, turned on the torch, and lunged at whoever the hell was on the veranda. At first, the bright light of the torch blinded me so I couldn't see much. Once my eyes adjusted, I discovered a bush turkey, an ugly black bird with a bright red head, perched on one of the veranda's wooden posts. It held my gaze for a few long seconds before it half flew, half fell down to the ground below and scuttled off into the darkness from whence it came.

"Get out of here, you mean-hearted bastard!" I screamed into the black night with more volume than the moment required.

Platypus Builders

The weight of the situation hit me the next morning. Mia was sick and may not have much time left. It was a catastrophe on a scale I couldn't fathom. Yet the smiley, bright-eyed dog who awoke beside me jumped down from the bed and charged outside for her morning roll as though it was just another day in paradise. The other realization which hit home was my urgent need to generate more income to pay for Mia's treatment. So I wrote out a list of my income-generating options:

1. Find another job
2. Go back to trash dashing five days a week
3. Pray

I wondered if option one, finding another job, was viable. After all, there was a large population of people in the Sunshine Coast region who needed stuff done. Surely there was another job out there for me if I was to open my mind. If you can dream it, you can do it, and all that. However, the only other advertised jobs I could find were for aged care assistants, and they all required extensive experience, qualifications, and either an Australian passport or a skilled migrant visa. Next.

Then there was option two, full-time trash dashing. Despite a tough start, I was getting used to life as a trash dasher. Yes, the clients could be rude, and I was working for a company associated with Ben Flinders, who reminded me of a young Hitler. However, it was strangely satisfying to return truck number thirteen back to the depot empty and intact at the end of each shift. And if the company was open to sponsoring me, the job offered me the potential to upgrade my visa to a skilled migrant visa after my working holiday visa expired in six months. I wondered if Raymond would put in a good word for me with senior management. As I contemplated full-time trash dashing, Mia half opened a red eye which she directed at me. She looked exhausted. There was the answer. Regardless of my visa challenges, I couldn't trash dash five days a week while I was caring for her. It was unfair to expect Mia to sit in the truck all week when she was feeling so sick.

So option three it was, praying. I'd travelled all the way around the world in search of home, and after a few short weeks in Australia, praying was all I had left. There was a lot I needed to pray for. I had to pray for enough income to pay for Mia's treatment. I had to pray I could find a way to feel at home in Australia. I had to pray the community wasn't involved in anything sinister. And the big one: I had to pray for more time with the one creature I loved most in this world. The last time I prayed was during a midnight mass church service last Christmas in York. Heidi's family had a tradition of attending their local church each Christmas Eve. They'd instructed Heidi and me to join them that year wearing formal attire, which implied we view religion as an exam of sorts. Heidi didn't blink an eye, but I felt claustrophobic the second my tie was done up. Reverend Povey, their local church minister, was a stern man with a deep frown line which split his forehead like lightning. He lectured the room about all the bad things that would happen to us if we didn't follow the advice littered throughout his sermon. As he whacked the pulpit to reinforce his points, he made the idea of smiling seem sacrilegious. And whenever he called upon the congregation to pray, I couldn't focus on a single word he said because his angry voice hurt my ears.

I clearly had a lot to learn about praying. In the meantime, I decided to try speaking my mind. “God, hi. It’s been a while. I hope you’re well. As I’m sure you’re aware, here on planet Earth things aren’t going great for Will Watson or my beloved dog Mia. Mia’s really sick ...”

My praying attempt came to a grinding halt as some uninvited tears erupted from my eyes. As I wiped them away, my laptop made a loud pinging sound to signal an email had arrived. I let it distract me from the all-too-challenging job at hand. The incoming email was a response from Miranda Minsky, the Pet Communicator.

> Dear Mr. Watson,
>
> I’m flattered you’d consider me qualified to communicate with your living dog. However, living dog communication is very different from talking with dead dogs. As an ethical pet communicator, all I can recommend is that you take your business elsewhere. My thoughts are with you and Mia during this difficult time.
>
> Sincerely,
> Miranda

I slammed my laptop shut. Something inside me had believed Miranda Minsky was the answer to something. However, she'd revealed herself to be just another waste of time. Of course, it wasn't her fault. I was the fool for allowing an inanimate website to create a favorable impression based solely on what I needed from it. Like so many billions of human sheep, I'd been susceptible to mercurial manipulation by the army of unscrupulous marketeers who were pulling the digital world's strings. I made a mental note never to use the internet again.

"Mutt Dog, let's go for a walk," I said.

Within seconds, Mia was by my side ready for action.

The two of us walked along the pathway connecting with the Serenity Trail, which was thankfully devoid of tricky humans that day. As we approached the platypus viewing platform, a crowd of people were congregating at the edge of the platform staring at the water below. True to form, the Whisperer was whispering to them while he pointed enthusiastically at the water. Mia pulled me in their direction so we could listen in.

"After extreme rain like we've experienced in recent months, the platypus will often have to rebuild its home," explained the Whisperer full of excitement. "They often lose everything and are faced with having to start all over again."

"They're brave little critters, aren't they!" exclaimed a loud American lady in the group.

"Brave they are," agreed the Whisperer. "But they're also pragmatic. You see, if you're a platypus and you've lost your home, your partner, even your bearings, what are you but lost? Like many animals, platypuses have this inbuilt ability to quickly accept their reality when they're lost. And at the very moment they do, everything starts making sense to them again. Would you believe I've watched platypuses rebuild their elaborate homes in only a day? And their new homes are usually much better than the homes which were destroyed by the rain. That's progress with a capital P in platypus terms. However, this miracle only ever happens after they lose absolutely everything and are forced to resurrect their lives from nothing."

"Maybe I should go to platypus school," said the same American lady with less volume.

One of the platypuses suddenly popped its head above the water and gazed around as though it was searching for something or someone. I wondered if it had heard the American lady's words, but it appeared to settle its gaze on Mia and me. Mia froze to the spot when she noticed we had the platypus's attention. After maintaining eye contact with Mia for a few seconds, the platypus dove back underwater leaving nothing but a ripple to remember it by.

"Come on, girl," I said.

Mia and I continued onward while the crowd remained fixated on the water below.

When we returned home, I reopened my laptop to reply to Miranda Minsky's email.

> Dear Miranda,
>
> A wise man once advised me we can rebuild our lives even stronger than they were from amidst the chaos of our disintegrating reality, or words to that effect. I'm emailing you from within the chaos, so I hope he's right. It's all I've got at this point.
>
> I understand why you'd want to decline my request. It makes sense. You're a dead dog specialist, whereas my dog is alive and I want her to stay that way. But what if there's an opportunity here amidst the chaos for both of us? What if your unique skill set means you can in fact speak with living dogs as well as dead ones? Wouldn't discovering that superpower be reciprocity in all

its glory? I hope I've spelled reciprocity correctly. It was always my alphabetical archnemesis at school.

Sincerely,
Will

Dark Waters

The next morning, I followed Mia out into the garden where she was engaging in her morning roll. Once she'd finished, she ran over to the garden shed and sat expectantly in front of it. I opened the door and entered the shed. It was a pigsty inside. There were piles of rusty garden tools and old sporting equipment, masses of unidentifiable rubbish, and a python by the name of Monty asleep on one of the rafters.

"You alright, Monty?" I asked as I stood on tippy toes so I could stroke his tail.

Monty raised his head, gave me an inquisitive look, then resumed his slumber like the lord of the manor. I left him to it and located what I was looking for—an ancient stand-up paddleboard leaning against the wall.

"You know how we had no plans today, girl?" I said to Mia who was watching from the doorway.

"Well, that's all changed. It's time we acquainted ourselves with this mysterious Lake Baroon, which has caused so much angst. Besides, I know you love an adventure."

Mia's ears pricked up with interest. I carried the paddleboard out of the shed and wedged it into one of the car's back windows through to the front passenger seat. Three feet of the board still hung outside the window, but I'd learnt that the local drivers did whatever the hell they wanted, so I concluded the overhanging paddleboard wouldn't be a problem. I opened the car's other back door and Mia jumped in. I remembered I'd need a paddle, so I charged back to the shed where I located an old wooden paddle behind the door. Monty half opened a lazy eye as I walked back out of the shed.

Within seconds of driving away, a brand-new black Range Rover emerged out of nowhere in my rear vision mirror. Of course. Ben Flinders. I drove on regardless, but he repeatedly honked his horn while he held up his hand up like an angry traffic controller. Remembering Raymond's advice about the importance of being nice to Flinders, I stopped the car on the side of the road and got out. He parked up next to me and wound down his window to ask, "What's that hanging out of your ass, Watson?"

I pretended to check my bottom for protruding objects. "I can't see anything, I'm afraid, but I'd say you know more about asses than I do," I answered without planning to push his buttons.

"Listen, Watson, I've had enough of your insolence," Flinders said as he got out of his car and walked over to the paddleboard, which he peered at with disdain. He pulled his mobile out of his pocket and held it up to take a photo of the paddleboard, presumably to be used as evidence to convict me with.

However, before Flinders could take the photo, an old man on a bicycle hurtled toward him with loud music blaring from his stereo. I recognized him as the same old man who'd nearly run me over a few days earlier, and he was as oblivious to humans as ever. The song playing on his stereo was an old song with a chorus which had always made me laugh as a child: "What's-a matter you? Hey! Gotta no respect? Shaddap-a you face!" With that upbeat music egging him on, the old man cycled straight at Ben Flinders with a determined grimace on his face. Ben Flinders froze to the spot like a drunk rabbit in the midst of a bender. A collision was inevitable. Ben Flinders obviously concurred as a large wet patch emerged uninvited on the front of his trousers. However, just before the inevitable collision, the old man swerved to avoid Flinders while shouting, "Out of the way, peck!" He missed him by inches before he continued on his way with the words "Ah shaddap-a you face!" dancing through the air toward the ears of a urine-soaked Ben Flinders.

"What the hell!" Flinders exclaimed as though a carrot had just been inserted somewhere less than comfortable.

"I only work here," I replied.

"You'll keep, Watson," he said as he jumped back into his car and sped off in pursuit of an eighty-year-old, music-loving cyclist.

Relishing our freedom, I drove the short distance to Lake Baroon, which was located at the bottom of a steep hill lined by thick rainforest. It was a pleasant surprise to discover a glorious lake glistening in the sunlight since the only words I'd heard spoken of it were complaints about its sordid origins. I unloaded the paddleboard from the car and carried it down to the water along a concrete access ramp. Mia followed without enthusiasm. She'd always had a minor phobia of water as a puppy which re-emerged whenever we approached strange new bodies of water she wasn't acquainted with. Unperturbed, I placed the paddleboard onto the water's surface. "On you get, girl," I said.

Mia remained glued to the spot with resolute determination on her face.

"We'll be fine, Mutt Dog. Besides, I can't leave you here all by yourself," I explained.

Once I'd picked Mia up and positioned her on the front of the paddleboard, I crawled aboard myself and pushed away from the shore. Mia's legs wobbled as she stared at the retreating shoreline while she gave me her best "I'm not happy with you" look. After paddling a few strokes on my knees, I stood up on the paddleboard. Initially, I imitated Mia's shaky leg routine which caused the paddleboard to rock from side to side without a semblance of stability. It was only when I took a deep breath and relaxed into the flow that I gained a degree of control. As I paddled away from shore, the sheer size of the lake became apparent. It was enormous. It also became clear that we were the only ones who were either brave enough or foolish enough to be paddling across its inexplicably dark waters.

The local wildlife was on display everywhere we turned. There were inquisitive pelicans lining its shoreline, engaged in conversation. There were eagles perched in the trees alongside the lake who were observing Mia and me as though they were considering whether we were prey-worthy. There were joyful little fish leaping out of the water all around us. And there was a tributary up ahead homing a forest of dead eucalyptus trees standing within the water, showcasing the lake's origins as a green, forested valley before it was flooded. While

I paddled through this Dead Tree Alley, as I named it, the ghostly arms of the deceased trees swayed in the breeze creating a high-pitched creaking sound which suggested they may break off at any moment. The risk of being crushed to death by a falling branch inspired me to speed up.

As I paddled, I noticed Mia was staring at the nearby shoreline, so I diverted us toward the rock-strewn beach she was focused on. When we hit the shore, I jumped off the paddleboard and landed on the rocky beach. Mia leapt off the paddleboard just after me, landing with a yelp half in, half out the water. Without missing a beat, she shook the water from her coat and sprinted off into the dense bushland lining the beach area. Within seconds, she was out of sight. The dead trees creaked their displeasure for all to hear.

"Mutt Dog!" I called out.

However, Mia didn't return from the bush. It was unusual as she was normally so obedient. With fear rising within me, I jogged up the beach and followed Mia's pathway into the bush. At first, I couldn't find her amidst the endless rows of tall gray eucalyptus trees, so I weaved my way deeper into the leafy world. Eventually, I found her about a hundred yards into the bushland, sitting on the ground staring up at a nearby eucalyptus tree.

"What is it, girl?" I asked as I approached.

Mia's gaze remained fixated on the tree, so I stepped closer to investigate. Around four feet up the side of the tree, I discovered some writing engraved on its side: "Beneath this lake lies the sordid truth."

"Let's get out of here *now*, Mutt Dog!" I exclaimed as I experienced an overwhelming feeling that we were in trouble.

Mia understood I wasn't joking. She ran with me back to the lake where I helped her aboard the paddleboard. Then I paddled as fast as I could back to the other side of the lake where the car was parked. As I paddled, I was terrified the paddleboard wouldn't remain afloat all the way across the lake's dark waters. The idea of falling into the inexplicable darkness below seemed to imply a certain death sentence. With stress permeating throughout my body, I tried to avoid looking directly into the water, which was noticeably blacker than on the outward journey. *Why was the water so dark?* I wondered.

Trash Truths

That afternoon, as I contemplated what lay beneath Lake Baroon from the safety of home, my phone pinged, signalling an email had arrived. I was surprised there was anyone in the world thinking of me. Against the odds, it was Miranda Minsky emailing back.

> Dear Mr. Watson,
>
> You're right.
>
> I've been helping dead pets for such a long time, you see. I have no idea whether I can help living pets and I've been content to leave it at that. However, your honest email made me realize I'm stuck in a rut of sorts.

> So I've changed my mind. I'm willing to experiment with your living pet. If you are happy for me to trial my skills on Mia, I'd be grateful to you. I couldn't accept payment, of course. And I propose we both have the right to end this project at any given moment. If you feel it's not helping, just tell me.
>
> If that's agreeable to you, I'll pop up the mountain to meet you and Mia. I only live in Maroochydore so that's easy. If you've changed your mind, I understand.
>
> Sincerely,
> Miranda

I wrote straight back.

> Dear Miranda,
>
> I haven't changed my mind. Do you have time to meet us tomorrow?
>
> Will

Miranda Minsky responded a few minutes later.

I can make that work, Will. Please send me your address. I'll be there at nine o'clock in the morning.

Before I could celebrate whatever Miranda Minsky was bringing into our lives, there was a knock at the door. I wondered if Miranda Minsky had telepathically transported herself up the mountain in response to my email, but I opened the front door to find Jude standing there, distressed.

"What's wrong?" I asked.

"I was just nearly run over by Ben bloody Flinders in his Range bloody Rover!" Jude exclaimed. "He saw me crossing the road and accelerated toward me. I had to leap out of the way to avoid being hit and probably killed."

"Oh my god! Are you alright?" I asked.

"I'm just furious," Jude replied. "The guy has a vendetta against me and I don't know why. Throw into the mix the fact he's a psychopath and it makes for an unpleasant situation."

"He needs to be locked up," I said.

"If Ben Flinders wasn't viewed as a 'person of influence' in Maleny, he'd have been incarcerated by now," Jude stated. "I'm sure New Zealand doesn't have anyone as evil as him living there."

"I reckon New Zealand probably has a Ben Flinders or two within their ranks just to ensure the kind-hearted people living there have a way to learn what they don't want to be like," I said.

"Poor bastards," Jude responded.

"Fancy a beer?" I asked.

"I'd kill for one," Jude said.

Jude sat down on the sofa while I fetched two beers from the fridge.

"How's the patient?" Jude asked as she stroked Mia.

"She's doing well, thanks," I answered. "I'm just working out how to pay for her treatment. The rubbish collection work isn't generating enough cash to make ends meet, and I can't find an alternative job I'm qualified to do."

"It isn't fair," Jude stated. "You've flown all the way around the world to start a new life and here you are being treated like a leper."

"I now understand how the convicts felt," I replied. "But I've started wondering whether I've ended up where I was always meant to be."

"How so?" Jude asked.

"Maybe I was never worthy of my dreams. My old boss sure didn't think so," I said. "Maybe I was always destined to be cleaning up other peoples' messes as penance for not cleaning up my own."

"I don't believe that, Will, and I don't think you do either," Jude replied. "Many successful people have worked as trash collectors to generate cash flow while their dreams were in transit. Did I mention Wolf collected trash for a few years prior to his possum-hunting days? He worked for a mob called Holy Crap Rubbish Removals."

"Small world! That's who I'm working for," I said.

"Too small a world," Jude stated. "Is Raymond still managing the team there?"

"He is," I said.

"And are the trash dashers still returning their trucks empty and intact without explaining what they did with the rubbish?" Jude asked.

"They are! Do you know what they do with it?" I asked.

"Wolf's not one to let sleeping dogs lie. He solved that mystery while he was working there," Jude responded.

"What did he discover?" I asked, full of interest.

"Well, one day, he followed one of the loaded trash trucks en route back to the depot," Jude explained. "Wolf said the trash dasher parked his truck on a quiet residential street near the depot. Then he unloaded all the trash in his truck onto the street in front of some poor sod's house before driving off."

"What a cunning plan," I said.

"That's one word for it," Jude replied. "Of course, you know who the council called to remove that same trash again. Wolf said the company's management viewed each and every piece of rubbish as a yield generator to be moved between different locations."

"I suspected some of the trash dashers weren't playing with a straight bat," I stated.

"Wolf believed it was coming from the top," Jude continued.

"Really? From Raymond?" I asked, surprised.

"No, from the king of trash himself, Dũng Heap," Jude answered.

I laughed. "Dung Heap? Is that his real name?"

"Yes. It's spelt with a curly symbol above the u," Jude explained. "Dũng moved here from Vietnam many years ago. The feedback he received from each and every small-minded local he met was that with a name like his, he was made for trash collection. Those thoughtless comments were made tongue-in-cheek, but he took them to heart. He's made a fortune because he took action when the local idiots tried to make fun of him."

"And Wolf thinks this Dũng Heap is to blame for the company's unethical business practices?" I asked.

"Yes—or at least, Wolf believes he knowingly turns a blind eye to ensure he maximizes his profits," Jude responded.

"What a shame Dũng has chosen money over doing the right thing," I said.

"We said the same thing at first," Jude stated. "But then we realized he's just one of billions of people doing the same thing. That's the way the system works, isn't it? It takes an unusually strong person to do the right thing when doing the right thing may cost them otherwise easy money."

"So what did Wolf do with his rubbish collections when he was a trash dasher?" I asked.

"Funny you should ask," Jude replied. "He turned the challenge into an opportunity, and I loved him all the more for it."

"Go on," I said with growing interest.

"Wolf realized there was residual value in the items he collected," Jude responded. "He's mighty handy in his man shed, so he brought the collected rubbish home at the end of each shift. He then recycled the items into things people actually wanted and sold them back to the public for a profit. Sometimes he even sold the recycled items back to the same people who'd once paid him to remove them. In a country where no one recycles a bloody thing, it was innovation in all its glory."

"What a genius!" I exclaimed. "What sort of things did he make?"

"Well, you need to understand that Wolf is a true artist," Jude replied. "Some of the things he creates are hard to understand at the time he makes them, but they start to make sense much later on. For example, he once integrated a bunch of electrical engines and wires to build a high-tech massage gun. It gave much deeper massages than anything available on the market at the time. It sure was a sight to behold. It looked like a *Star Wars* gun from the eighties."

"Did it work?" I asked.

"In the prototesting stage, it worked beautifully," said Jude.

"And after prototesting?" I asked.

"Well, what happened to O'Hara was really unlucky," Jude replied.

"Grumpy O'Hara, the one who only cares about his cows?" I asked.

"Yes. O'Hara bought the massage gun from Wolf to help with his bad back," Jude explained.

"What happened?" I asked.

"The story I heard was that O'Hara asked his wife to try it out on him as soon as he got it home," Jude replied. "The problem was she turned the massage gun straight onto its highest setting. Apparently, O'Hara's body vibrated so violently, half his teeth dropped out."

"That's not ideal," I responded as a picture emerged in my mind of O'Hara's teeth dropping out as he grazed on his lush green grass alongside his precious cows.

"Come to think of it, that's when he started liking his cows more than humans," Jude said.

"That makes a lot more sense now," I replied.

"But that incident was most unusual," Jude stated. "Most of Wolf's creations were treasured by the people who bought them."

"I love this recycling idea," I said. "Being a park ranger was always about helping the environment, but I'm wondering if recycling may be even more fruitful on that front. Imagine how many trees could be saved."

"Here's an idea then," Jude added. "Wolf's sitting at home twiddling his fingers with time on his hands. Did I mention he's killed all the possums? So he'd love it if you brought all the rubbish you collect around to our place at the end of your shifts. Wolf can then transform them into beautiful and useful things to be sold, and the two of you can split the profits. There may even be enough in it to pay for Mia's treatment."

"Shall I speak with Wolf directly about it?" I asked with excitement.

"Nah," Jude responded. "Wolf's not a talker. He prefers it when I do the thinking and talking for him. He'll love this idea because I love it. When I say he's in, he's in."

"Are you sure Wolf would want to go into business with someone he's never met?" I asked.

"Wolf's a possum hunter, he's not picky," Jude replied.

Miranda Minsky

The next morning, at the second the clock changed from one minute before nine to nine o'clock, there were three gentle knocks at the door. They were so quiet that I wondered if I was imagining them.

When I opened the door I found a petite, purple-haired woman wearing a multi-colored ensemble of mismatched clothes standing on my doorstep. Her bright-pink, fluffy top clashed in the most awful of ways with her brown overalls and yellow Doc Martens boots. And her deep purple hair cascaded onto her shoulders in a tidal wave of uniqueness. I had an overwhelming desire to put on a pair of sunglasses in her presence. She smiled warmly and said, "Will?"

"That's me," I said. "Miranda?"

"That's my earthly name, yes," she replied.

"Come on in," I said as I opened the door.

Mia charged over the moment Miranda Minsky entered our home. After a few welcoming licks, she lay on her back at Miranda's feet ready for tummy stroking. It was a first. I'd never seen her do that with anyone except me before. Miranda bent down to stroke Mia's tummy as though she knew her already. "What a beautiful girl you are, Mia—both inside and out," she said.

"Can I get you a coffee, Miranda?" I asked.

"Yes, please," she replied.

"I'll meet you on the sofa," I said as though Miranda Minsky already knew where the sofa was.

"See you there," she responded.

By the time I'd made the coffee, Miranda was seated on the sofa, notebook and pen in hand. She put on a pair of sharp-rimmed blue glasses which clashed with her purple hair, her clothes, the sofa, and everything else. I sat down beside her, while Mia lay at our feet.

"Thanks for making an exception to meet us, Miranda," I said. "It means a lot."

"Hold that thought until you've gotten to know me," she replied. "I'm not everyone's cup of tea, or coffee for that matter, and I'm officially driving in the dark here. I've never communicated with a living dog before. Never. So let's both assume I'm an idiot, and hopefully at least one of us will be pleasantly surprised."

"I can do that," I said as I noticed Miranda Minsky was wearing a necklace with the word "Believer" written in the middle of a kaleidoscope pattern.

"I like your necklace," I said. "Can I ask what you believe in?"

"I believe in all the things most humans can't see," she stated. "That's where the real fun starts."

Mia nodded as if to reinforce Miranda's point.

"So how's the dead dog communication business these days?" I asked.

"It's thriving," she replied. "So many humans need help."

"You mean they need help in communicating with their deceased dogs?" I asked.

"So they tell me," Miranda responded with a shrug of her shoulders. "Nothing is what it seems in this world."

"I'm learning that," I said.

"Now, for me to even take a stab at helping you," Miranda said, "I need more information. But not the type of information you'll be used to being asked about. I'm going to have to ask you some strange questions, really strange questions. Are you OK with that?"

"I'm actually more interested now," I replied.

"Are you ready, then?" Miranda asked as she eyed me up and down as though she was uncertain if I'd ever be ready.

"Let's do this," I replied.

"OK. First question: does Mia ever seem to know exactly what you're thinking?" she asked.

"Often," I responded.

"Good," Miranda said as she made notes in a language which didn't look like English. "Next question: does Mia ever seem to know things you wouldn't expect her to know about the world in general?"

"Often," I replied.

"So far, so good. But it's the next question that really matters," Miranda stated.

I shifted forward to the edge of my seat.

"When Mia knows what you're thinking, or knows things she shouldn't know, does it tend to happen in a particular location, or around certain people, or in any other noteworthy situation?" Miranda asked with gravity.

"I don't think so, no," I responded after some thought.

"Oh bother," Miranda replied. "That's less than useful, isn't it?"

"Sorry," I said.

"It's OK. There are different pathways we can take," Miranda replied. "Does Mia enjoy rolling?"

"She loves it!" I exclaimed.

Miranda stood up off the sofa and lay down on the carpet next to Mia. "Does she roll like this?"

she asked as she wiggled her bum from side to side like she was disco dancing. "Or like this?" she asked as she appeared to be escaping a flea infestation colonizing her body. "Or like this?" she asked as she lay almost stationery apart from her head which bobbed from side to side as though she was listening to R&B music through headphones.

"It's the first one," I stated.

"Great!" Miranda exclaimed as she jumped back up and returned to the sofa. "That means she's a joy exhibitor of the first order. It also means we have a chance, a teeny-weeny, miniscule chance, of communicating with her when she's ready."

"When she's ready?" I asked.

"I can help build the telephone but only Mia has the twenty cents we need to start the conversation," Miranda said.

"It actually costs fifty cents for phone calls these days," I added.

"I'm going to have to start charging more," Miranda responded with a sad shake of her head.

"I thought you weren't charging for this job," I said.

"Exactly! It's time I upped my rates," Miranda replied as she wrote more illegible notes on her pad. "I'll be back when we have the information we need to take the next step. In the interim, here's what I need you to do."

"Go on," I said.

"Every time Mia seems to know what you're thinking, or anything else that's hard to explain with human words. I want you to email me when and where it happened, as well as anything else that comes to mind," Miranda explained. "Include all details, no matter how strange. In fact, the stranger the better. We need to capture data, data, and more data. Once we're swimming in the data, I'll have figure out what on earth to do with it. Till next time."

Without another word, Miranda Minsky gave Mia a final belly stroke, then she marched back out the front door.

"Thank you!" I called at the closing door, but she was already gone. Miranda Minsky had entered our lives in all her glory.

Help From Above

The next morning, I arrived earlier than usual at the trash depot so I could thank Raymond for providing me with the part-time roster. When Mia and I arrived at his make-do office, he was typing away at his computer. "Morning, Will. Morning, Mia," he said when he saw us. "How is she, the poor thing?"

"She's her usual buoyant self," I replied. "We just need to keep it that way."

"I'm glad you're here, Will. I want to introduce you to someone," Raymond stated as he picked up his mobile and dialled a number.

"He's here now," Raymond explained to whoever was on the line. "See you in a minute."

"If this is about Ben Flinders, in my defence I was only driving down the road to the local lake. My hire car was too small for the paddleboard," I explained.

"I don't know anything about that, so let's keep it that way," Raymond said. "This is about business. Dũng Heap, the big business owner, wants to meet you."

"Really?" I asked, suddenly nervous.

"Dũng enjoys getting to know his staff. He was keen to meet you after I told him about your challenges with Mia's health," Raymond explained. "Here he is now."

A brand-new Ferrari pulled up outside the reception shed, and a short, well-dressed man with slicked-back hair emerged from inside the vehicle. He walked over to the shed with a confident swagger. When he entered the room, he removed his sunglasses to reveal a boyish face and a beaming smile.

"Dũng!" exclaimed Raymond as though he was in the presence of royalty. "Thanks for popping by."

"Good to see you, Raymond. You must be Will Watson," he said as stepped forward and firmly shook my hand.

"Nice to meet you, Dũng," I replied.

"I must say I know your story well," he said.

"Thanks for your interest, Dũng. I'm going to do everything I can to help Mia recover," I replied.

"I meant *your* story, Will Watson. The one you're starring in," he continued. "It's one of the oldest stories the world has ever known."

"Which story is that, Dũng?" I asked, perplexed.

"The story in which you arrived in this great southern land with nothing but the shirt on your back and the mask of a smile on your face, all the while holding tight to the dreams you believed would come true," Dũng Heap responded with a knowing nod.

"I suppose I did," I replied.

"However, nothing has turned out as you'd hoped, has it?" he continued. "You've started to believe the system is rigged against you, while everyone else is finding life as breezy as a seaside picnic."

"Now you mention it..." I started.

But Dũng Heap was on a roll. "I know your story because it's my story too, Will Watson. I arrived here from Vietnam with nothing, just like you. And look at me now." He stood taller and breathed deeper to illustrate his point.

"You're looking well," I responded, unsure which particular compliment Dũng Heap was fishing for.

"No, I mean just look at me now," Dũng Heap reiterated. "I'm a wealthy man who has risen from the bottom of the pile to the top. Can you even see me up here from where you're standing?"

Dũng Heap was losing his charming vibe all of a sudden.

"I'm doing my best to," I replied.

He looked me up and down as if to assess my likelihood of forever remaining a bottom dweller at the base of the heap he'd so successfully conquered. "I'll tell you what I'm going to do, Will Watson. I'm going to help you. No one helped me when I had nothing, but I'm a big enough man to know it's the right thing to do. Just look at the state of you and your dog."

I wondered if Dũng Heap was after an Academy Award nomination, but I chose to remain silent.

"So here's what I'm going to do for you," he continued. "I'm going lend you truck number thirteen on a personal basis. That way, you can return your hire car and save all those pesky fees."

Dũng Heap paused to let his offer sink in. Before I could thank him, he was off again. "My generosity doesn't stop there, Will Watson. I'm also going to pay you triple rates from now on to help with paying for your dog's cancer treatment."

I nearly fell over when I heard that. Dũng Heap stopped talking for a moment to gauge my response.

"I can't believe it!" I exclaimed. "Thank you! What a beautiful gesture."

"It is," Dũng Heap agreed as he carefully considered his next words. "There's just one thing I ask in return."

"Anything," I said like a fool.

"I need you to promise me you'll respect and support Ben Flinders and the village association," he explained with a tinge of sadness. "They're more important to the success of this business than you may realize."

Dũng Heap stepped closer, as though he was peering at me through a large magnifying glass. "If you can do what I say, Will Watson, I'm confident we'll be able to sponsor the skilled migrant visa you need to stay in Australia longer term. You see, I understand your plight."

"Of course, Dũng, I can do that," I replied, ignoring the stress rising within me.

"I know you'll do the right thing, Will Watson," he said. "Now, gentlemen, I must leave you to it. I have mountains to climb."

Dũng Heap shook Raymond's hand and nodded at both of us before he turned and swaggered back to his Ferrari. Then he sped off.

"I'm glad you got to meet the great man in person," Raymond stated. "He has a way with people, doesn't he?"

"He certainly has a way about him," I replied.

"Will, this morning's training is on pronunciation. You're already at the top of a mediocre class on that front," Raymond explained. "So you can get started with today's job when you're ready."

“Thanks, I think,” I responded as I walked out of Raymond’s office.

The rest of the trash dashers were congregating outside the shed, chatting amongst themselves.

“Hawaiian Shirt!” exclaimed Murph. “Were you sucking up to the big boss again?”

“Good one, Murph,” I said as Mia pulled on her lead, signalling she wasn’t in the mood for any of the trash dashers’ insults.

“Listen, Hawaiian Shirt,” said Beefy as he stepped forward with a sole nostril flaring. “We’ve had enough of you being a pussy. Either work five days a week like a real man or piss off back to England. Tell them we don’t need the royal family anymore, while you’re at it.”

Despite Mia’s protestations, I stepped closer to him. “Thanks for the feedback, Beefy. I’m sure Dũng would love to hear about your disdain for people from other countries, otherwise known as racism. Good luck with today’s lesson on pronunciation. For your information, when you want to inquire how someone is, it’s ‘How are you?,’ not ‘How ya gayin’?’ The world’s gay population deserves more respect than that, don’t you think?”

Beefy’s face dropped when he realized he’d been made to look foolish, which was reinforced by the harsh laughter of his fellow trash dashers. He gave them a hard stare, willing them to stop.

"Oh come on, Beefy," added Murph. "Lighten up, mate."

Despite the buildup of frown lines on his face, Beefy forced out a high-pitched, crowd-pleasing chuckle as I turned to leave. However, we all knew he'd stew on that conversation for a long time.

My job sheet revealed the day's collection job was the pickup of an old fiberglass swimming pool a few miles away in Buddina.

"How are you feeling, girl?" I asked Mia once I'd helped her into the truck.

She lay down on the front seat and closed her eyes. By the time we arrived at the Buddina address, she was snoring loudly.

"You wait here, Mutt Dog," I said as I stepped down from the truck.

Mia didn't raise her head from her reverie.

The house had an immaculate front garden and a beige brick frontage, care of the seventies, as so many local houses did. I knocked on the front door, but no one answered. After waiting on the front porch for a couple of minutes, I heard splashing coming from behind the house. I walked around to the back where I discovered a family of four playing volleyball in their swimming pool.

"Hellooo!" called out the mother as she whacked the ball over the net to win the point before high-fiving her daughter. "Are you Mr. Rubbish Collection Man?"

"That is indeed my nickname," I replied with a smile. "I'm here to collect a fiberglass pool if you could please point me in the right direction."

"We'll just get out then," she responded.

I assumed I'd misunderstood the implication of her words. Surely she couldn't mean I was there to collect the pool she was splashing about within.

The four of them stopped playing their volleyball game and climbed out of the pool. They walked over as they towelled themselves down with the vibe of people on holiday at an exclusive beach resort. The mother and father must have been young parents as they only appeared to be about ten years older than their prepubescent son and daughter.

"We're so glad you could make it today, Mr. Rubbish Collection Man," the mother stated. "We have a new shiny pool arriving this afternoon."

"So you want me to remove that pool *there*, the one in the ground?" I asked, incredulous.

"That's the only pool I can see, mate," interjected her husband. "Why, can you see another one that we're missing?"

"It's just that to remove a pool, it needs to be empty and above ground," I explained.

"That's why we hired the best at great expense," the husband continued, as he shook his head toward the ground in an attempt to clear his ear of water. "You're here to figure out how to do it so we don't need to think about it."

As I contemplated what to do, I remembered Dũng Heap's triple pay offer and Mia's expensive vet bills. I gazed over at the swimming pool, trying to decide whether it was a friend or foe. "No worries, mate," I eventually responded, knowing it was the only right answer for all of us. "If you could please clear your stuff out of the way, I'll get on with it."

The family finished towelling off and removed the volleyball net and ball, then they retreated inside their house where the games would no doubt continue. I stared at the pool, willing it to explain how to remove it from within the ground, but no answers came.

I returned to the truck to top up Mia's water. She was still asleep, but she sat up when she heard me. "It's another challenge for the ages, Mutt Dog," I stated. "The question is: how can I remove a pool which is still installed and full of water?"

Mia stared at me as though I was speaking a foreign language she'd like to understand one day. As she did, an idea suddenly occurred to me. What if I turned the filter to backwash? I could let it drain the pool for me, then I could crack the base and lift out the broken pieces with the hydraulic lift. Mia smiled as though she was the one understanding something important. I followed her lead as a complex job had become beautifully simple. And it was. I had the pool emptied within half an hour, and within another half an hour, the fiberglass pool was in broken pieces inside the truck. Mia watched on like a proud parent.

Riding high after a successful trash collection mission, I waved at the husband who was throwing darts at his veranda wall. He didn't return the wave. In fact, he appeared somewhat upset that I'd successfully removed his pool as requested. The next dart he threw missed the dartboard.

With the truck full, I drove it back up the mountain to Jude and Wolf's place so Wolf could work his magic on the pool's remnants.

Jude came over to greet me. "You don't mess around, do you?"

"We're all going to do well out of this arrangement," I said.

"I believe you, and Wolf does," Jude replied. "I'll go wake him up to tell him he finally has some work to get on with."

"You do that," I said, wondering why Wolf was asleep in the middle of the day.

Once truck number thirteen was unloaded, I drove it back down the mountain to the depot where the hire car was parked out the back. Fortuitously, there was a car rental office across the road, so I was able to return the hire car that very afternoon. Mia and I then walked back across the road to collect truck number thirteen, which was empty and intact and ready to drive us home.

The Serendipitous Mongrel

After that week's trash collecting at triple pay, I jumped out of bed on the Friday morning with enough cash in my pocket to pay for Mia's treatment. But first, I owed a purple-haired pet communicator a data gathering update.

> Dear Miranda,
>
> An observation to report. I may be imagining it, but whenever Mia is near water or I am thinking about water, some of her thoughts seem to somehow jump into my mind. Or I may have a screw loose. That wouldn't surprise me.
>
> Will

There was a knock at the door the moment I pressed send. It was Jude. "I just wanted to let you know that Wolf is in the middle of reconstructing the pieces of that swimming pool you dropped off into something, well, more creative. Do you want to come and have a look?"

"I'd love to," I replied. "Can Mia come too?"

"Of course, it's a bring your partner affair," Jude stated with a smile.

The three of us crossed the road to Jude's house, where a loud banging sound echoed all around.

"As you can hear, Wolf's putting his back into it," Jude said.

"And every other body part, by the sound of it," I added.

Jude's place was like a peace and love commune from the sixties. There were multiple ramshackle homes scattered around the property, along with six campervans which appeared to have been parked decades earlier and not moved since. There were people I'd never met before residing within each of the campervans, but it was unclear who they were or what they were doing there. Their long beards, dreadlocked hair, sun-wrinkled faces, and bemused expressions suggested they were time-travelling hippies who'd arrived in the modern world from an earlier era and didn't like what they saw. Four of them were smoking weed while rocking from side to side in a hammock hanging between two orange trees. Jude waved at them, but they were too engrossed in doing nothing to reciprocate.

"Who are they?" I asked.

"We don't really know," Jude replied. "They arrived during one of Wolf's possum-purging parties and they've stayed ever since."

"Aha," I said.

"Have you seen our veggie garden?" Jude asked as we walked past an old tennis court.

"No, and I haven't seen your tennis court either," I responded.

"We'd rather eat than have a hit of tennis these days," Jude explained as she led me onto the court.

There were neat rows of tables lined up across the court. On top of each one were troughs homing a vast array of brightly-colored vegetables full of health-giving nutrients.

"You must eat like royalty," I added.

"It's the upside of there being no possums left. Wolf has a lot more time on his hands these days, so our veggie intake has risen considerably. He's in the shed, this way," Jude said as she pointed toward a wooden structure at the back of the court.

Jude opened the shed's heavy wooden doors, and we walked inside. When the door slammed shut behind us, the bright light of day quickly dissipated as a noisy cloak of darkness enveloped us.

Thankfully, a sliver of daylight forged a lonely pathway into the shed through a shoe-shaped skylight above. It created just enough light to reveal the silhouette of a yeti, or a caveman, or an unusually hairy man, who was hammering wildly at something inexplicable on a large wooden table. He appeared ignorant of our presence as he pounded away.

"Wolf!" exclaimed Jude. "Wolf!"

The busy beast eventually stopped what he was doing and stared at us as though we'd just interrupted his favorite film at the crucial moment. "I thought you wanted me to work!" he shouted. "Well, I'm working, aren't I?"

"I've brought Will around to see what you do with the items he'll be dropping off," Jude explained with more kindness than Wolf's response seemed to warrant.

"Will? What's Will?" asked a confused Wolf.

"This is Will," Jude explained. "He's our neighbor. Remember, he's the one who dropped that old pool around that you're pummelling to death. He's the one who works for Raymond at Holy Crap Rubbish Removals."

Wolf was suddenly interested. For the greater good, he put down his ridiculously large hammer before he wandered over to where we were standing. He perused me up and down as though he was inspecting a possum carcass with a view to cutting it up for dinner.

"I've heard great things about your creative endeavors, Wolf," I said as I held out my hand.

Wolf didn't appear to have noticed my outstretched hand, or if he did, he chose to leave me hanging. He stood in silence as he digested the situation. Then, just when I thought he was going to remain mute, he directed some words in the vicinity of my feet. "Are those *bastards* still dumping everything they collect outside random properties so they can keep earning collection fees on 'em?"

I assumed my feet wouldn't know the answer, so I spoke up. "They are. I saw one of them do that the other day."

Wolf considered my words for what felt like an eternity. Jude remained comfortably silent while we awaited his next thought, whenever it was ready to drop by. "Here's what you should do at the end of each shift," he finally responded with gravity. "You drive by the streets near the depot to recollect all the dumped crap you can find, then bring it here. You hear me? Bring it *all* here! We'll be the ones to make a profit for doing the right thing, rather than those crooks who are making a fortune by wrecking the planet. You hear me?"

I did hear Wolf's words, but I was, I think the technical Australian term is "shitting myself," in his presence. However, I noticed Mia was looking relaxed as she watched Wolf talk, so I knew he was more friend than foe. "I like your idea, Wolf," I said. "Funnily enough, I've been provided with access to one of the company's trucks in the evenings, so your plan is easy to execute."

Wolf appeared stumped by the word "execute." Or maybe he was contemplating a different meaning of the word, a meaning I didn't want him to contemplate when I was standing in his dark shed, near his massive hammer. "I wonder why they gave you one of their trucks," Wolf eventually replied. "Did they mention the village association by any chance?"

"They did, yes!" I answered. "How did you know that?"

"Because they're corrupt bastards," Wolf stated. "They're trying to buy you like they buy everyone else. They'll be assuming your price is cheap since you're a foreigner who's got bugger all options to earn a crust. You're a sitting duck around those lowlifes."

"Oh, Wolf," Jude interjected, "Will doesn't want to hear any of your conspiracy theories. He just came around to see what you've done with the pool."

Without another word, Wolf walked over to a nearby light switch and turned it on. A ceiling light gate-crashed the darkness with welcome levity. I could suddenly see everything clearly, including Wolf and the thing he was hammering away at. I wasn't sure what to be more shocked by. The bright light certainly didn't complement Wolf's complexion, which was by its very nature dark and hairy and incomprehensible. Then there was the thing he was working on. Where are the words I'm looking for to describe it? In a moment of kindness, I'd call it an avant-garde work of modern art which pushed the art world's boundaries in directions no one could have foreseen. However, in the cold light of day it looked like a light aircraft had crash-landed into a tree, and the tree had come out the victor.

"What do ya think of it?" asked Wolf with more interest than I'd have liked.

"Well, it's interesting," I responded. "What do you call it?"

"It's working title is 'The Serendipitous Mongrel,'" replied Wolf the wordsmith.

"What an apt name," I said.

"Do you know what I like best about it?" Wolf asked.

"Tell me," I said.

"The way the white, the gray, and the black intermingle with one another like acquaintances who want to get along as friends, but eventually discover they're just too different to make an authentic friendship work," continued Wolf, full of pride. "Just look at those conflicted colors to-ing and fro-ing around the charcoal pattern in the middle. I've never seen a pool with a charcoal buildup on its sides like this before, but it's only served to compound the beautiful, artistic effect I was aiming for."

"You're an artist to be reckoned with," I stated as I prayed someone would turn the light back off.

"And that's how we can repurpose the crap no one wants into something better," Wolf stated like a lawyer concluding his case for the defence. "*Bring it all here.*"

After agreeing to Wolf's suggestion, Mia and I left Wolf and Jude to bathe in the glory of his unique creation. When we exited the shed, the bright light of the sunny day provided welcome respite from the weight of the darkness Wolf appeared to thrive in.

Mia was due at her first vitamin C treatment that morning, so we wandered directly into town.

As we walked up the street toward the vet's surgery, we came across Mad Jack, who was once again charging his shiny Apple devices at a public charging point.

"So you weren't put off using council resources, then?" I asked.

"Needs must," Mad Jack stated. "But I'm always on the lookout for assholes unanimous."

"Yes, Ben Flinders seemed rather worked up the other day," I said. "What was that all about?"

"Flinders dislikes anyone who has witnessed his bad behavior over the years," Mad Jack replied.

"Such as?" I asked.

"Have you ever wondered how a village as small as Maleny can afford all these expensive luxuries we all consider so normal? Have you ever seen a homeless man charging the latest Apple technology at a public charging point before?" he asked as he checked over his shoulder.

"Now you mention it, no," I replied.

"Between you and me, it would be more convenient for the village association if I were to sail off into the homeless sunset," continued Mad Jack.

"I can relate. What has the village association done?" I asked.

"I haven't survived this long by being stupid," he responded as he resumed working on his computer.

"Well, good to see you, Jack," I said as Mia and I continued on our way.

When we arrived at the vet's surgery, a sharp-nosed, elderly woman with a gigantic wolfhound was walking out. I held the front door open for her, and she walked through it without thanks or acknowledgment. Mia looked up at me with an annoyed expression.

Michelle was standing behind the reception desk when we entered the otherwise empty reception room.

"Are you a one-woman band this morning, Michelle?" I asked.

"I am," she responded. "We keep losing receptionists. The girl who was working here texted this morning to say she's been offered better money to work elsewhere. That's the third one we've lost this year for the same reason. I thought we were paying a fair market rate, so I'd love to know where they're all finding these rivers of gold."

"When you find out the river's address, please send it to me," I replied.

"Are you able to fund Mia's treatment without the help of an act of God?" Michelle asked.

"We're covered for now, thanks to my employer helping out," I responded.

Michelle led us into her consulting room. After Mia's usual efforts to hide and escape, Michelle successfully attached the vitamin C drip to one of her front legs. It took half an hour to administer the treatment, so she left me sitting with Mia while she sat at reception. Mia calmed down as soon as Michelle left and didn't appear bothered by the drip. I sat down on the ground beside her and held her front paw which didn't have the drip attached. She closed her eyes and drifted off to sleep. I also closed my eyes and relaxed into a nap while the rhythmic drip lived up to its name. A short while later, when I was trying to pull myself away from the ledge of deep sleep I was teetering on, the warning engraved in the tree beside Lake Baroon drifted into my mind like a ghost from another world. When I opened my eyes, Mia was staring at me with an expression which suggested I'd begun a conversation which she found interesting.

"What is it, girl?" I asked.

As Mia looked at me, I experienced an overwhelming fear that bad things were happening around us, as well as a feeling that Lake Baroon's dark waters were connected. No, it was more than a feeling. It was knowledge. Before I could make any sense of it, Michelle returned to the room.

"Well done, Mia," Michelle said as she removed the drip from Mia's leg. "Your bright eyes tell me the vitamin C is already working."

Once she was free, Mia jumped high into the air as though she'd won the dog lottery. She then charged toward the door, dragging me through reception like a husky pulling its sled. "Thanks, Michelle!" I called out. "Please email me the bill."

The vitamin C therapy gave Mia the energy boost equivalent of consuming a gallon of coffee. She pulled hard at her lead, encouraging me to find somewhere for her to expel her excess energy. We walked over to a field adjacent to the Serenity Trail, where I let her off the lead. With all that excess energy coursing through her veins, Mia sprinted across the field before she took a running leap and dove head first into some long grass. A few minutes passed and she didn't re-emerge, so I walked over to investigate. I couldn't find her anywhere, but I discovered a trail of downtrodden grass on the other side which indicated she'd kept running. Who could blame her?

"Mia!" I called out, but she was nowhere to be found.

I followed her trail across the field where it weaved its way around some eucalyptus trees into a nearby paddock which was being grazed by a herd of Black Angus cattle. That's where I found Mia. She was sitting in the middle of the field—and she wasn't alone. A young calf, which must have only been a couple of months old, was standing in front of her, staring into her eyes. Mia sat motionless in front of the calf, seemingly deep in conversation. I didn't call out. I just watched in awe as my beautiful dog freely gave her love to another creature who no doubt needed it. When their conversation drew to a close, Mia walked over and sat down beside me so she could observe the calf from a distance. By then, it had returned to its mother and was mooing intently as though it was enlightened about something important.

little c BIG D

When I awoke the next morning, Mia was sprawled diagonally across the bed in a deep sleep while she snored and wagged her tail with excitement. A gentle knock at the door disturbed our peace, so I rolled out of bed to investigate. I opened the door to find Miranda Minsky standing on our doorstep wearing a yellow, wide-brimmed cowgirl hat lined with long pink feathers.

"Come on in, Miranda," I said.

"This is me emailing back," she explained as she remained stationery on the doorstep.

"I like your style," I responded.

Mia ran out of the bedroom wearing her best smile. She threw herself into her signature sliding maneuver before coming to a belly-up halt at Miranda's feet.

"What a fun party trick, Mia!" Miranda exclaimed as she stroked Mia's tummy. "I've never seen a living dog greet someone so creatively before."

"How do the dead ones do it?" I asked.

"Well, it's easier for them to be creative because they aren't constrained by having an earthly body," Miranda replied. "I met a Chihuahua the other day who serenaded his owner to 'I Want To Hold Your Hand' without his owner realizing it. All she noticed was a drop in room temperature and goose pimples on her arms. They're the tell-tail signs your departed dog is showing you affection from the other side."

"Are you coming in?" I asked.

"No," Miranda stated. "I'm hoping you two will join me for a short road trip."

"Where to?" I asked.

"I'll explain on the way," she said as she turned to leave.

"OK, we're coming," I replied.

Mia charged after Miranda as though her life depended on it. I followed.

Miranda Minsky's vehicle was a hippy van with a painting on the side depicting three joyful dogs running through a field of pink and purple flowers toward a deep-blue pond. The words "Pet Communicator: I speak with dead pets" were painted in modest black letters on the van's back door.

"I'll give you three guesses where we're going," said Miranda as we drove away.

"A pet cemetery?" I asked.

"You watch too many horror films," she responded.

"To meet one of your other clients?" I asked.

"No way," Miranda replied. "What if you told each other what you really thought of me?"

I laughed. "I've got it. We're going to your home so you're in your element when creating the ideal dog communication conditions."

"You're close, but I must report an epic fail," Miranda replied. "When you emailed to tell me you could hear Mia's thoughts whenever you were near water, it was a breakthrough. It was the data point I needed."

"So where are we going?" I asked.

"To the source," Miranda said. "We're going to the ocean so it can work its wonders for us."

"The ocean?" I asked.

"Yes. Most dead dogs are receptive around water," she explained. "I think Mia may be similar, and I suspect a few of the dead dogs I'm connected with may step in to help. But it's only an idea so we need to test it out like any unproven theory."

"What do you think of that, girl?" I asked Mia.

She gazed at me with her early morning sleepy eyes which didn't give much away.

"Have you considered which questions you'd like to ask Mia?" Miranda asked.

"The idea of communicating with her has overridden all practical questions like that," I said. "I just know she knows more."

"More than what?" Miranda asked.

"More than me, more than humans," I said.

"Well, that isn't hard, is it?" Miranda asked.

"Are you suggesting I'm an idiot?" I replied.

"No, but I'm outright saying the human race doesn't know its ass from its elbow," she said. "Give me a dead dog over a living human any day."

"So what do you talk with the dead dogs about? Maybe you could give me some pointers," I added.

"You name it. I've had conversations with Labradors about philosophy, with schnauzers about politics, with border collies about economics, and with dachshunds about psychology," Miranda responded. "But do you know which subject dead dogs are almost always the most passionate about, the most informed about, and the easiest to talk with about?"

"The dog food industry, and what really goes in their food?" I asked.

"Their owners," stated Miranda. "Dogs love their owners on a level most humans can't comprehend. They watch their every move, day in, day out, with remarkable focus. That makes them the world's leading experts in what their owners are really like. You know, the no bullshit version."

"That makes sense," I replied. "Mia's with me all the time. She's always watching me."

"And do you know the other subject I've noticed dogs are remarkably chatty about?" Miranda asked.

"Space travel?" I joked.

"The people their owners interact with," Miranda continued. "If you want to know what's really going on beneath the surface of any relationships in your life, just ask your dog."

"You're raising my expectations here," I said. "It sounds like Mia has the answers I've been searching for."

"My bad," added Miranda. "Here's me talking freely about communicating with dogs, but I'm once again generalizing. I'm talking about dead dogs. Talking with Mia is an experiment with no guarantee of success."

"I get it, terms and conditions apply," I said.

"There's only one term and condition here, Will," Miranda responded. "And only you can figure out what it is."

Miranda parked her van near Mudjimba Beach. The moment I opened the door, Mia launched herself to the ground and sprinted along the sandy pathway.

"She definitely has a water-centered soul," Miranda stated as we followed.

By the time Miranda and I caught up with Mia, she was rolling on the sand as though she was dancing to a tune only she could hear.

"So what's the plan?" I asked.

"Do I look like I know what I'm doing?" Miranda replied. "I'm hoping Mia, and possibly a dead dog or two, will show us the way."

"Why don't we go for a stroll along the beach then?" I suggested. "Mia loves that. It may inspire her."

"Good idea," Miranda said as she kicked her shoes off with joyful disdain. She rolled up her white jeans, threw her cowgirl hat into the air and charged into the shallow water while laughing. Mia followed her into the ocean and was soon swimming a few yards from shore while Miranda splashed water into the air. It was like watching two dogs at play. Miranda had a half-steely, half-wild expression on her face which challenged me to have as much fun as she was, so I followed her into the shallows. She responded by kicking seawater all over me, soaking me through. It was game on. I kicked water back at Miranda while Mia galloped in and out of the water like her old energetic self.

A well-dressed Asian couple walked past as we played. The man held his camera up in the video recording position with his trigger finger at the ready.

"Come join us!" shouted Miranda as she kicked water in his direction.

However, the man jumped backward and held his camera behind his back like a vulnerable animal being threatened by an unpredictable force of nature. "Be careful, please!" he exclaimed. "This is the latest iPhone."

"And this is the latest in virtual reality!" replied a buoyant Miranda.

Unimpressed, the man whispered something in his wife's ear before they turned and marched off in the opposite direction.

"Too bad!" called out Miranda. "See you when you're ready."

After our splashing game concluded, the three of us returned to the dry sand, soaked but happy. We then walked along the beach for hours. As Miranda and I talked, she appeared to grow dog fur. She was boisterous and loving and kind—and everything good about dogs. As we walked, I gazed at the water lapping at our feet and stopped looking at Miranda's human face. The longer we talked, the more certain I became that I was in the company of a canine. Was I out of my mind? Possibly.

"We're at the right place, Will," Miranda stated. "I can feel unusual energy circling around your lives."

"Our lives?" I asked.

"Yes," she replied. "You and Mia are sitting on top of a gigantic ant's nest of questions. More than your usual Joe. That's pretty exciting, eh?"

"If lost ants are your thing," I said.

"Look at those apartments over there," Miranda said in an abrupt change of subject as she pointed at some buildings on the foreshore. "They must have incredible ocean views, don't you think?"

"Yes, imagine waking up to this view every day," I replied.

"But how many people can you see on their balconies appreciating their views?" Miranda continued.

I looked up at the row of apartment buildings lining the beach. "There's no one there—not a single person."

"And yet, all those thousands of people paid a fortune for their ocean views, no doubt believing they'd spend a lot of time appreciating them. Just think about the many retirees this area is famous for, with all that time on their hands," she said.

"You're right. I wonder why none of them are on their balconies on a stunning day like this," I replied.

"Because they've forgotten to appreciate all they have," Miranda stated. "Every single one of them—for one simple reason."

"What's that?" I asked.

"They're now looking for something else to fill the gap in here," Miranda continued, touching her heart. "Living humans have this constant need to search for new, shiny things to make them feel better about themselves. It's a real issue-avoidance strategy that stops so many people from finding the answers they need, which are usually located on their doorsteps—along with their dead dogs."

I nodded. I sensed there was something in Miranda's words for me. Was Australia my expensive new balcony with a shiny view? Before clarity arrived, Mia rubbed my leg and looked up at me with thoughtful eyes. I paused to listen to her, but I couldn't hear or feel her thoughts. I was starting to feel exhausted by the long beach walk as well as the weight of unfulfilled expectations it was creating.

"Will, we're not alone," Miranda suddenly whispered in my ear.

"I assume you aren't referring to the other humans walking along the beach," I replied.

"Three golden retrievers have dropped in from the other side," she explained.

I instinctively looked around despite knowing I wouldn't be able to see three golden retrievers in the vicinity. "They're here to help Mia?"

"They are," Miranda responded. "A male, a female, and their daughter have reconnected in the afterlife to help Mia communicate with you in human words. They seem to think it's important."

When we returned to the sandy section in front of the pathway entrance leading back to the car, Miranda asked me an unusual question. "Will, how did you learn the alphabet as a child?"

"My mother attached magnetic alphabet letters to a whiteboard," I responded.

"What do you think your mother would have done if you didn't have a whiteboard?" she asked. "For example, if you were at the beach?"

"She was a creative lady, so I'd imagine she'd have written the letters in the sand," I replied.

Miranda Minsky stood motionless as she smiled a smile of significance.

"What harm can come from giving it a go?" I asked.

"The motto of the enlightened human," Miranda responded. "Why don't you cover A-J and I'll cover K-Z."

"Done," I said as I began drawing a gigantic A in the sand.

Within minutes, Miranda and I had written out an alphabet in the sand. Mia watched on with interest.

A passing family laughed at us. "Where are your kids, mate?" asked the father.

"We don't have kids. We're conducting an experiment which may change life as we know it," I responded.

The man looked me up and down as though I was insane before he walked away in silence.

"We're scaring the locals," said Miranda.

"Or educating them," I added with a grin.

Mia sat down in front of the alphabet and looked at the sandy letters with mild interest. Then she turned to her left and thousand-yard stared into the distance.

"She's noticed the family of deceased golden retrievers beside her," Miranda stated. "They're communicating."

"Can you understand what's being discussed?" I asked.

"No," Miranda stated. "They're communicating with her like living dogs do."

"What do you mean? What's the difference between living and dead dog communication?" I asked.

"Once dogs pass to the other side, they can often communicate using human words in their owners' language," Miranda replied. "It's an adapted spiritual response that allows them to connect with and understand their owners from the other side. It's remarkable really. In contrast, living dogs communicate through pheromones, secretions, barking, whining, body posture, and many other methods humans aren't even aware of."

"So why are these three dead golden retrievers communicating with Mia like living dogs?" I asked.

As Miranda pondered my question, Mia stepped closer to the letter A in the sand. She stared at it before she gazed to her left and right as though she was in the middle of an engaging conversation. Then she moved on to the letter B and did the same thing.

"Clever, eh?" Miranda said. "They're teaching her how to read the alphabet. That's why they're communicating like living dogs. They know Mia can't yet communicate like a dog who's passed over, so they're talking her language while they teach her English words."

I remained silent. My eyes confirmed that Mia was indeed stepping from letter to letter and appeared to be guided in the process. It was what I couldn't see that was creating some internal confusion. Hard as it is to admit, while my heart believed what was happening, my head had questions.

After Mia had lingered and listened in front of each letter of the alphabet, she circled back to various letters. It was almost as if she was practicing word construction with the help of her guides. She directed a smile at the empty spaces near her every time she connected a few letters. Once she'd finished whatever it was she was doing, she trotted back to Miranda and me, and sat down in front of us full of expectation.

"Are the dead dogs still here?" I asked Miranda.

"They're hovering in the background in case Mia needs their help. So what's your first question for her?" asked Miranda.

"Mutt Dog, do you understand me?" I asked.

Mia sat there motionless, still gazing up expectantly. She seemed to have answered my question in the negative along with my internal questions about the likelihood that three dead dogs had popped across from the other side to teach her English. Miranda sat beside Mia on the sand and gave her a belly rub, then Mia returned to where she'd been sitting in front of me.

"Ask her again a little slower, Will," Miranda suggested.

"Mia, do you understand me?" I asked, slowly pronouncing each word.

After considering my words, Mia stood up and ran over to the letter Y, the E, and the S, before returning to where she'd been sitting.

"Oh. My. God! Did you see that?" I asked as my doubts evaporated in an instant.

"She's a special one, Will," Miranda responded.

"Mia, do you know what type of animal you are?" I asked.

Mia once again charged off toward the letters. She ran to the D, the O, and the G, before returning to sit down in front me. She then turned her head to the side and jumped back up as though she'd remembered something. She ran back to the letters to continue. This time, she approached the W, the I, the T, and the H, before she paused. Then, she trotted over to the A and waited. A few seconds later, she ran to the B, the I, and the G, before pausing again. Then she walked over to the D which she plonked herself down in front of.

"Dog, spelt with a big D?" I asked.

"She's telling you something important, Will. The dead dogs are encouraging her to make this point," Miranda explained. "You may need to ask her another question to understand what she's saying."

As I gazed at the letter D, a question popped into my mind.

"Is there a word which you think deserves a lower case letter, Mutt Dog?" I asked.

Without skipping a beat, Mia jumped up and charged back to the letters. She ran to the C, the A, the N, the C, the E, and the R, before returning to sit in front of me.

"You're saying cancer should be spelt with a lowercase c?" I asked.

Mia smiled at me before she lay down at my feet, exhausted.

"OK, big D for Dog, little c for cancer it is," I responded as I wiped a stray tear from my face. The ramifications of that moment didn't fully hit me until a long time afterwards.

Mia remained motionless on the ground, breathing heavily.

"She's spent, Will," Miranda said. "She's done so well, but it's time to get her home for some well-earned rest."

"She has," I replied. "Please thank her teachers on my behalf."

"They've already popped back to the other side. Believe me, they know how much this means to you," Miranda replied.

"How do you feel, Miranda, now you've proven you can indeed build a phone to communicate with living dogs?" I asked.

Miranda Minsky considered her response long and hard. "I think the main reason I've been so focused on dead pets is because I've always wanted to learn more about the afterlife. But every time I've learnt more about the world of the dead, all I'm really left with is more questions. The truth is, sitting here watching Mia communicate with you about the things that matter in this world feels like the first *real* moment in my entire career. I think I've been focused on the wrong team."

"Well, welcome back to the land of the living, Miranda," I said, knowing I was talking to myself as well.

Miranda Minsky let her tears run at that point—and run they did. Mia ran over to comfort her by leaning her body up against hers. I sat down beside Miranda and put my arm around her shoulder while she cried in the salty breeze.

The Congregation

From that day onward, Miranda Minsky became a regular feature in Mia's and my life. Every Monday and Wednesday, we met Miranda at the beach for dog communication sessions; every Tuesday and Thursday I worked as a trash dasher; and every Friday we visited the vet for Mia's vitamin C therapy. The routine was a welcome lubricant to the flow of time.

On the next beach outing with Miranda, I decided to learn more about how Mia enjoyed spending her time. Not knowing how much time she had left made me focused on helping ensure she enjoyed every single day. Miranda and I drew an alphabet in the sand and sat down nearby. Mia knew the drill and sat up ready for a question.

"Mutt Dog, what are your favorite things to do?" I asked.

Mia ran to the B, and the E, before she paused. Then she ran to the W, the I, the T, the H, and waited for a few seconds. She then ran to the Y, the O, and the U, before she sat down in front of the U as if to emphasize her point.

"That one wasn't a surprise," said Miranda. "If I ever met a dog who adores her owner, it's Mia."

"What else, Mutt Dog?" I asked.

Mia ran to the T, the A, the L, and the K. After considering where to go next, she ran to the W, the I, the T, and the H. Then, after another pause, she ran to the A, the N, the I, the M, the A, the L, and she finished at the S.

"Talk with animals?" I asked.

"Mia's telling you she can communicate with all animals, Will," Miranda interjected. "More than that, she *wants* to communicate with them. I've never met a dog like her before. Most dogs are focused on their owners and other dogs, but Mia seems to have a bigger part to play."

"A part to play in what, though?" I asked.

"We'll find out when the time is right," Miranda replied.

It didn't surprise me that one of Mia's greatest joys was communicating with other animals as she was always doing it, or at least trying to. But ever since we'd been reprimanded at Mary Cairncross for breaking the No Dogs rule, we hadn't visited any national parks where she could freely meet other animals for a friendly chinwag. As Mia's words sank in at the beach that day, I had an idea.

After parting ways with Miranda, Mia and I returned home and walked down to the Serenity Trail at a time when the Whisperer was conducting one of his tours. Sure enough, he was showing a group of tourists where the platypuses lived. He waved at Mia and me as we joined the group, most of whom were staring at the still water below, willing it to ripple with life. When a platypus finally popped its silky head above the water a few minutes later, there was a communal sigh of relief, followed by the clicks of evidence gathering in the form of photo taking. After the tour ended and the group departed, I stuck around to talk with the Whisperer.

"Another satisfied group?" I asked.

"People are predictable," responded the Whisperer. "If you offer them hope that something may possibly happen, they'll focus on that one thing and nothing else. And if that one thing does happen, they'll feel so incredibly relieved they were right to hope in the first place—relieved they weren't revealed to be wrong, or even worse...foolish."

"So when a platypus doesn't reveal itself on cue for a photo, do you have disappointed tourists on your hands?" I asked.

"You'd better believe it," replied the Whisperer.

"So here's an idea for you then," I continued. "How do you feel about diversifying your hope-raising activities?"

"What do you mean?" he asked.

"I mean, extend your tour to include other animals," I responded. "So if the platypuses are asleep or otherwise engaged, you don't need to suffer the heavy weight of unfulfilled tourist expectations."

"It's a novel idea," replied the Whisperer. "But I'm a platypus specialist, I always have been. You can't teach an old dog new tricks."

"What about dogs who aren't so old?" I asked as I peered down at Mia, who was following the conversation.

"This is about wildlife, not dogs," the Whisperer responded without interest.

"What if this particular dog has the specialist skillset you're lacking? What if this particular dog can communicate with wildlife?" I asked.

"I'd say you've drunk too much creek water, mate," the Whisperer responded.

"Maybe you're right," I said. "But then again, maybe not. What if I've started seeing things clearly for the first time? Why don't you join us for a short walk in the bush?"

The Whisperer looked me up and down as though I'd lost my mind. It was obvious he was fighting an internal battle between following his heart and mind, but I wasn't sure which organ was on my side.

"Oh bloody hell, OK," he finally responded. "But I've only got half an hour."

The three of us walked in silence along the Serenity Trail, then veered off left toward the creek. Mia walked beside me with purpose. I recalled how much she used to love chasing deer when we lived in Yorkshire. It didn't bode well for a smooth mission. As if she'd read my mind, Mia broke ranks before I could hold her lead tight and sprinted off up ahead. She was soon out of sight. The Whisperer shook his head as if it was all the proof he needed that it was a big old waste of time as he'd expected. Once we hit the creek, we walked alongside it as we searched for Mia, but she was nowhere to be found.

"Sorry about this," I said. "The good news is the creek is flowing well. If you're a platypus, it's the equivalent of a five-star hotel around here."

The Whisperer peered at the creek, then back at me, then back at the ground. I knew he was close to calling time on our adventure. Just before he did, we heard a strange collection of sounds which were almost happening in tune with one another, but not quite. The Whisperer and I walked over to investigate.

Up ahead, Mia was sitting in the middle of a circle of the most unlikely group of animals. She was surrounded by two wallabies, three kookaburras, four possums, and a platypus who was poking his head above the water in the nearby creek.

"What the...," said the Whisperer.

"You took the words right out of my mouth," I added.

The inexplicable group of animals didn't appear to have noticed our presence. They were all watching Mia intently as though she was the hired entertainment on an otherwise dull day. She gazed into each of their eyes with her customary warmth and appeared to be enjoying hanging out with her new friends.

"What's she doing?" asked the Whisperer.

"I'd say she communicating with them," I replied. "But they're communicating on a deeper level than we humans can understand."

"I thought I'd seen everything, but I stand corrected," stated the Whisperer. "What do you think they're saying to one another?"

"I reckon they're sharing the secrets of the universe we're all so desperate to understand," I responded.

"Do you think Mia would mind if a group of tourists occasionally watched her doing this?" the Whisperer asked.

"I'm sure she'd be overjoyed to show people how special each of these animals is," I said. "But let me get back to you on that. Mia's her own boss so I'd like to check with her first."

"You two sure roll in your own unique way," responded the Whisperer.

"Thanks," I said.

We waited until the congregation had concluded and Mia returned to us. However, the other animals didn't want to part ways with her. The wallabies hopped over and waited beside Mia in expectation of something else happening or being communicated. The possums ran over and stood on their back legs as though they were about to start dancing. And the kookaburras landed on a low-hanging branch nearby, ready for whatever was coming next.

"Do they believe *we're* the zoo animals?" asked the Whisperer.

"It would seem so," I replied.

"What should we do?" the Whisperer asked. "How does a zoo animal deal with the heavy weight of expectation being watched creates?"

"By mirroring the species of animal watching them?" I suggested.

"You're talking like a human," said the Whisperer. "No, I reckon these creatures value the differences each of them brings to the party. Take the kookaburras for example. These guys are the bush's alarm clock. They lighten everyone's mood throughout the day. No other creature can do that."

On cue, the kookaburras burst into wild laughter as though he'd cracked the funniest joke they'd ever heard. I joined them. Eventually, the Whisperer did as well.

"Then there are the wallabies," the Whisperer continued. "These guys are the bush's community builders. The strong bonds they develop in their mobs are nothing short of extraordinary. Watching them interact with one another is like watching an episode of *Friends*, only far more interesting."

As if they'd understood every word, the two wallabies hopped closer to one another to rub each other's noses.

"And the possums are the bush's talkers and comedians," continued the Whisperer. "They provide the humor the kookaburras find so hilarious and can generally be found nattering about something."

In response, the four attentive possums clicked at one another, confirming they agreed with the Whisperer.

All of a sudden, a rifle shot exploded and a bullet shattered a nearby tree trunk, as well as the moment. The animals scattered off in different directions, and Mia looked up at me with her eyes full of stress.

"That's a first," said the Whisperer. "I've never encountered a shooter around here before."

"Let's get the hell out of here," I added.

The Whisperer, Mia, and I jogged back through the bush, but we didn't encounter anyone along the way. When we arrived at the Serenity Trail, we turned left toward the town center. Up ahead, someone was walking in that same direction—a tall, dark-haired man wearing jeans and a white shirt who had his back turned to us.

"Oh great," said the Whisperer.

"Who is it?" I asked.

"It's Ben bloody Flinders, of course," the Whisperer replied. "Let's hang back. He's been trying to shut down my tour guiding activities for years as he thinks it's out of keeping with the vibe of the area. You know, with us living in the countryside surrounded by wildlife and all."

"He's a real piece of work," I said.

As I spoke, the figure up ahead stopped in his tracks as though he had supersonic hearing and was unhappy with my prognosis. We stood still and held our breath, but we'd been noticed. Ben Flinders did an about-face and stared at us with aggressive intent. Like the gun-slinging showdown scene in a B-grade Western film, he parted his legs, put his hands on his hips, and willed us forward.

“I reckon we’d best change direction about now,” stated the Whisperer.

“You do that, but I’m done with allowing bad people to make my day worse,” I replied. “I’m heading that way regardless of who’s standing in my path.”

“Good luck with that,” said the Whisperer as he turned to leave.

Mia and I strode toward the one person who could make our lives even harder than they were—the one person who represented all the difficult stuffed frogs in my mind, who just happened to be standing in our pathway. Even from a distance, it was obvious he was angry.

“Your nose out of joint again, Flinders?” I asked when the distance between us narrowed to around ten yards.

“Pardon, Watson?” he seethed. “It sounded like you spoke to me with that insolent tone again. But that can’t be right, I said to myself, considering this cretin’s future in this country depends on his being nice to me.”

As Ben Flinders once again threatened me, I’d had enough. Enough of bad people making the world a worse place. Enough of bad things happening to good people and creatures. Enough of being afraid.

“Ah yes, the narcissist’s guide to all the ways the world revolves around them,” I responded as I stepped closer. "It's a classic read if you're a narcissistic prick."

"You, you, you...," he started.

"Yes, it is me. Well done," I responded.

Ben Flinders vocabulary wasn't able to keep up with his fast-paced emotions. As I waited for him to get his words out, I had time on my hands, so I was able to take in the beautiful surroundings. A small brown lizard grinned at me as it ran across the footpath.

"Here's what's going to happen," Flinders eventually stated. "At the next village association meeting, I'm going to tell them all about your growing portfolio of business interests in the region. Then we'll arrange to shut them down one doomed enterprise at a time."

"What are you talking about?" I asked.

"I saw you dropping off your trash at Jude's property which can only mean Wolf is intending to illegally recycle it despite his disastrous track record," he replied. "That one will be straightforward to erase from the face of the planet for the greater good when we investigate whether you've set your business up in accordance with the Corporations Law. And I happened to overhear you mention your bizarre business idea with the Platypus Pussy. That one will be easily wiped out when I shut him down for his lacklustre approach to licensing."

"Oh, and one more thing," Flinders continued. "Dũng Heap will be at the next village association meeting. I'll look forward to updating him on your inability to follow simple instructions. Dũng's a great guy but he doesn't tolerate lowlifes. Your inglorious days as a trash collector will be over when he learns the truth about you. Do you know what else that means? You won't be getting that skilled migrant visa you so desperately need, so it's almost time to book that plane ticket out of here. Your limp-wristed search for home is leading you straight back to whatever shithole you emerged uninvited from. What a shame, eh?"

Ben Flinders then gave birth to something that almost sounded like a laugh. It was an ugly, ill-humored noise which couldn't have sounded less authentic if it had tried. However, rather than rubbing salt in an imagined wound as he'd intended, he inspired me to join him with the real stuff. I roared with laughter because Ben Flinders and everything he stood for was so damned funny.

"Laugh away, Watson," he responded. "It just proves that what's so obvious to the rest us is true."

I didn't wait around to hear his parting insult.

"I'll see you at the village association meeting, Ben *bloody* Flinders," I shouted over my shoulder as Mia and I headed home.

Stuffed

When Mia and I arrived home that afternoon, I sat down on the veranda's top step and closed my eyes. As I did, an unwelcome image of Austin the Aussie reared his ugly head in my mind. I tried to upgrade his face from Ben Flinders's, but it was useless—the two of them were one and the same. Austin was pointing at a whiteboard with a list written on it entitled "The final glorious steps to eradicate Watson from Australia." It included:

1. Demotivate Watson by shattering the basis of every enterprising idea he has before they have a chance to grow into action. Good work on that front, Ben Flinders.
2. Laugh at Watson at every opportunity and in the most

condescending of ways to ensure he feels small and worthless. Well done, everyone. Beautiful work.

3. Ensure Watson understands that he exists at the bottom of the social hierarchy and will never advance any higher. Excellent job, Holy Crap Rubbish Removals. Five-star effort.
4. Make sure Watson believes he has zero chance of being granted the skilled migrant visa he needs to remain in Australia. Ben Flinders, once again you've outdone yourself.

It was the final item on his list that really excited Austin the Aussie. He jumped up and down as he pointed at the words:

When Watson's dog Mia passes away, it will be the knockout blow. Can everyone please ensure Watson has no meaningful human connections by the time that happens? We don't want a single person or animal making that loss any easier for him to bear. With any luck, we'll be bidding Watson farewell within days of his dog's passing. I'll have the champagne ready.

Austin broke into an impromptu dance as his excitement about my impending departure was too much to contain. I opened my eyes so as to evict the green maniac from my mind.

I wondered what Emmanuel would think of my imagined versions his creations. Without planning to, I pressed dial on my phone.

The phone rang a few times before a woman answered. "Hello."

"Hi. Is Emmanuel there, please?" I replied.

"Who may I ask is speaking?" she asked.

"It's his foster son, Will," I replied.

"Oh right," she said. "Will, my name is Veronica. I'm a nurse. Emmanuel is here with us in Inverness Hospital because he had a heart attack yesterday."

"Oh my god!" I exclaimed. "Is he alright now?"

"He's weak but conscious, Will," she replied. "The doctors believe he's got a decent chance of pulling through."

"Can I speak with him, please?" I asked.

"You can, but only for a couple of minutes. He needs his rest," she replied.

"Understood," I said.

"If it isn't the yeti from the south," said a weak voice I recognized well.

"How are you feeling?" I asked.

"Like a bowling pin that was knocked down with all the rest in a brutal strike against humanity," he stated.

"I'm not going to say I told you so," I replied. "What were you doing when it happened?"

"Sitting and waiting in the cold," he stated. "Isn't that the story of my life?"

"You were searching for Nessie?" I asked.

"Yes, but none of that matters anymore," he responded.

"Why not?" I asked.

"Because whether Nessie's real or imagined doesn't make the slightest bit of difference when you're lying motionless in a hospital bed while your maker is considering calling time. It's all the same at this point. If you believe something's real, it's as real as anything else," he explained. There it was...the answer to the question I'd long wanted to ask Emmanuel about the significance of imagined stuffed frogs. It wasn't the answer I was hoping for.

"Hi, Will," interjected Veronica the nurse. "I'm afraid that's all the chatting Emmanuel can cope with today."

"Thanks for looking after him," I added, "and call me on this number if you need to speak with the closest thing Emmanuel has to a family member."

"Emmanuel gave us your phone number when he was first admitted, but he asked us not to bother you," she said.

"Please bother me if anything changes," I replied.

"OK, Will," she said. "Bye for now."

After I hung up, I experienced overwhelming guilt that I was on the other side of the world and unable to afford the airfare to travel to Emmanuel's bedside. Australia was starting to feel like it was cut off from the rest of the world.

As I rocked myself from side to side, I recalled a memory of Emmanuel from a few years earlier. He'd just finished creating one of his precious stuffed frogs when Heidi and I popped into his shop in York to say hello one afternoon. When he noticed us, he walked over to greet us with his latest stuffed frog in hand. Then he did something curious. He started talking to us as though he was the stuffed frog he was holding. "Hello, you two," he said as he held the frog up in front of his face.

"Who have we here?" I asked.

"I'm Frederick the Fortune-Teller," he responded as he held the frog out to shake our hands with its tiny hand.

Heidi rolled her eyes, but I stepped forward for a closer view of Frederick. He was dressed like a gypsy with a red head scarf wrapped around his head. His arms were crossed as though he was deep in thought.

"It's a pleasure to meet you, Frederick," I replied. "What can you tell us about the future then?"

Emmanuel paused before he answered on behalf of Frederick. "The one thing I can promise you is you'll get the life you deserve. All the good and bad that enters your life is yours, and yours alone."

On cue, a few tears arrived for all the previously unappreciated good things Emmanuel had brought into my life—including his overly chatty stuffed frogs.

A Foreign Language

The next morning, I struggled to wake Mia up. She was snoring too loudly to hear me talking, so I stroked her as she slept. As I did, I noticed the lump on the side of her body was growing and she'd been licking it. The fur had all fallen off to reveal a bright red mass of soreness for the whole world to see. I looked away from the lump, willing it to be anything but real. Mia awoke an hour or so later. She returned my gaze with alarm in her eyes.

"It's OK, girl," I said. "You just slept in. We all do it."

We were due to meet Miranda at the beach, however I knew it had to be just Mia and me that morning. Miranda was an integral part of our team, but I needed to ask Mia one particular question without anyone else around. I texted Miranda, *Can we postpone today's beach session, please? I'll explain later. Will.*

She texted straight back. *Of course. I hope you are both OK.*

When we arrived at Mudjimba Beach, Mia jumped down from the truck and charged along the sandy pathway with far more energy than we both knew she had. As she rolled, I drew an alphabet in the sand. The letters G and Q were fast becoming my sand alphabet nemeses. Every time I drew either letter the wind blew sand over them making them illegible, so with the help of a stick I drew them deeper until they were almost readable.

"Mutt Dog, when you've finished rolling, I have a couple of questions for you if I may," I said.

Mia sat attentively in front of me.

"Thanks, girl," I responded. "Can I ask: what were you talking about with the kookaburras, the wallabies, the possums, and the platypus yesterday?"

Mia contemplated my question for a minute before she trotted over to the B, the A, and the D. Then she paused ahead of running over to the P, the E, the O, the P, the L, and the E. After checking we were alone, she sat down in front of the E.

"Who are these bad people, Mutt Dog? What are they doing?" I asked.

In hindsight, I shouldn't have asked two such big questions at once. I was making dog communication errors left, right, and center.

Mia again considered my words before she jogged over to the P, the E, the L, the I, the C, the A, the N, and the S. She then paused for moment before she ran to the K, the N, the O, and the W.

"The pelicans know?" I asked. "I assume you means the pelicans down on Lake Baroon."

Mia gave me a look which could only mean, "Have you seen any other pelicans around here, genius?"

"Well done, girl," I responded. "That's a great start."

I took a deep breath and considered whether the next question I wanted to ask really needed to be asked. "Next question, Mutt Dog," I continued with more seriousness than Mia was used to hearing from me. "You may have noticed your owner is a little...lost. Where do you believe my home is in this world?"

Mia jumped up and ran straight over to the I, the N, the S, the I, the D, and the E. Then she paused before she ran to the Y, the O, and the U.

Inside me. I vividly recall the strangeness of my emotional response as I digested Mia's answer. You'd think I'd have felt somewhat stupid to have learnt this from my dog. However, I experienced only one emotion when Mia told me the truth about my relationship with myself. Relief. I was relieved to know that everything I was feeling about my life could possibly be fixed with some tinkering on the inside. Of course, that assumed I had the right tools and I knew what to tinker with.

Mia lay down on the sand as a wave of tiredness hit her. I sat down next to her.

"Thank you, Mutt Dog," I said. "It must be frustrating for you to have such a dunce of an owner. Truths which are obvious to you are like a foreign language to me."

Mia gazed at me with loving eyes which explained in a million ways that in her eyes I was wrong to think so badly of myself. I was perfect to her just as I was, and if the rest of the world didn't love me in the same way, that was their loss. And another thing, her eyes continued to explain: you're the best dog owner in the whole goddamn world, don't ever forget it. And one final message while we are talking like this...I'll always be your dog regardless of what happens in this world.

The Mystery Pickup

The next morning, I was due back at the depot for another day of trash dashing. Mia was slow to get moving, but once she was up, there was no convincing her to rest at home.

When we arrived at the depot, the other trash dashers were waiting outside Raymond's office, ready for morning training. Mia and I wandered over to join them.

"Speak of the devil!" exclaimed Beefy when he saw me.

"That's just my nickname," I replied.

"Hawaiian Shirt, have you *really* been doing special favors for the big boss?" asked Murph.

"Yeah, are you heaping it on the Dũng?" asked Beefy with a school-boy smirk.

The rest of the nameless trash dashers laughed with harsh abandon at the rather obvious implications.

"Hey, guys," I responded, "here's a tip: when you're cracking jokes, don't be so blatant. Humor comes more from what's *not* said."

"What?" blurted out a perplexed Beefy. "Nah, mate, not saying something ain't funny. I can just imagine you as a stand-up comedian in front of an audience not saying a single word, then running home crying to mommy when no one laughed. Where can I buy a ticket to *that* show?"

The group was off again with more forced laughter. Raymond heard the raucous outburst from inside his office and joined the group. "Morning, gang," he said.

He was greeted with a few caveman-like grunts.

"Let's get on with this morning's training," Raymond continued. "Today, we'll be learning how to read between the lines. It will help you understand what a client is really saying. You know, the subtext."

"The sub what?" asked a perplexed Beefy.

"The subtext, Beefy," responded Raymond. "Here's an example: if a client asks you to remove your shoes before you enter their home, what are they really saying?"

"That they'd like you to take your shoes off?" asked Beefy.

"That's what they're actually asking," continued Raymond. "But what they're really saying is that they're afraid you'll mess up their home when you enter."

"Well, I'd like a word with the bastards about that," added a fired up Beefy.

"How's this helpful for us, boss?" asked a bored Murph.

"It's about reading the signals to ensure we're providing the best all-round client service," answered Raymond. "In the shoes-off-at-the-door example, we can learn from what was said that the client is on the highly strung side. So the best way to manage this type of client is by being ultracourteous and focused on not making a mess."

Beefy fell silent as did the rest of the group.

"Here's another example," continued Raymond as he held my gaze. "What's the subtext to this comment? Please respect the village association as they are important for business."

Beefy put his hand straight up. "I've got it, boss!"

"Go on then," said Raymond.

"Our business is in a secret partnership with the village association aimed at enriching both parties," Beefy offered up.

Raymond shifted on his feet, uncomfortable with the answer. "That wasn't what I was looking for. The subtext was that we should be prepared to say yes whenever a member of the village association asks us to do something. That's our one and only job...to say yes. Consider them an important client we need to keep happy at all costs."

Murph put a sympathetic hand on Beefy's shoulder.

"That's it for today, guys. Give 'em heaps," concluded Raymond as he handed out the day's job sheets.

My job sheet listed an unidentified item to be picked up from the village association's "entertainment venue" in Maleny.

By the time I was driving back up the mountain, it was pouring with rain. I was still surprised by how little space there was between the rain drops in Australia. In the UK, the rain followed a well-worn pathway of continuous drizzle released by apathetic gray clouds. It was different in Australia. The clouds were intense and angry, and hurtled the rain down to earth in fits of rage. I'd had similar experiences with the respective peoples from both countries.

After locating the village association's "entertainment venue," which was actually the Hairy Lemon Pub in the center of Maleny, I parked the truck. I hopped out while Mia rested in the vehicle.

Upon entering, I discovered the pub was as empty as you'd expect at ten o'clock in the morning. The only sound I could hear was the clunking of heavy machinery being operated out the back.

"Hello?" I called out as I pushed open a door behind the main bar.

No one answered, but the machinery kept grinding away. With only that noise to guide me, I walked through a small kitchen area which ended at a scratched fridge door. I pulled the handle and the door opened to reveal a refrigerated room enclosing hundreds of tall, thin cylinders surrounding a cube-shaped freezer which was rotating on top of a spinning machine.

Without warning, a huge hairy hand deposited itself on my shoulder. It had my attention. "Who are you, mate?" asked a giant of a man wearing a beer-stained singlet and thongs. Straight away, I recognized him as the unmusical noisemaker from the bogus Make Australia Green Again Music Festival.

"I'm with Holy Crap Rubbish Removals," I managed to blurt out. "I'm here to collect *something*."

"Oh yeah," the giant responded. "Follow me."

I followed his enormous footsteps as he escorted me out the back of the pub.

"These are yours to take," he said as he pointed at five large metal drums lined up alongside some rubbish bins. Their lids were all welded closed so it was impossible to tell what was inside.

"Can I ask what's inside these bad boys?" I asked.

"Nah, mate, you can't," he responded as he stepped on my foot and almost broke every bone in it.

I yelped like a small dog, but the giant didn't remove his gigantic foot.

"What was Raymond thinking trusting you like this? Murph and Beefy don't ask unhelpful questions," he continued, annoyed. "Here's what you need to do. Take these bins away and bury them somewhere no one will ever find them like the good little trash dasher you are. And guess what else you need to do?"

"What's that?" I asked through the pain.

"Absolutely fucking nothing," he stated as he removed his offending foot. "You just need to get the hell out of here. Can ya manage that, mate, can ya?"

"I'll give it my best shot," I replied.

I tried picking up one of the metal bins, but it didn't budge.

"I'll give you a hand with that, mate," said the suddenly helpful giant as he threw one of the bins over his shoulder as though it was a small child ready for a game. He tossed it into the back of truck number thirteen, then he returned for the rest of the bins. The truck groaned under the weight of inexplicability.

As I drove away from the pub, I was unsure what to do with my mysterious cargo. Eventually,

I decided to drop the bins off at Jude and Wolf's place since Wolf was convinced he could use pretty much anything to recycle into his unique art.

Jude came over to greet me as I drove up their driveway. "Are you OK?" she asked with concern.

"I'm surviving, thanks," I replied. "Why?"

"It's just that Wolf said he's been experiencing strange feelings from the items you've been dropping off," Jude answered.

"What kind of strange feelings?" I asked.

"I'll let Wolf tell you about it when he's awake," Jude responded. "He's sleeping in because he's finished working on the items you brought him. For all of our sakes, please keep them coming. Anything to stop that man's hands from becoming the devil's playthings, or rather, sleep things."

"Funny you should say that," I said. "I've got some steel drums to drop off for Wolf right now. The only problem is I'm not sure what's inside them. I'd like to be here when he opens them if that's alright. I'm curious."

"Of course," Jude responded. "We'll yell out before Wolf opens them."

"Thanks. I must dash. Mia and I have somewhere we need to be," I explained.

The Pelicans

After driving the truck back home, I jogged over to the garden shed and opened the door. Monty the python lay on the workbench and peered at me like a teenager who'd been caught sleeping in.

"You're looking well, Monty," I said. "I assume you've been snacking on the tasty mice this region is famous for?"

Monty resumed his slumber like a teenager who intended to keep sleeping for another few months. I walked past him to where the stand-up paddleboard was stored, picked it up, and threw it into the back of the truck. Once Mia was aboard, I drove back down the driveway. As I pulled out onto the road, the old man with the stereo was cycling past. I may have imagined it, but when he noticed me, he appeared to slow down so he could turn his stereo up. However, he still refused to acknowledge me in any way. As he cycled past, the words, "I don't care what you say anymore, this is my life," blared loud in my direction.

Once the old man was out of the way, I drove the short distance down to Lake Baroon. It was windy, so we arrived to discover one-foot-high waves were rippling across the lake's surface with remarkable regularity. Who knew waves were a thing on lakes?

"We'll be fine, girl," I explained to Mia who looked terrified. "We'll just head out for a short paddle to ask the pelicans what's going on around here."

Mia and I got out of the truck and walked down to the lake access point where the waves appeared even larger. I placed the paddleboard onto the lake's surface and watched it rock from side to side as though a watery earthquake was occurring. Despite the water's warnings, I picked Mia up and placed her at the front of the board, then I crawled onto its rear. The rocking motion prevented me from standing up, so I paddled out onto the lake in the kneeling position. As we ventured away from the safety of the shore, the sky filled with sooty clouds. Maybe the water was reflecting its darkness upward, or it was the other way around, but it was soon as dark as dusk despite it being early afternoon.

"I wonder where those pelicans hang out in dicey weather like this," I said to Mia. The moment

I asked the question, the answer popped into my head. Without a second thought, I steered the paddleboard toward Dead Tree Alley. Inexplicably, the waves seemed to shift their direction toward Dead Tree Alley at the same moment and with more velocity than I'd have liked. In short order, a powerful wave emerged out of nowhere, picked up the paddleboard and carried us forward with it. Mia's legs wobbled in protest, as did mine. Beyond not knowing how to surf, our main problem was the speed with which we were travelling as the wave continued to accelerate. The tall, dead eucalyptus trees loomed up ahead like burly gatekeepers within an obstacle course of ghostly truths.

Once we entered Dead Tree Alley, things turned hairy fast. I thrust the paddle deep into the water behind the paddleboard and swerved right just in time to avoid being slammed into a thick-stumped tree with sharp branches sticking out at neck height. I celebrated not being decapitated by slinging the paddle across to the other side to avoid the next impending collision. After a few more swerves and near misses, I noticed we were hurtling toward the rocky shoreline which the waves were crashing into and reverberating backwards from. With growing desperation, I tried to steer us out of the wave's pull, but it refused to let us go. As the inevitable collision with the shoreline approached, I knelt down and pulled Mia toward me. I swiveled around in front of her, then I curled my body around hers. As I held her tight, Mia's leg shaking stopped for a brief moment while we hovered in suspended animation. Seconds later, we smashed into the shoreline. The paddleboard came to a grinding halt while the ball of skin and fur otherwise known as Mia and I continued flying through the air. After hurtling a few yards, gravity reared its ugly head and we crash-landed onto dry land. I expected the sharp rocks to rip me apart, but all I experienced was shock as I skidded along some sand while Mia rode me like a paddleboard. Once we grinded to a halt, I opened my eyes to find Mia lying on my chest smiling at me. She was fine. Beyond a few bruises and age-exacerbated aches and pains, I was as well.

Mia disembarked and I stood up to survey the scene. The thick bushland behind us appeared to be untouched by humans. There was a dirt road beside us which led through the bush into the lake as though amphibious vehicles had been driving in and out of the water. The road was overgrown indicating it hadn't been used recently, yet it had the well-loved look of a mainstay country road. It didn't make any sense. Why would anyone drive into the lake?

Mia remained seated on the beach, staring up at some nearby trees where a squadron of twenty pelicans were peering down at us. Each pelican had colonized a separate branch, which they were squatting on like proud home owners with an excellent knowledge of property law.

"Well done, Mutt Dog, you found them!" I exclaimed.

Mia gave me a look which could only mean, "No shit, Sherlock."

In short order, one of the pelicans flew down from its branch and landed on the ground beside Mia. It opened its beak to communicate with its brethren through a series of movements and squawks. Soon, another pelican landed on the ground, then another, and then another. Within a couple of minutes, all twenty pelicans had surrounded Mia in a circle on the ground—just as the wallabies, possums, kookaburras, and platypus had done. Mia didn't appear to be doing or saying anything, but the pelicans intermittently opened their beaks as though they were communicating with her. This went on for at least an hour. Then, after a short nod at Mia, one the pelicans flapped its wings and took off, and the others followed. Within seconds, all the pelicans had flown back to the same branches from whence they came, where they resumed observing us from above.

With Mia's pelican communication session over, my mind turned to paddling back across the lake. However, the waves continued to pound the shoreline with oceanic velocity, making it clear we weren't getting out of Dead Tree Alley that evening. It was a quandary. No one knew where we were, which meant no one was coming to save us.

Mia nudged me, indicating she had something to say. I jumped up to write out an alphabet on the beach area. The sand was hard and rocky so I needed the help of a stick to make the letters legible.

Once I'd finished, I thought long and hard about the right question to ask. "Mutt Dog, what are the bad people trying to cover up?"

Mia didn't need to think. She walked over to the C, the A, the K, and the E.

"Cake?" I asked, perplexed. "What type of cake?"

Mia considered my question before she walked over to the Y, the E, the L, the L, the O, and the W.

"Yellow cake?" I asked, stumped.

I contemplated some potential rational explanations. Maybe someone had hidden something valuable in a cake at one of the village association gatherings. Unlikely. Or maybe the village association had discovered the recipe to a delicious cake which was making them millions of dollars. No way—those people didn't know the meaning of wholesome or legal. As I unsuccessfully pondered

Mia's mysterious words, I lay back and fell asleep where we were sitting.

When I awoke, the sun was rising. I'd slept all through the night. Mia was curled up beside me, which was why I was so warm on an otherwise chilly night. As a slither of sunlight on the horizon reanimated the dark world in which we found ourselves, I noticed the waves had stopped crashing into the shoreline. The water was calm. I breathed a sigh of relief. Remarkably, the pelicans were still squatting on their tree branches above. They'd somehow slept all through the night in the standing position without losing their balance. It was either more comfortable than it looked, or they were determined to assert their branch ownership rights come hell or high water. As I sat amidst the stillness of that early morning, I didn't want to be anywhere but where we were. I wondered if this was what being at home felt like.

Once Mia woke up, I helped her mount the paddleboard and relaunched it for the journey back across the lake. A currawong sang a soothing song as I paddled through the dark water which no longer frightened me. In fact, as I looked into the lake's black water, I was momentarily grateful that I couldn't see through to the other side. Being stuck in the land of unanswered questions above the waterline had forced me to notice what a beautiful place it was—a promised land where natural beauty reigns supreme. For the first time since arriving in Australia, I'd found something I was searching for. Then we arrived back on the other side of the lake.

Leonard the Lonely

Our impromptu night of camping took its toll on Mia. Maybe it was the cold or lack of sleep, but she had zero energy that morning. As a result, she opted to stay at home when I headed off for the day's trash dashing. She curled up in a crumpled heap in her basket and drifted off to sleep.

As I drove away without Mia by my side, I felt as empty as the broken water tank I'd collected from O'Hara's place, and just as split down the middle. The bright blue sky above appeared colorless, anticolorful even.

When I arrived at the depot, the trash dashers were waiting in a circle for Raymond to arrive for training.

"Morning, Hawaiian Shirt!" said Murph. "Listen, we've got a question for you."

"What's that?" I asked, on edge.

"Where are *you* dumping your trash at the end of each shift?" he replied.

"What's it to you if one of us does the right thing?" I asked.

"We have business standards to uphold, mate!" he exclaimed.

"Back in a jiffy," I stated.

I walked into Raymond's office where he was busy working on his laptop. "Morning, Raymond," I said. "Do you mind if I teach today's professional training on business ethics?"

"Good idea. I'm under the pump here. Here are today's job sheets and the training notepad," Raymond responded as he handed them to me without looking up.

I marched back outside to the trash dashers. "Guys, I'm running today's professional training, and the name of the lesson is 'An Introduction to Business Ethics.' Feel free to take notes."

Beefy let out a harsh attempt at a derogatory laugh, and the rest of the trash dashers followed his lead.

Unperturbed, I threw the infamous training notepad onto the ground before I knelt down and wrote two words at the top of the page: "Ethical" and "Unethical." The trash dashers crowded around like preprogrammed robots ready to receive their next orders.

"Who can give me some examples of ethical business practices?" I asked.

My question was met by an aggressive silence.

"It's OK, I'll help you out," I continued as I wrote out the words "Honesty," "Trustworthiness," "Acting in Clients' Best Interests," and "Protecting the Environment."

"Are you taking the piss?" asked an angry Beefy. "Protecting the environment isn't an ethical issue, moron. That's up to the government, not us."

"Thanks, Beefy," I responded. "You got the right answer, albeit it to the wrong question. That brings me to the second list."

"You're the wrong question, mate," seethed Murph.

"Let's populate the 'Unethical' list. I expect some enthusiastic responses to this one," I said as I wrote down "Avoiding Responsibility," "Bribery," "Bogus Contracts," and "Double Dipping Rubbish Collections."

Beefy unleashed some more perverted laughter before he added, "As if we'd double-dip? Do the words 'in perpetuity' mean anything to ya?"

"Thanks for providing yet another example of what not to do. You're a gifted man," I stated.

"Thanks," responded a proud Beefy.

"The big boss will hear about your shithouse behavior," interjected Murph. "Your days in this country are numbered."

"What a wonderful point to conclude with. All our days are numbered, so let's make them count by doing the right thing," I said, as I handed out their job sheets for the day.

"What a turdwad!" an unnamed trash dasher exclaimed as I walked away.

My job sheet revealed I was due to pick up some old furniture from a house in Maroochydore. I drove to the pickup address, said hello to the client, collected their dusty old furniture, then left. As the furniture landed inside the truck's belly, echoing back the rumblings of a job well done, I felt nothing.

Before driving back up the mountain, I collected the items the trash dashers had predictably dumped outside some nearby properties at the end of their shifts. As agreed, I stopped in at Jude and Wolf's place to deliver the load en route to home. When I arrived, Jude was mowing their front lawn on an ancient ride-on mower with a top speed of about half a mile an hour. "That looks like a solid stash!" she called out. "It's good news for the lord of the slumber."

"Is he around?" I asked.

"He's asleep I'm afraid," Jude replied. "By the way, Wolf can't open those steel bins you dropped off as they're properly welded shut. But Mad Jack has a brand-new jackhammer which should do the job. He's popping around in a couple of days to help out."

"How on earth does Mad Jack carry a jackhammer around with him?" I asked.

"There's more to that old goat than most people realize," Jude stated without going into detail.

"Well, I'll make sure I'm here to witness the grand opening," I responded. "Did Wolf mention anything about those feelings he experienced the other day?"

"Not really," Jude replied. "He just asked if that swimming pool had been owned by members of the Rural Fire Service, but I didn't know."

"OK, thanks, Jude," I said, feeling uneasy.

When I returned home, I walked inside to discover Mia was still asleep in the same position as when I'd left.

"How are you feeling, Mutt Dog?" I asked.

She opened her eyes and peered at me, but she didn't raise her head.

"Hopefully the next vitamin C booster will help," I added. "In the meantime, you're to take it easy, you hear?"

Mia closed her eyes and drifted back to sleep, so I sat down on the sofa without my partner in crime to talk to. Within minutes, loneliness engulfed me like a hungry version of one Emmanuel's stuffed frogs. I imagined him to be called Leonard the

Lonely. He had a habit of sitting perfectly still while he waited to chow down on lonely souls at their most vulnerable. That fat bastard didn't need to eat that day, but he saw his opportunity. The truth was he'd been eyeing me up as a potential meal for months. I visualized him opening his massive, warty mouth and swallowing me down whole without even chewing. Who could blame him? I was as alone and lonely as a person could be. But there was a more concerning question Leonard's presence raised...if this was how I was coping with Mia being tired out by her illness, how was I going to survive losing her?

My thoughts drifted to Emmanuel. I felt an urgent need to talk with him, but I remembered he was weak and tired as he was recovering in hospital. Regardless, I decided to call him to tell him everything would be alright. The truth is, I needed to believe the same thing. I pressed dial on my phone.

The phone rang a few times before Veronica, the same nurse I'd previously spoken to, answered with her kind but efficient voice. "Hello, Will."

"Hi, Veronica. How's Emmanuel doing?" I asked.

"The doctors have just sedated him," she replied. "A few minutes ago, he was ranting and raving about a stuffed frog, if you can believe it."

"Oh, I can," I replied. "Did he happen to mention its name?"

"Now you're testing me," she responded. "Was it Lionel? No, something like that though."

"It wasn't Leonard, by any chance?" I asked, knowing the answer.

"That's it, Leonard! How did you know that?" she asked, surprised. "Leonard the Lonely, I think it was called. Isn't he imaginative? Once he started shouting at us that this Leonard the Lonely was running rampant and needed to be pacified, the doctors gave him a sedative to calm him down. He's sleeping it off as we speak."

"Lucky him," I replied.

Both Sides Now

Mia and I were due to meet Miranda at the beach the next morning. Mia remained exhausted so I carried her from the bed to her basket, then I carried her to the truck and placed her basket on the front seat. She closed her eyes and resumed her slumber like a baby who didn't care where she slept as long as she had room to curl up.

Miranda was waiting for us at our normal meeting point at Mudjimba Beach. I opened the passenger door and half expected Mia to launch herself onto the sand as she always did, but she remained asleep. I picked up her basket and carried her down to the beach. Miranda's facial expression momentarily fell into despair when I approached carrying my motionless dog. She took a deep breath and forced a smile for all three of our sakes. "Morning, you two!" she beamed. "How is my favorite hound and hound owner this morning?"

"We're having a slower start to the day, but we're doing okay, thanks," I answered with a smile. "How have you been?"

"Fair to muddling, but all the better for seeing you two," she responded.

We walked down the sandy track onto the beach which was being caressed by soft sunshine that sparkled off its metallic grains.

I placed Mia's basket down on the beach. Miranda and I sat down beside her.

"So tell me, Miranda, what's on your mind?" I asked.

Miranda held some sand in her hands, which she let slip through her fingers. "I'm thinking of making a career change."

"Why?" I asked. "I thought you were enjoying pet communication."

"I was, until I met you two. The truth is, I've felt like a fraud ever since the day Mia revealed her ability to communicate," Miranda confessed.

"I thought that had only proven your talent as a pet communicator extraordinaire," I responded.

"I didn't do anything, Will. Believe me, it was all Mia," Miranda said. "I was just in the right place at the right time to witness something miraculous."

"But you inspired the whole thing," I replied. "The only reason it happened is because Mia and I listened to your valuable advice."

"Maybe, but I don't feel like I'm doing enough," Miranda explained. "I want to help dogs like Mia thrive *in this world*."

I wasn't sure what to say, so I remained silent. Mia opened her eyes and slowly stood up in her basket. She gazed around at the nearby sand.

"It looks like Mia's got something to say about it," I said as I stood up to draw an alphabet in the sand.

Mia waited patiently. Once I'd finished writing out the letters, she hobbled over to the G, the E, and the T. She then paused before she walked to the A. And then she walked to the D, the O, and the G, before returning to her basket into which she collapsed.

"Maybe it's time you got your own dog, Miranda?" I suggested.

Miranda laughed. "Oh course it bloody is! I've been doing all this work to help the dog population at large, but I've never owned my own dog. I think I've avoided it because I've witnessed so much pain experienced by dog owners when their dogs cross over to the other side."

"Well, the good news is when your dog does have to cross over, it won't stop you from communicating. You can happily coexist on both sides," I responded.

"But it's not the same, is it?" Miranda replied as she stroked Mia. "If I've learnt one thing as a pet communicator, it's that dogs love us in ways humans can't love one another. How many humans do you know who are always happy to see you, always loving, always positive, always loyal, always constant?"

"The sum total of zero," I answered. "So do you think owning your own dog may be the only change you need to make?"

"No," Miranda stated. "I still want to do more with my life than I'm doing right now. I'm not sure what that means, but I'll know when the right path presents itself."

"Welcome to my world," I replied.

After parting ways with Miranda, I drove the truck back up the mountain. It rained in short sharp bursts along the way which thankfully washed away the truck's smelly gunk which had built up over recent days.

As I was about to turn into our driveway, I came face-to-face with the infamous music-loving, human-hating cyclist. He was kneeling on our driveway while he perused a flat bike tire with his stereo playing "Bridge Over Troubled Water" on a lower volume than usual.

"Hello," I said as I wound down the window.

The old man didn't appear to have heard me as he remained silent.

"Hello," I said again as I climbed down from the truck.

As I stepped closer, he suddenly noticed me and jumped up into a martial arts stance as though he was facing up to an aggressive enemy.

"It's OK," I said. "I'm not here to do you harm."

The old man relaxed and put his hand behind his ear, which he appeared to be scratching. "What's that?" he asked.

"I just said hello," I responded.

"These bloody hearing aids are more trouble than they're worth," he added.

"Did you just turn your hearing aid on?" I asked.

"What's that?" he asked.

"Here, let me check," I said as I stepped closer.

The old man once again jumped into a defensive stance, ready to protect himself from all and sundry. I held my open hands in the air to show him I wasn't going to hit him, then I slowly moved my hand to where his hearing aid was perched behind his ear. He watched my every move as though I might turn on him at any moment. Upon inspection, it was apparent his hearing aid was turned off, so I fiddled with the control switch until a soft start-up tone could be heard. "Is that better?" I asked.

"What's that?" he replied with a shake of his head.

"Shit. I thought I'd turned it on," I said.

"Listen, mate, swearing around your elders is unacceptable," he responded.

"You can hear me?" I asked.

"Of course I bloody well can," he replied. "And what a shock it is to hear again, only to discover we've been inundated by posh-speaking Poms with catastrophic dress sense. Can you turn my hearing aid back off, you bastard?"

From his stony facial expression, it was hard to tell if he was serious or joking.

"I have the same problem," I added. "Everywhere I turn, I hear this angry nasally accent which sounds like a question is constantly being asked, when in fact it isn't, but probably should be. Do you know how to turn the volume down on that, please?"

The old man gave me a hard stare which lasted a full minute. I'd once again misjudged my audience, or as Raymond had highlighted, my lack of audience. As the old man contemplated his response, I half expected him to karate kick me in the head. But then he surprised me. "Billy Baxter," he said as he held his hand out with a smile.

"Will Watson," I replied as I shook his hand.

"Have I seen you before?" he asked.

"I don't think you have," I responded, "although you've nearly run me over a few times."

"Shame I missed," Billy Baxter said with a wink.

"Why don't you bring your bike in?" I suggested. "I'll try to fix that flat tire of yours."

"Alright then," he said as he picked his bike up off the ground and pushed it forward along with a bike trailer which was attached to its rear.

Billy Baxter followed me toward the garden shed. When we walked inside, we discovered Monty the python was napping on the bench.

"Sweet Jesus!" exclaimed Billy Baxter. "He's a big one, isn't he?"

"People say that to me all the time," I said.

"Look, I'm not interested in your dick size, thanks, mate. It's just not my thing," responded Billy Baxter.

"Noted," I replied.

I moved Monty's not insignificant tail aside in order to rummage around on the bench. He slid away to continue his nap in a quieter corner of the shed. After a short search, I located an old bike tire repair kit someone had left behind.

"So why are you helping a grumpy old man, Will?" Billy Baxter asked.

"You grumpy? Surely not," I said.

"We both know that's a lie," he responded.

"I'm just being neighborly," I stated. "Also, I appreciated it when you gave Ben Flinders a scare the other day."

"Shame I missed the bastard," he responded.

"So that was an intentional lesson for him?" I asked.

"Does it look like anything I do is intentional?" Billy Baxter replied.

"Yes," I said.

"Well, it's one of the joys of being old and deaf. People treat you like you're an inanimate piece of furniture. So I've decided to act like an inanimate piece of furniture, but with a will of my own. Do you know how confusing that is for most people?" he asked.

"So it's all about getting the last laugh?" I asked as I glued the tire repair patch onto his bike tire.

"There's more to it than laughing," Billy Baxter responded. "I'm showing the bastards in this twisted community that I'm still an individual. As long as I'm alive and kicking, people like Ben Flinders can shove it."

"You're not the only one who feels like that," I said as I went in search of a tire pump.

When I returned with one, I noticed Billy Baxter's impressive bike trailer had shiny suspension forks on each of its four tires. "What do you use that trailer for?" I asked.

"You'd be surprised by how many animals need a lift around here," he stated.

"Animals?" I asked.

"Whenever an animal is injured on the road, I give them a lift to the vet or a wildlife charity," he responded. "The local Range Rover drivers wreak havoc, so someone needs to pick up the pieces."

"Yes, some locals don't give animals the respect they deserve," I agreed as I pumped air back in the repaired tire.

"And then some," Billy Baxter responded with a sad shake of his head.

"Hey, Mia's due at the vet's tomorrow," I said as an idea occurred to me. "She's being treated for cancer. Do you think we could borrow your bike and trailer for the day to transport her into town and then onward? She's not well enough to walk at the moment, and I know she'd enjoy the fresh air."

"I'll go one better than that," responded Billy Baxter. "I'll cycle her into town myself, and I'll bring along a spare bike for you."

"Thanks, we'd both like that," I stated as I finished pumping the tire up. "Sir, your bike is ready to hit the road again."

"You're alright for a Pom," Billy Baxter said as he turned his hearing aid off and cycled back down the driveway.

Dog Taxi

When the early morning sun attempted to awaken me from a deep slumber the next day, I heard a soft voice whispering nearby.

"Watch the rose open its petals,
Revealing to the world a beauty,
Too powerful for the human eye to understand,
Just because the light asked it to open up,
Knowing being open is better than being closed,
For both the rose and the light alike,
Don't be afraid of the light, my dear."

I opened my eyes. Jude was sitting on a chair beside the bed. She was smiling at Mia who was still asleep by my side. "Morning, sleepyheads."

"Morning, Jude," I replied. "Sorry I didn't hear you come in."

"You and Mia both need rest at this difficult time," she responded.

"Can I get you a cup of coffee?" I asked.

"No, thanks," she stated. "I just popped over to tell you the news."

"Oh yes?" I responded.

"Wolf heard from Mad Jack that at the next village association meeting, they're planning to pass a rule stating that everyone who's been living in Maleny for more than fifteen years has to either accept a formal role in the village association or be banished from the area," Jude explained.

"How can they do that?" I asked, incredulous.

"That's the question we've all been asking for years," Jude responded with a solemn shake of her head.

"But why fifteen years?" I asked.

"There's only one local event of significance that occurred fifteen years ago," Jude replied.

"The flooding of Lake Baroon," I stated.

"Bingo," Jude said.

"Jude, what was that land used for before it was flooded?" I asked.

"That's the million-dollar question," Jude responded. "It's been the subject of intense debate between Wolf and me for years. Mind you, we've never attended a village association meeting so we're not in the know. But we're unusual. Most people in this twisted community are scared into attending that corrupt meeting every damn year.

They'll all know exactly what happened down at Baroon."

"Do you have any theories?" I asked.

"All I know is the village association bought that land from Ben Flinders's family about ten years before it was flooded," Jude replied. "God knows what they used it for during that time. You'll have seen the size of the dead trees in the lake. It was impossible to view the property at the time as they installed towering security fences around it to ensure no one entered. A few local kids once tried to climb over that fence. It cost them a trip to hospital when they were electrocuted by an electric current well in excess of what's legally allowed. A girl named Michelle permanently lost all feeling in one of her hands that day."

"You don't mean Michelle, the vet?" I asked.

Before Jude could respond, there was a loud knock at the door. It was Billy Baxter wearing his cycling helmet and pointing at his ear.

"I've got it, Billy," I said as I turned his hearing aid on.

"Reporting for dog taxi duties, sir," Billy stated as he saluted.

"That's not Maleny's wobbliest cyclist, is it?" Jude called out.

"That's not Maleny's prettiest girl, is it?" replied Billy as he stepped inside.

"You old dog!" Jude exclaimed.

"You haven't aged a day," Billy continued.

"You only last saw me yesterday when I nearly ran you over because you wouldn't move out of the bloody way," Jude stated.

"You see, I never lie," Billy responded.

"That makes you unusual in these parts," Jude said. "Have you heard about the village association's latest shenanigans?"

"My hearing aid only has a limited battery charge," Billy answered. "I can't waste it hearing about those lowlifes."

"Being an ostrich won't help us anymore, Billy," Jude stated with growing seriousness.

"So when's the next pile of shit due to hit the communal fan?" responded Billy, without asking what Jude was talking about.

"At the village association meeting tomorrow," answered Jude.

"Good to know. I'll turn my hearing aid off that day," said Billy.

Jude shook her head, disappointed.

"Let's wake Cinderella up so we can take her to the ball," suggested Billy.

Mia was fast asleep despite all the talking. I knelt down to stroke her. She eventually opened her eyes, surprised to discover Jude and Billy in the living room.

"Come on, girl," I said as I picked up Mia within her basket.

Billy and Jude followed me down the steps to where Billy's bike was waiting along with a spare bike in the trailer. I gently placed Mia and her basket inside the trailer where she laid her head down while continuing to watch events unfold. Billy mounted his bike while I climbed onto the spare bike.

"What a curious spectacle you three make," Jude said. "Just when I thought things couldn't get any stranger around here, you go and prove me wrong."

"This is what you missed out on, Judey," responded Billy as he pretended to flex an arm muscle. "If only you hadn't met Wolf, you'd have had a shot at real happiness."

"See you tomorrow, Will," Jude said, ignoring Billy's jibe.

The three of us started cycling down the driveway, but Billy suddenly slammed on his brakes. "I nearly forgot!" he exclaimed as he pressed play on his ancient stereo. With "We are the Champions" blaring at a louder volume than I was comfortable with, we drove out onto the street. Billy shouted at the universe, "I've had my share of sand kicked in my face, but I've come through," with a voice more out of tune than a broken record doused with petrol and set fire to. Jude was right—we couldn't have been less normal. But for some reason, I had an uncontrollable grin on my face.

Billy led the way, and I cycled behind. Mia's bemused expression indicated she was only buying into whatever was happening because she was too tired to fight it. Billy's cycling technique could at best be described as free-spirited. It involved steering his bike in whichever direction he felt so inclined and praying. Each time I thought he was going to crash into a fence or a hedge, he miraculously swerved back onto the road just in time. Whenever a car tried to pass us, Billy resumed his pretence of not being able to hear their loud horns, abusive shouting, and revving car engines. Hearing aid on or off, Billy remained blissfully at peace on his own journey no matter what was happening around him.

Around halfway to town, a black Range Rover appeared behind us and hovered with ominous intent.

"Let's pull over, Billy!" I called out. "It's Ben bloody Flinders."

Rather than stopping, Billy gave me an enthusiastic thumbs-up. However, I felt uneasy. It didn't take a genius to know that blocking Ben Flinders in his Range Rover was a red rag to a bull. Predictably, Ben Flinders reacted by accelerating forward and connecting his hard front bumper with the rear of my bike, pushing me forward against my will. Within seconds, the distance between my bike and the trailer Mia was riding in decreased to a couple of inches. Enough was enough. Ben Flinders could hurt me, but I wouldn't tolerate anything happening to Mia. "Back off, you bastard!" I shouted as I leveraged my growing momentum to veer off to the left-hand side of his vehicle. Ben Flinders was wrong-footed by my swift change of direction, so he slammed on his brakes to ensure I couldn't loop back around his car. However, as his vehicle decelerated, I was already standing on my bike pedals and braking hard. By the time he slowed his Range Rover to a halt, I was in the perfect position to accidentally connect my ample bottom with his shiny side mirror. It snapped off without a fight and hung from the side like a limp-wristed hand which had lost an arm wrestle. When Ben Flinders noticed the damage done to his precious vehicle, he shrieked some no doubt obscene words from within his sound-insulated cabin. Like Billy Baxter, I couldn't hear a word, so I just smiled and waved at him as he got out of his car to survey the carnage. When I caught up with Billy, he was oblivious to the whole incident. His devil-may-care attitude was proving contagious, although I'm not sure the devil was happy about it.

By the time we arrived at the vet's surgery, Billy was in need of a break. "I'm not as young as I used to be!" he exclaimed as he parked his bike out the front. "But I delivered the precious cargo as promised."

"That you did," I said.

Mia showed her appreciation with a smile.

"We'll be back in half an hour or so, Billy," I explained.

"Your carriage will await," Billy replied with a bow.

I carried Mia inside the vet's surgery and placed her basket on the ground in the waiting area. Michelle poked her head around the door from her consulting room. "Morning, Mr. and Mrs. Watson."

"Still no receptionist?" I asked.

"No, I think someone in this town is trying to make life difficult for me," she replied. "Bring her in, Will."

I carried Mia into the room and placed her down next to the vitamin C drip in the corner. She didn't try to hide this time.

"Michelle, how long have you lived in Maleny?" I asked as she attached the drip.

"Only forever," she replied. "Would you believe I grew up here?"

"I'm sure it's changed a lot since you were a kid?" I asked.

"Yes and no," Michelle responded. "The biggest change happened when the lake was flooded. Since then, it's been the same tune playing on repeat."

"Did you happen to see the property underneath Lake Baroon before it was flooded?" I asked.

"No, but my attempted peek at it as a teenager cost me the feeling in this hand," Michelle responded as she held up her left hand. "That'll teach me for being young and inquisitive."

"I'm sorry to hear it," I said.

"Still, I haven't had it as bad as some," Michelle continued with a distracted air.

"Who do you mean?" I asked.

"Do you know Mad Jack?" she replied.

Before I could answer, an elderly woman walked into reception carrying a white Persian cat who was meowing wildly.

"Will, can you please stay with Mia for the rest of her therapy?" Michelle asked. "I'll be back shortly."

"Of course," I responded as I stroked Mia's head.

Mia was more lively from the moment the vitamin C started flowing into her. She gazed up at me with happy eyes which told me she was appreciating all everyone was doing for her.

"You're graceful even now, Mutt Dog," I said.

However, my feelings were far from graceful. The truth was my blood was boiling. The gentle, beautiful creature I loved most in the world was fighting for her life while bad people like Ben Flinders were walking around perfectly healthy when all they did was make people's lives worse. Why does the world work like that?

Once Mia's vitamin C therapy was finished, I settled up the vet bill. "What were you saying about Mad Jack before, Michelle?" I asked.

"You know, Will," she answered, "one thing I've learnt around here is not to ask questions. Someone always gets upset."

"They only get upset because they've got an issue they want to hide or ignore," I responded. "Asking questions is a healthy thing to do, and I'll be doing more of it from now on. The people of this town best prepare themselves."

"You sound like a superhero from a bygone era," Michelle said with a half-nervous laugh.

"Thanks, but I'm more like the sidekick to a superhero," I replied.

I carried Mia back outside where Billy was dancing on the street to "Dancing Queen." It was a sight to behold. He was jumping around like a drunk kangaroo in need of directions. He was twisting and turning like a tailless platypus swimming in ever decreasing circles. And he was jigging sideways like a special needs possum with an unfulfilled love of dad-dancing. The passers-by stared at him in disbelief before crossing the road to avoid walking in his vicinity. When he noticed us approaching, Billy zigzagged over carrying Mia's basket. For her benefit, he sang a few words as he helped her aboard the trailer: "Ooh see that girl, watch that scene, digging the dancing queen."

"Where to next, kind madam?" Billy asked Mia once the song had ended.

"Do you know the creek near the platypus viewing platform?" I asked.

"I recall playing in it as a youngster back when the world was a simpler place," Billy responded.

"Let's head there," I said.

"An off-road adventure it is, then," Billy replied as he pirouetted towards his bike like a long-term, out-of-work ballet dancer.

Billy cycled onward and I followed. His stereo seemed to have a mind of its own. As he cycled, it started playing an unrecognizable tune which sounded like reggae-inspired African tribal music with sea shanty vocals in the background. When we reached the roundabout where we were meant to turn right, Billy veered left. Mia gave me a look from the trailer which could only translate into, "What the hell is going on?"

"Billy, that's the wrong way!" I called out.

Billy gave me a silent thumbs-up before he continued toward wherever he was going in high spirits. As we cycled into the busy part of town, many passers-by stared in our direction. Some were shocked but most were laughing. A group of children ran to the side of the road and cheered us on. "Go Team Doggy, go!" they exclaimed. A line of bystanders raised their hands in an impromptu version of The Wave as we passed by. Mia sat up in her basket for a better view while Billy waved at the children as though he'd always been a local celebrity.

Without warning, Billy then veered right despite there not being a road that way. Unperturbed, he cycled toward the street curb which he swiftly mounted with an abrupt bump. Mia was momentarily launched into the air before she landed back in her basket, while a family jumped out of the way as Billy cycled across a busy footpath. I followed the pathway cleared by Billy's wake as he cycled toward another group of unsuspecting people who were queuing at a café serving takeaway coffee on the street.

"Watch out!" I shouted at the innocent bystanders.

In unison, the coffee queuers jumped out of the way to avoid being wiped out by the rogue cyclist known as Billy Baxter. Their quick thinking had ensured their survival but that was already old news. By then, Billy had veered left and was hurtling down a side alley beside the café. I also swerved left as I shouted "Sorry!" at the shocked coffee queuers who were regathering themselves after their near-death experience. Billy and Mia were already out of sight since the alley ended only a few yards ahead. I cycled around the corner to discover a paved garden area inhabited by a few coffee drinkers who were escaping the hustle and bustle of the main street. However, the hustle and bustle had found them anyway—and its name was Billy Baxter. One coffee drinker watched in horror as Billy cycled away wearing his coffee as a shirt stain. And a middle-aged woman screamed a scream of pure terror when she noticed Billy was hurtling toward her. He swerved just in time, missing her by inches. The woman continued to scream as I cycled past in pursuit of an old man and my dog.

"Everything will be alright!" I called out to the screaming woman, but she was too busy being terrified to hear.

As the distance between us grew, Billy cycled through an unkempt garden connecting with the back of the paved area. His African tribal music echoed across the treetops with the rhythm of progress. Once he reached the end of the garden, Billy veered right through an adjacent field. I saw my opportunity to catch up with him by turning into the same field at an earlier exit. However, the grass in that part of the field was long and the surface uneven, so I was forced to slow down to a dawdle. By the time I reached the downtrodden grass Billy and Mia had left in their wake, they were no longer in sight.

With growing frustration, I followed the flattened grass which zigzagged left and right before it carved out a few circles and then continued onward. Against the odds, it looked like Billy was heading in the vague direction of the platypus watching platform. Surely he wasn't heading where he'd intended to? As if answering that question in the affirmative, Billy's pathway abruptly swerved off to the right where it crossed the creek. The lack of footsteps on either side of the water suggested he'd somehow cycled through the rocky creek without dismounting his bike.

Up ahead, I heard an unusual mix of bird songs and animal noises like you'd expect to hear at a zoo. I made a mental note to ask Billy Baxter where he'd bought his hearing aid from. As I followed yet another sharp directional shift, the growing volume of animal voices suggested I was getting closer to the source. So I stopped cycling, leant the bike on a tree, and walked ahead to investigate.

Amidst a clearing in front of the platypus viewing station, Mia sat in her dog basket. All around her were native animals of varying shapes and sizes who were staring at her intently as though they were in the middle of a deep conversation. There were wallabies, kangaroos, koalas, possums, kookaburras, currawongs, bandicoots, and pademelons. On the nearby creek bank, a paddle of platypuses watched on with interest as they wagged their tails within the water. Billy was observing the gathering from a nearby grassy vantage point in respectful silence. As if that wasn't a big enough shock in itself, up on the platypus viewing platform a group of tourists were watching events unfold with excitement. The Whisperer was talking them through the scene below. "So what we're witnessing, folks, is something most unusual in the animal kingdom. This unique golden retriever, Mia, is bringing all these animal species together through her mysterious communication abilities. It's almost like watching a religious congregation, eh?"

"What are they discussing?" asked a South African lady wearing a brand-new Akubra.

"That one's above my paygrade," the Whisperer responded. "All I can say for sure is that's belief we're witnessing. Just look at how calm and steadfast those normally busy creatures are when they look at Mia. Each and every animal down there is feeling connected to her through something they believe to be true."

"Lucky them!" exclaimed the same lady as she took a photo of the animals.

Billy suddenly stood up from where he was seated. I wondered if his hearing aid was turned on or off. "Can't you see?" he called out to the South African lady, but he was really addressing the entire group of tourists.

"What's that, Billy?" asked the Whisperer.

"They're here to teach us!" exclaimed an enthusiastic Billy Baxter as he circled his hands emphatically to ensure everyone was aware he was referring to Mia and the animals congregated around her. "We humans think we know it all. We believe the other species on this great planet should bow down before us in awe of our superior knowledge. But here we are. One dog is able to do all this, and all we can do is watch on in amazement. Do we really know as much as we think we do?"

"That man scares me, Mommy!" a little girl could be heard exclaiming within the group of tourists. Her mother shielded her eyes, while the rest of the group turned their gaze away from Billy Baxter. Once they'd regathered themselves, they resumed taking photographs of the inexplicable spectacle below so they could upload them to social media in the interest of growing their followers.

With a shrug of his shoulders, Billy sat back down, and the animals continued their congregation in relative peace.

Once the tourists left and the animals disbanded, I wandered over to Mia. She was as bright-eyed as she'd ever been and in high spirits. As I stroked her head, she leant in. "You can tell me later, girl," I said. "Just know I couldn't be prouder of you."

As she looked up at me, I knew she was returning the sentiment.

"Shall we head home, Billy?" I suggested.

"You betcha," responded a smiley Billy Baxter.

Wolf Escapes

While I was stroking Mia that evening, I noticed her main lump was growing and it was red raw. There were also smaller lumps popping up all over her body, and she'd started coughing regularly. I was shocked by how fast the cancer was spreading, and how little the vitamin C treatments were doing to hold it back. I gave her dinner, but she only ate a couple of mouthfuls so I tried handfeeding her. She ate a few mouthfuls more out of politeness than hunger, then she placed her head on my lap before she drifted off to sleep. I didn't move from that spot on the ground all night. The idea of interrupting her rest and our time together seemed wasteful.

When I awoke the next morning, Mia was snoring loudly with her head still resting on my lap. Despite the pain caused by sleeping in the upright position, the rhythm of her snoring was as soothing to my ears as the sound of the ocean. A knock at the door interrupted the moment. I placed Mia's head on a pillow and attempted to reanimate my body. When I hobbled over to the door, I was greeted by Jude with the wild, unkempt morning dreadlocks you'd expect from an authentic hippy. "Morning, Will. Just to let you know, Mad Jack has popped around with his jackhammer. He and Wolf are about to open those stubborn steel bins you dropped off the other day."

"Great, I'll come and watch. Mia needs some quiet time anyway," I replied.

Jude and I wandered across the road where a jackhammer could already be heard hammering away within Wolf's shed. We entered the front door to discover Wolf communicating using extravagant hand gestures while Mad Jack annihilated some sandstone rocks with a shiny miniature jackhammer. He turned it off when he noticed Jude and me walk in.

"Morning, Wolf, Jack," I said. "That's a serious piece of kit."

"Only the best for Maleny's lowest-profile homeless person," responded Mad Jack.

"So what's the plan?" I asked.

"The plan is to obliterate the tops off those bloody bins," explained Wolf as he attached an extension cord to the jackhammer. "We should be able to reach it now. You two ladies wait there."

I ignored Wolf's jab.

Jackhammer in hand, Mad Jack stepped toward the steel bins like a soldier approaching the front line of battle. Wolf knelt down and put his arms around one of the bins so Mad Jack could hammer away without it moving away from the blast zone. Mad Jack pressed the green button on the jackhammer and directed it in the vicinity of the bin's welded metal lid. After a few near misses, the jackhammer connected with the bin lid, generating a sharp, abrasive noise amidst a fit of sparks. I covered my ears, and Wolf gave me a look which insinuated I was less of a man for wanting to be able to hear longer term. Mad Jack's entire body shook as the jackhammer attacked the metal, but the bin lid remained stubbornly attached. After a few more minutes of jackhammering without progress, Wolf signalled to Mad Jack to turn the machine off. "Let's swap positions!" Wolf called out. "I want to crack this motherfucker open myself."

Without a word, Mad Jack handed the jackhammer over to Wolf before he positioned his arms around the steel bin, ready for whatever was coming. Wolf smiled a knowing smile as he pressed the green button. He held the revved-up jackhammer high above the bin before he thrust it upon its lid with all his strength. The bin let out a shocked screech indicating Wolf was winning the battle, possibly even the war. So Wolf did it again. He lifted the jackhammer high and forced it down onto the bin lid. With that next surge of force, the bin lid cracked open along the welded lines without any fuss at all.

What happened next seemed to occur in slow motion. Wolf turned the jackhammer off and stepped closer to inspect the open bin. When he saw what was inside it, he turned and screamed "Run!" at all of us. Mad Jack was a little slow on the uptake, but Jude and I didn't need to be asked twice. All three of us charged toward the shed's exit as though our lives depended on it. As we sprinted across the tennis court, Mad Jack made up for lost time and was soon at the front of the pack. Then I stopped running. "What are we running *from*, Wolf?" I called out in the direction of the shed.

There was no response, as Wolf was busy walking backwards out of the shed while staring at the steel bins as though they were armed foes ready to attack. "Stay back! *Way back*!" he shouted over his shoulder.

"Let's wait behind the house," Jude suggested as she headed in that direction.

Mad Jack and I followed. We crouched down and waited behind the house. A minute later, still nothing had happened.

"What on earth is going on?" I asked.

"*Those bastards!*" Mad Jack exclaimed.

"Where's Wolf?" Jude asked.

"I'll go check on him. Wait here," I said.

When I walked around the house, I found an even wilder-haired-than-normal version of Wolf sprinting away from whatever was inside the steel bins. "Get in the car now!" he shrieked as he pointed at a rusty yellow car parked near the end of the driveway.

We all did as Wolf suggested. The four of us climbed into Jude and Wolf's rickety old car which didn't look like it had passed a roadworthy test in the past decade. Without a word, Wolf retrieved a key from behind the sun visor and accelerated down the driveway. He then turned right and drove like a madman along Bald Knob Road, en route to anywhere else.

"What about Mia!" I exclaimed.

"No time. This is a life and death situation," Wolf responded.

"What's in the bins?" I asked.

"Do you know anything about atomic number ninety-two?" Wolf asked as the car skidded around a bend in the road.

"What does that mean?" I asked. "Wolf, Jack, can you please explain what just happened?"

Wolf didn't appear to have heard me as he was busy accelerating over the middle of a roundabout.

We were all momentarily launched into the air, which provided some peaceful respite from the inglorious uncertainty of the moment.

"Those bastards!" Mad Jack reiterated as the car crash-landed with an abrupt thud.

"Who, Jack? Who?" I asked.

"There have been so many," Mad Jack continued without elaborating.

"Let's take a step back, Jack," I said, after taking a deep breath as Wolf accelerated toward another sharp bend in the road. "When did the bad stuff start?"

"More than a quarter of a century ago, when I was the president of the village association," Mad Jack answered.

While Mad Jack was getting his thoughts together, Wolf was mistaking the brake for the accelerator, and the back of the car was skidding across the road toward a large ditch. Rather than slowing down, Wolf reacted to our impending doom by pressing the pedal all the way to the metal. The car's tires spun wildly as the car dovetailed all over the road, but it appeared to be too late to stop whatever was coming. As our number was being called out from above, the only pictures which ran through my mind were of Mia's smiling face letting me know everything would be alright.

At the moment the vehicle was about to crash into the ditch, the car's spinning tires regained a semblance of traction on the road—and Wolf regained a semblance of mental control. Somehow, against the odds, the car hung onto the road, and we had more time to look forward to. However, Wolf didn't celebrate our survival. He just accelerated onward.

"So you were the president of the village association, Jack?" I asked, once I was able to speak again.

"Yes," he replied. "Maleny was a poorer place in those days, but it had a soul."

"What changed, Jack?" I asked.

"What a question!" Mad Jack responded. "Well, things went tits up after Ben Flinders's father, Bob Flinders, attended one of our village association meetings. I'll never forget it. He waltzed in unannounced and requested all the attendees sign a nondisclosure agreement about a lucrative business opportunity for the region."

"So you signed it?" I asked.

"I did, we did. Bob Flinders was the wealthiest man in town, and most of the locals hero-worshipped him at the time," Mad Jack replied.

"What was the opportunity?" I asked.

"Bob explained that he'd discovered some valuable resources on his property down at Baroon," Mad Jack explained with reluctance.

"What *type* of valuable resources, Jack?" I asked.

Mad Jack fell silent as he considered whether to continue. "Bob explained that he'd discovered a shitload of yellowcake throughout the property."

Yellowcake. Just as the pelicans had told Mia.

"What *is* that?" I asked.

Mad Jack paused as though he was trying to recall what it was. "It's uranium, plain and simple. Bob Flinders had discovered an enormous uranium ore deposit on his property."

"I thought uranium mining was illegal in Queensland," I stated.

"It was at the time," replied Mad Jack. "That's why Bob Flinders presented us with a cunning deal."

"What type of deal?" I asked.

"He suggested a profit-sharing agreement based on us agreeing he could mine his property for uranium with the community's help. He talked about how his plan would boost jobs and growth, the only two things the village association cared about," Mad Jack responded.

"How did that help him if uranium mining was illegal?" I asked.

"The law didn't matter to Bob Flinders," Mad Jack answered. "He paid a German industry expert called Claus with similarly non-existent ethics to install a top notch uranium enriching facility at the pub. By the time he'd finished building it, Claus apparently described it as idiot-proof. He's been proven correct. Anyway, Bob then started selling the enriched uranium on the international black market for a massive profit. When I say massive, the numbers were astronomical."

"Oh my god!" I exclaimed as I realized what was inside the bins.

"Wolf, I need to get back to Mia right now!" I shouted.

Wolf was still focused on escaping at the expense of everything else.

"Jude, we need to turn back now," I pleaded.

"Will, you may have noticed Wolf has started thinking for himself," Jude replied as she stared out the window. "God help us all."

Jude was right, we had bigger problems brewing. As we descended the mountain, Wolf was still accelerating, which combined with gravity, was propelling us forward at an insane speed. The old car's speedo was broken, but we must have been travelling at a hundred miles an hour. However, the more immediate problem was that we were travelling on a single-lane country road, so we had to contend with the other drivers on the road.

"Hang on, Jack," I continued. "As the president of the village association at the time, are you saying you agreed to Bob Flinders's illegal uranium mining plan?"

"No way!" Mad Jack exclaimed with a violent shake of his head. "I fought against it with all my energy, but Bob Flinders was a step ahead of me."

"How so?" I asked.

"He'd already bribed all the weaker hands in the village association," Mad Jack explained. "So when I opposed his uranium mining plan, they called a vote for a new president at Bob's request. Guess who put themselves forward for the president's role?"

"Ben bloody Flinders," I seethed.

"Yep," Mad Jack responded. "Ben was a young man at the time, but he'd already mastered the art of corruption thanks to years of training by his old man. He'd also mastered the art of being a total asshole."

"Yes, he's a true master," I said. "So you were kicked out?"

"Not just kicked out," Mad Jack replied. "The village association vowed to make my life a misery if I stayed here. And they've been remarkably true to their word."

"I'm sorry to hear it," I responded.

I suddenly noticed that Wolf was riding on the bumper of a ute in front of us. Rather than braking like a normal driver, Wolf was pushing the ute down the mountain against its will. "Speed up, you daft bastard!" he exclaimed as he honked his horn and hit the steering wheel in a not-quite-right-in-the-head kind of way.

However, the daft bastard in the ute didn't enjoy being pushed down the mountain against his will, so he slammed on his brakes to make his point. When the car decelerated, Wolf reacted by accelerating against the opposing force. The ute driver was clearly of the same older school of thought as Wolf, so he reacted by braking with all the ute's might. For a brief moment, the two opposing forces were roughly balanced, and the two vehicles continued forward at around the speed limit. However, the ute's screeching wheels were burning more rubber than they had to burn, and Wolf's car's engine was revving in ways it was never meant to rev. Something had to give. It wasn't a surprise when Wolf's old engine exploded in a cacophony of unheeded sparks.

Unready to concede victory, Wolf kept pushing down on the accelerator in the hope of a more collaborative response. However, nothing happened. The car slowed to a limp drift before it grinded to an inglorious halt, freeing the ute driver to resume his onward journey minus the nutcase behind him. The ute driver soon realized he'd won whatever game he and Wolf had been playing in the most satisfying of ways. In a final victorious gesture, he wound down his window and wound up his middle finger for Wolf's educational benefit. Wolf stared at the erect finger standing loud and proud as he boiled within an internal cesspool of embarrassment.

"Pull the car to the side of the road, you daft bastard," Jude instructed her defunct husband.

Wolf followed Jude's orders. We all knew he'd probably resume doing so from that moment until the end of his life. He hunched over the steering wheel exhausted by his escape efforts while an overpowering stench of burnt rubber stagnated within the vehicle.

"Jack, one thing I don't understand is why Ben Flinders agreed for his property to be flooded if he was running a lucrative, albeit illegal, mine down there," I stated.

"I was out of the loop when that happened," Mad Jack responded. "But you can rest assured he didn't make that decision for the good of his health, or anyone else's for that matter."

"I've got a question too," interjected Wolf as he lifted his head from the steering wheel with renewed urgency. "Why do some of the rubbish items Will dropped off at our place have charcoal on them?"

"That's above my paygrade, I'm afraid. I've been shut out of the system for the past twenty-five years," replied a sad Mad Jack.

"Well, Jack, it's time you reintroduced yourself to the system and its twisted puppeteers," I said.

"What do you mean?" asked Mad Jack.

"The village association meeting is scheduled for this afternoon," I responded. "I'll be attending in order to have a chat with the powers that be about rewriting Maleny's story in a more positive, more legal way. Will you join me?"

"You want to go back into the danger zone? You do know what that stuff is?" asked Wolf as he pointed up the mountain.

"I finally know what it is and what it represents," I responded. "But we need to take responsibility for telling others the truth about Lake Baroon, the village association, and the illegal uranium enterprise. It's time we used our voices. It's time I used *my* voice. Besides, Mia is sitting in the middle of it all. I'm going back, whatever you decide."

"Hear! Hear!" interjected Jude. "We're with you, Will."

"Me, too," added a circumspect Mad Jack.

Wolf remained silent. He stared at the steering wheel as though it may deliver him a more palatable answer. When none arrived, he nodded, following Jude's lead.

"How are we going to get back to Maleny?" asked Mad Jack. "It's a good ten miles from here.

If you haven't noticed, almost all the traffic is heading down the mountain."

"Let's attempt to hitchhike. Otherwise, we walk," I responded.

Everyone concurred in silence and exited the vehicle. Then we began walking back up the mountain along the side of the road. Our group made remarkable progress considering the average age of my fellow travellers was mid-seventies. Mad Jack led the way, walking with more purpose than I'd seen from him. I followed, while Jude and Wolf brought up the rear. Jude was holding Wolf's hand tightly. Wolf appeared grateful, and the two of them encouraged one another onward with the occasional glance or gesture.

After fifteen minutes of walking without being passed by a single ascending vehicle, a loud clunking engine could be heard approaching from behind. It sounded like a collector's model from an earlier era. I turned around to discover a compact, painted van was advancing up the mountain toward us. As it got closer, it looked strangely familiar. I tried to recall where I'd last seen a hippy van with a colorful picture painted on its side. Then the answer hit me—and what a relief it was. I waved as Miranda Minsky pulled up beside us.

"Someone call for a taxi?" she asked with a beaming smile.

"You're a living miracle, Miranda," I stated.

"Jump in, guys," she responded.

"Miranda, this is Jude, Wolf, and Jack," I said as the four of us climbed into the van.

Miranda waved at the three of them and they nodded at her.

"They're all Maleny locals and we've had quite a day," I continued.

"So far, Will. So far. There's more to come," Miranda replied with a knowing nod.

"By the way, what are you doing here?" I asked. "And how did you know we were in trouble?"

"Funny you should ask. This morning, I was working with a well-connected French bulldog on behalf of her owner," Miranda responded.

"Dead or living?" I asked.

"Dead," she answered. "Anyway, she instructed me to get up the mountain to help my friends ASAP. I ran out of there that minute and drove straight here."

After being speechless for a moment, I said, "Thank you, Miranda, and please thank that genius French bulldog when you next see her."

"She's sitting on the back seat right now," Miranda stated. "You can thank her yourself."

Wolf gave Jude a look which translated into, "We've got a nutcase on our hands."

Jude ignored Wolf and said, "Thanks, French bullie. We sure needed your help today."

Wolf went back to minding his own business.

"Miranda, before we go any further, there's something you need to know," I said.

"Go on," she replied.

"We opened some bins containing uranium waste earlier. The village association is enriching uranium at the pub, so it's dangerous back in Maleny," I explained.

Miranda Minsky didn't react in any way to the news which would have scared most humans. "And?" she asked.

"So you're not bothered to be risking your life?" I replied.

"I'm more bothered by the mundanity of averageness which seeps into my life like a cancer on a daily basis," she responded. "Caring about the people and animals in my life is the fun stuff. I wouldn't drive back down this mountain if you paid me."

I nodded in appreciation of the force of nature that is Miranda Minsky.

When we arrived back into Maleny, I said, "Miranda, Mia's at home. Can we collect her, please?"

"Of course," Miranda replied as she turned right at the roundabout which led home.

A couple of minutes later, we were parked on our driveway. I jumped out of the van and sprinted inside, but Mia's basket was empty. I searched all through the house for her. I checked under the bed, in the cupboards, and under the house. I couldn't find her anywhere. My heart raced. *Where on earth could she be?* I wondered. Miranda joined me on the veranda.

"She's not here!" I exclaimed.

"She's somewhere, Will," Miranda responded. "You just have to think like Mia."

"How?" I asked.

"Well, from what I know about Mia, I'd say she'll have been focused on protecting those she loves," she answered.

"But there's no one else here," I stated.

"Are there any other creatures nearby she knows?" Miranda asked.

"Yes!" I exclaimed. "In the shed."

After sprinting to the shed, I threw open the door. There was Mia curled up beside Monty the python on the floor like two old friends who were relaxing in one another's company. They raised their heads when I entered as if to ask what all the fuss was about.

"Mutt Dog, you need to come with us," I explained.

Mia gazed at Monty with concern on her face.

"Monty will be fine!" I exclaimed as I picked Mia up and carried her to the van where Miranda was holding the door open.

"You're good at thinking like a dog," she said.

"I've been taught by the best. Back in a jiffy," I added.

I jogged back to the shed where Monty was still curled up on the floor. After stroking his head, I picked him up, placed him on my shoulders, and returned to the van. Miranda was still holding the door open. "Another fellow traveller," she said.

I placed Monty inside the boot before I got into the van.

"Where to next?" Miranda asked.

"The village hall, please, driver," I said.

Miranda reversed out of the driveway, and we were soon en route to Maleny's town center. A couple of minutes later, I thought I heard knocking coming from outside the van, but I decided I was imagining it. Then it happened again.

"Miranda, can you stop the van for a second, please?" I asked.

Miranda pulled over and I opened the van's door to discover an out-of-breath Billy Baxter on his bike. "Billy!" I exclaimed. "Are you alright?"

"Too right, I'm alright," he responded. "My hearing aid is turned up to eleven. I'm coming to speak my mind at the village association meeting for the first time in, well, forever."

"I'm glad to hear it," I replied. "The world needs you to use your voice, and your hearing for that matter. But Billy, we've discovered a uranium operation here in Maleny. It's dangerous in town. You should get back home."

"I'm eighty years old, Will," Billy Baxter stated. "Do you think I care about dying? It's not living which is the challenge."

"Alright, Billy," I said. "Leave your bike there and jump in."

"Another fellow traveller," I explained to Miranda as Billy climbed in.

"The more, the merrier," Miranda said with a smile.

A few minutes later, we arrived in Maleny, where most residents were wandering toward the village hall, next to the library. Miranda Minsky parked the van in the library car park and everyone got out. I carried Mia, who was all out of energy, and called out, "You wait there, Monty!" to a sleepy python who was already enjoying his next nap.

The Village Association Meeting

The seven of us entered the village hall through the front door. The hall was full, with upwards of a hundred locals sitting in rows of plastic chairs. Up the front, Ben Flinders was seated at a long table flanked on either side by three people. On his left was Dũng Heap, Wilma, my landlady who I hadn't seen since the day I moved in, and then a nondescript, middle-aged man wearing a nondescript suit. On Ben Flinders's right was O'Hara, whose water tank I'd collected; the uniformed man who'd complained when I took Mia to Mary Cairncross soon after arriving; and the man whose pool I'd collected while he was still swimming in it. It was a smorgasbord of Maleny's chief dickheads in the one spot.

We sat down toward the back of the hall. I made sure Mia had her own seat so she could view what was happening, then we waited like everyone else. The room was silent like a group of school children who'd been told off one too many times to feel safe opening their mouths ever again. I waved at the Whisperer who was seated a few rows away. He raised his eyebrows, suggesting he was prepared for the worst. Wolf gave Jude a look which indicated he was uncomfortable, and Jude gave Wolf a look which indicated she concurred. Then Ben Flinders stood up and held his hands high as though he was about to start conducting an orchestra. The room waited with bated breath as he prepared to open his exceptionally large mouth.

"Welcome all to the annual village association meeting where we discuss all we're doing to make Maleny even greater again," he said while making eye contact with as many people in the audience as he could.

I ducked behind a tall-haired woman in front so he couldn't see me.

"As some of you may recall from previous meetings," Flinders continued, "we need all of you to sign nondisclosure agreements, otherwise known as NDAs. A couple of our girls are walking around with them right now. Just to be clear, the rule is: no NDA, no meeting."

Mad Jack gave me a pointed look. One of the girls who used to work at the vet's reception was collecting NDA signatures nearby. She was closing in on us fast.

"NDAs are a normal part of business as they allow us to discuss sensitive issues without being worried you'll tell other village associations about them," explained Flinders with his most condescending tone. "You see, not everywhere can be as great as Maleny. It's all about protecting and building our competitive advantages."

Most people were happily signing the NDAs without even reading the words on the page. The girl from the vet's reception soon arrived at our row, ready to collect our signatures. She handed Wolf the clipboard with the NDAs and a pen. I watched over Wolf's shoulder when he signed it as "Hugh Jass." I suppressed an overwhelming desire to laugh as he turned the page over and passed it to Jude. She followed Wolf's lead by signing hers as "Dixie Normous." When it came to my turn, I signed it as "Ben Dover." Miranda withheld a giggle as she signed "Jenna Tools" on hers. And Mad Jack hadn't been watching over anyone's shoulder, but his signature was so incoherent that there was no way anyone was going to know who he was. He passed the clipboard back to the girl with a wink which threw her off her game. She was so focused on getting away from Mad Jack that she forgot to check our signatures. I gave

Mad Jack a low five which he accepted without understanding why.

"Now, let's talk business," stated Ben Flinders with a forced smile fuelled by smarmy intent. "Let's start with the finances. Baz, over to you."

The nondescript, middle-aged man stood up as though he'd been called to attention.

"Thanks, Ben," he responded. "I have good news. After some rightsizing, rebalancing, hedging, and optimizing of our digitalization strategy, we were able to grow the top line while reinvesting back into our balance sheet and profit and loss account. With that said, we had a few challenges to navigate, but we were able to lean into them and leverage them to our advantage."

I wondered if anyone else had any idea what this sap was talking about.

"So net-net-net," Baz continued, "we ended the financial year with a $55 million surplus thanks to careful financial management and the foresight of those who came before us."

I nearly fell off my chair when I heard that, and then I involuntarily stood up from my chair.

"Doesn't anyone want to know why the village association is so minted?" I asked the room in general.

Ben Flinders focused his steely gaze upon me. "As Baz explained, careful financial planning is the reason. I assume you're grateful for that, Watson, since you've tried your hand at pretty much everything around town to earn a dodgy crust. Lucky someone around here can make the numbers balance, eh?"

Mad Jack jumped up out of his seat. "Don't you all realize what's going on?" he asked the room.

"Oh, sit back down, Jack," Flinders commanded. "Your time in the sun passed when most people here were in diapers. Go back out to pasture when you belong."

"You...you, asshole!" Mad Jack exclaimed. "My time in the sun passed when your father bribed everyone in the village association to kick me out so you could mine uranium down at Baroon."

There were a few surprised gasps around the room, but most people rolled their eyes skyward suggesting they already knew this information, and by the way they couldn't care less.

"That's ancient history, Jack," Flinders responded. "Just like you."

"Do you all realize what's being processed out the back of the pub as we speak?" Mad Jack asked the room with growing urgency.

No one responded or even looked in Mad Jack's direction. Most people stared at their laps, willing him to stop highlighting the inconvenient elephants in the room and general vicinity.

"I'll tell you what it is," Mad Jack continued with growing verve. "It's the bloody uranium! It was stock-piled there from the days of mining the Flinders' property down at Baroon. They're enriching it at the pub, people. Do you all understand what that means? Enriched uranium is radioactive for god's sake!"

"OK, here's what we'll do for you, *Mad* Jack," Flinders interjected. "We'll ask the audience how many people believe their lives are at risk, and how many believe you're a nutcase who should be locked up."

Mad Jack reacted by sitting back down just as Ben Flinders had hoped. He hid his face from the crowd.

"So, folks," Flinders continued, "who here believes we're sitting in the middle of a potential nuclear holocaust which could kill us all?"

The only people to put their hands in the air were the six humans in our group, the Whisperer, and Mia would have raised her paw if she could have. The rest of the room remained as unmoved as Lance Armstrong when he was first questioned about doping.

"Let's follow this through to the end," Flinders continued. "How many people believe Mad Jack is a silly old codger who should be locked up?"

Everyone in the room apart from us and the Whisperer threw their hands up in a one-handed wave of humiliation. A couple of older folk up the front sniggered viciously at Mad Jack's public denouncement to reinforce the point. Mad Jack buried his face in his hands.

Mia gave me a look which could only mean, "This is embarrassing." The moment she did, an idea popped into my head, or rather, a picture of the truth. I suddenly understood what the cunning deceivers on the stage didn't want us to know—and what a monstrous secret it was. However, before I could say anything, Billy Baxter was up on his feet.

"Hey, Flinders, you owe Jack here an apology," Billy stated calmly.

"For recognizing that he's wasting our valuable time? I can't see your point, Baxter. I recommend you turn your hearing aid on so you know what you're talking about next time," Flinders said with a crowd-pleasing wink of condescension.

Billy stood taller and took a deep breath. "Enough! You owe Jack an apology for treating him like dirt for so many years. While you're at it, you can apologize to me for the same thing."

"Oh, let me guess," responded Flinders. "Do you want me to apologize for the lack of customized, local cycle paths for geriatric cyclists with balance challenges?"

"No," stated Billy. "I'd like you to apologize for trying to run me over about a hundred times. I'd like you to apologize for spreading fear throughout our community since the moment Baroon was flooded. And I'd like you to apologize for scaring me into turning my hearing aid off for so long. Actually, scratch that last one. That was my fault for not standing up like this before now."

Ben Flinders rolled his eyes as he chuckled with the authenticity of a politician on vote day.

Without thinking it through, I stood up alongside Billy Baxter. "While we're at it, let's talk about the real reason Baroon was flooded and why you've been terrorizing this town ever since," I said to Flinders.

"Well, this should be amusing," he responded with less ease.

"Flinders, why is Lake Baroon so black?" I asked.

Ben Flinders shifted nervously on his feet while a few members of the crowd turned around to inspect my face for signs of insanity.

"I'll tell you why," I continued with growing volume. "Because the village association hatched a plan to flood Baroon Valley fifteen years ago to save the expensive mine closure costs. By flooding the uranium mine once all the uranium had been stockpiled at the pub to be enriched at a later date, the problems posed by the mine's ongoing presence could be forever covered up without the huge costs of rehabilitating the land. That's why the lake is so black. The water still contains dangerous chemical sludge which has festered there for decades."

"Watson, the problem with your story is it lacks credibility—just like you," Flinders responded. "Can someone please call the Department of Home Affairs to let them know we have a rogue foreigner terrorizing our poor community? Tell them the Maleny Village Association Chairman says the lout needs to be deported straight away—preferably to somewhere he'll suffer."

"Hang on," Dũng Heap interjected at a most unexpected moment. "I'd like to hear more about Will Watson's theory."

"Hi, Dũng," I said. "The other reason the village association agreed to flood Baroon was so they could receive the chunky water supply fees from Brisbane's council each year. The lake water supplies around half of Brisbane's drinking water, so it's been a bounty for the region. Clever, eh? Flood your illegal uranium mine to cover it up, save the closure costs, and then generate millions of dollars from the water, which is hiding your problems from the rest of the world."

"So you're saying Lake Baroon has been supplying polluted water to Brisbane?" Dũng asked as he stood up, powered by an aha, or rather an oh-shit moment.

"That's exactly what I'm saying," I replied.

"Hang on, surely a water inspection would have revealed this by now?" continued Dũng.

"Yes, if it had actually happened," I responded as the weight of Dũng's dot connecting resonated around the room. "However, our infamous village association is adept at hiding the things they want to remain hidden. Who is our local water inspector anyway?"

Ben Flinders diverted his gaze from mine.

"It's O'Hara!" called out an elderly man in the crowd. "O'Hara has been our water inspector ever since Baroon was flooded. Come to think of it, that's around the time he started living a life of luxury with the fattest cows in the district."

O'Hara stood up beside Ben Flinders. "Do you really think we're all corrupt?" he shouted at the crowd as an uninvited vein started throbbing on his forehead.

"I know you are," responded Billy Baxter as he pointed at O'Hara with aggression. "Whenever I cycle down to Lake Baroon when you're meant to be testing the water, I can see you sunbathing on the grass like the unethical bastard you are."

"Now I know you're lying," replied a surprised O'Hara. "It's not possible to view that grassy patch from the road, you silly old crank."

"That's right," added Billy. "That's why I cut a hole in the fence with wire cutters. I'm sick and tired of being told by the crooks of the world to mind my own business. I've seen you, *mate*. Every word Will spoke is correct."

"Do you all understand the gravity of the situation?" I asked the crowd. "Brisbane's main water supply has been contaminated with dangerous chemical waste thanks to Maleny's corrupt village association. Let me spell that out for you...Lake Baroon's polluted water is the cause of the gastro problems experienced by Brisbane's residents. Can you imagine being poisoned by the drinking water you trusted to keep you alive and well? If we weren't all using rainwater tanks here in Maleny, we would have been just as affected."

I paused and looked around the room. Most people were looking as uncomfortable as if I'd just called their mothers ugly, but they remained silent.

Mia gazed up at me with pride in her eyes, and another thought hit me.

"I wish that was the end of it, but it's not," I said to the room.

"What else do you want to accuse us of?" Flinders asked. "Murder is about the only thing you've not covered. Why don't you live up to your surname, Twatson, I mean Watson, and dazzle the crowd with a truly spectacular accusation that will keep everyone on the edge of their seats. Because that's what this is, isn't it? You've finally got an audience after a lifetime of being a friendless, homeless loser—and you're relishing every sad moment in the limelight. It's just a shame your joy is coming from attacking others with your baseless lies. Once the government hears about your long list of illegal business activities, rest assured we'll be saying good riddance to the bad rubbish you are."

As Ben Flinders belittled me, I made an instinctive assessment of what sort of man Dũng Heap really was and took a deep breath. "Dũng, why don't you explain to the crowd what else has been happening in our community?"

Dũng sat still in a state of confusion as he considered how to respond. "Will Watson," he finally said, "Murph was right about you. You're a sanctimonious wanker, and you're fired."

Ouch—it was my second firing within a few short months. That meant my skilled migrant visa had gone up in smoke. The fragile, lost version of me who'd landed in Australia would have covered his face while trying to walk away from that scene without anyone noticing. However, the me who stood there that day had had enough of not being counted as a living, breathing human with a voice of my own.

"Dũng," I continued, "you've been a great boss to me, and I'll always be thankful for that. More to the point, I know a good person when I see one.

There's one, and only one, up there on that stage. You're better than the people standing alongside you. I'm sure of it."

Dũng crossed his arms and appeared unmoved. Eventually, he stood up, and I prepared myself to be fired again. "Will Watson, you are a foolishly brave man," he stated. "Just like I once was when I lived a simpler life back in Vietnam—before I moved to this country and cruel people laughed at my name, my family's name. For all you half-wits who think my name is funny, let me let educate you. Dũng means bravery in Vietnam, and the accent mark above the 'u' in my name denotes a rising pitch. My name should sound like it's being sung from the rooftops. It's time you Aussies learnt that. It's time I remembered that."

Ben Flinders gave Dũng a hard stare which would scare children.

"I'm my own man, Ben Flinders, and it is time you understood that," Dũng continued. "The truth is, the village association has been paying us to illegally remove their uranium waste each year. When Ben Flinders realized our price to perform this high-risk operation was higher than he was willing to pay, he proposed a reciprocal business arrangement. It involved paying us the quoted amount to remove the waste, but he insisted the village association charge us an additional 20 percent levy on all our legitimate business in the region. He calculated the levy so it would offset our entire charge for removing the radioactive waste. In other words, he proposed getting what he wanted from us for nothing. And here's the most shocking part of the story...I accepted his crooked proposal. If I didn't, I knew Ben Flinders would do everything in his power to ruin my business."

Ben Flinders stepped closer to Dũng and whispered something in his ear.

"I don't care anymore," Dũng said out loud. "I was an honorable man in Vietnam, Ben Flinders, but ever since you entered my life with your corruption it has spread like a virus throughout my organization. I'm not proud of the man I see in the mirror anymore. Enough already. It's time the truth was told. I've needed this for a long time."

Ben Flinders sat back down like a naughty schoolboy.

"So we started removing the village association's uranium waste as agreed," continued Dũng. "Of course, we expected our core business would suffer because of the higher prices we were charging thanks to the additional levy. However, we were very wrong. It turns out people in this part of the world enjoy paying more for services as it makes them feel like they're more important or something. You Aussies are weird. Anyway, as our business grew, the village association started making money out of our dirty agreement—lots of money. Let me translate that for you: we were removing their illegal uranium waste while we were paying them for the privilege. Well, I must say, this, how you say, capsized my goodwill for the village association."

Dũng paused so the weight of his words could resonate around the room. I expected the crowd to gasp in dismay before jumping to their feet to demand justice for their community, but the crowd reacted by doing the sum total of sweet fuck all.

After a full awkward minute of inaction, the elderly lady I'd seen with her cat at the vet's stood up toward the front of the audience. "Mr. Heap," she stated, "I'll be honest. Nothing you say is a surprise to me. But think about it for a moment. Your business is booming while Maleny is the richest, most welcoming, and best-maintained regional town in Australia. Where's the harm in this fruitful partnership?"

"That's an awful big question, madam," responded Dũng. "So I'll give you two answers. There's the harm it's done to me and my team from not earning our income honestly and honorably. That's been eating away at our souls, even if some of us don't realize it."

"Hear! Hear!" I called out.

"Then there's the bigger issue," Dũng continued, "which is that this is just the tip of the iceberg. Corruption has become a normal way of doing business in this community. Once the village association realized how much money our levy was making for them, they rolled out similar levies covering most businesses in this town. So they're making millions of dollars for doing nothing in addition to all their illegal uranium income. We've all become slaves to these crooks who are abusing their power. Why have we accepted such unethical and disrespectful behavior? The business owners in the audience will know what I'm talking about..."

Dũng paused and gazed around the room, giving the other local business owners their moment to stand up and be counted. We all awaited the rush of angry voices. However, it soon became clear that the business owners scattered around the room were busy thousand-yard-staring into the distance. Not one of them said a word. So Wolf stood up instead, this time without preapproval from Jude. "Dũng's right," he stated. "This town is rotten to its core. Even the Rural Fire Service is in on it."

Dũng looked confused and remained silent.

"That's right," Wolf continued with growing confidence. "These guys have been burning bushland for years. I'm bloody sure of it. Even some of the items I recycle have been coated with charcoal particles. I'm angry about it."

"Take it easy!" exclaimed the uniformed man seated on the stage who had told me off for walking Mia at Mary Cairncross. "Yes, we occasionally burn stuff, but we're only human. We get bored sometimes."

"Oh right," Wolf responded. "Well, stop burning stuff, you hear me? Our bushland deserves better."

Wolf sat back down. Jude gave him a look encouraging him to remain seated and silent henceforth.

Ben Flinders stood up amidst the crowd's confusion about Wolf's interlude. "We've heard enough complaints today, don't you think?" he asked the crowd before he turned to look Dũng in the eye.

Dũng remained stationery as he met Ben Flinders's furious gaze.

"I hope all you moaners and whingers feel better for getting your pitiful worries off your chests. But the truth is, our system works beautifully for all of us. So let's get on with enjoying our status as Australia's most welcoming town. And let's be honest, the only reason we're so bloody friendly is because we're so bloody wealthy. You're welcome by the way," Flinders said with a bow.

"I don't think you understand, Ben Flinders," Dũng interjected. "When I said enough is enough, I meant the game is over. For god's sake man, you're responsible for supplying polluted drinking water to millions of people. I'm going to tell the authorities. That means jail time for you and the other village association members."

"The authorities are here already, Dũng," responded Flinders. "Constable Watkins, what say you, sir? Have you learnt of any illegal behavior here today?"

A well-fed, middle-aged man with slicked-back hair wearing a large Rolex stood up within the crowd. "No, sir, nothing suspicious afoot here."

I stroked Mia under my chair. She was still dozing in and out of consciousness, but she opened her eyes and gave me a pointed look. An idea popped into my head as soon as she did. I marched up to the front of the room, much to Ben Flinders's dismay.

"Sit back down, Watson," he instructed. "We don't have time for any more of your shenanigans. We have real business to get on with."

"Real business is exactly what I'd like to discuss," I said.

"Carry on, Will Watson," interjected Dũng. "We're all listening."

"Thanks, Dũng. So look at who we've got sitting in the room with us today," I said to the room. "We've got Mr. Dũng Heap, the king of trash and a successful entrepreneur. We've got one of Australia's leading recycling experts, Wolf. Wolf, what's your surname by the way?"

"I'm more a one name type of guy—like Kylie," Wolf explained to the room.

"Nice," I responded. "And we've got the Whisperer, one of the country's leading wildlife tourism experts."

The Whisperer waved.

"And that's just scratching the surface of this town's immense talent pool," I continued. "Now imagine a future for Maleny in which we let go of the problems of the past and position this town to become part of the solution."

Ben Flinders pretend-yawned loudly.

"How, Will Watson? How can we be part of the solution?" asked Dũng.

"Here's my idea...let's build Maleny into Australia's most sustainable town," I stated. "Dũng, your business could be at the center of this change because you collect the items people don't want anymore. If you're open to it, I could help you transform the business into a sustainability leader. We have the ideal team in this community to make this work. Wolf has already started recycling rubbish into things people can use again. Why not get the whole town involved in an innovative recycling operation?"

The room fell silent, and Wolf lowered his head.

"Oh brilliant! A plan which depends on employing unemployable Watson and that useless old codger!" exclaimed Flinders. "You may as well close the town now if that's your vision for the future."

"People would travel here to see what's possible when a community lives in harmony with nature," I continued. "They could even sign up for a musical bicycle tour of the local bushland with cycling legend, Billy Baxter."

"Too right they could!" exclaimed Billy with a fist pump.

"Can't you see?" I continued. "The answers are here in this room. We can clean up and put all this corruption behind us...if we just work together."

I gazed around the room, which was no longer silent. In fact, there was the slight murmuring of people talking about my idea. A few seconds later, I noticed a curt nod from a young woman in the front row, which triggered a short, sharp nod from an old man nearby. That nod was witnessed by a teenager across the room who involuntarily joined in the nodding action. Before I knew it, the murmuring had turned into real-life discussion about real-life ideas, and the nods were taking control of more people in the crowd.

Dũng was deep in thought for a few minutes before he joined in the nodding action with more enthusiasm than your average nodder. He then stood up with his arms held high as though he had something important to say. "Will Watson, you once again surprise me. I concur that this sustainability idea is indeed the answer, and I pledge henceforth to be a part of the solution. Ben Flinders, how you say, you can shove your uranium and corruption up your unethical ass."

"Let it burn on the fumes of your own bullshit!" called out Wolf.

In response, Ben Flinders diverted his gaze from the crowd as he called someone on his mobile. The room fell silent to listen in to his presumably important phone conversation in the midst of a most unusual moment.

"Big Man, listen carefully," Flinders instructed with more volume than was necessary. "I need you to make Project Nuclear Bomb happen right now. The U-gun is under the bar. You know what to do."

He went quiet while Big Man considered his response.

"That's right," Flinders continued. "Blow the whole fucking town up!"

Big Man clearly had something else to say as Ben Flinders stopped talking for a glorious moment.

"Just wear the protective suit if you're worried about dying, you dropkick," Flinders responded as he hung up.

Ben Flinders turned back to face the crowd with a beaming smile. "There you have it, folks. If I can't have this town, no one can have it."

Truth or Truth

As the room digested the awful reality laid before them, a range of reactions could be observed. Most of the older folk jumped out of their seats and sprinted for the exit with more speed than you'd expect, causing a gray-haired traffic jam at the door. In contrast, most of the younger folks photographed Ben Flinders on their phones before they posted updates on their social media accounts hashtagged "Psychopath on the loose," followed by "Someone please help us!", and finally, "Top ten best things to do when the world is ending."

Constable Watkins pulled out a pair of handcuffs and approached Ben Flinders, who swiftly karate-kicked him in the head, knocking him to the ground. As Watkins pulled himself up off the floor, Ben Flinders charged out the back door, which no one had noticed even though it was in plain sight, and disappeared.

Our group remained still amidst the growing wave of chaos breaking around us. The Whisperer came over to sit with us, while Mia remained fast asleep. The exhaustion was once again too much for her.

"Shall we drive out of here?" Wolf asked.

"Where to?" asked Jude. "Unless we can travel at the speed of light, we aren't escaping from whatever is coming."

"I'm tired of running from the living," added Miranda Minsky. "Maybe we are where we're meant to be."

"Escaping is overrated," I added.

The last few locals filed out of the hall, leaving us in peace.

"Here's an idea," suggested Billy Baxter. "If Ben bloody Flinders has pressed the button which ends it all, what's the point in running or worrying or reacting in any way? Why don't we just relax and play a game? We may as well enjoy our remaining time."

"Good idea, Billy," responded Jude. "Let's play Truth or Dare. I used to love it as a child."

"Truths are all we have left," added the Whisperer.

"You're right. Let's play Truth or Truth," said Jude.

"I'll go first," suggested Billy Baxter, full of enthusiasm. "Jude, why did you choose Wolf over me? When we were youngsters, I was better looking, wealthier, and more fun. I've never understood."

"Here's the truth, Billy," Jude stated as she took hold of Wolf's hand. "You were too busy being all of those things to communicate your feelings to me at the time. You see, Wolf was straight with me. I'm a simple woman who needs a straight talker in my life."

"If only I'd cut the bullshit and learnt how to talk to women as a younger man," Billy stated as he dropped his head.

"If only I was that straight-talking man still," interjected a circumspect Wolf. "My truth is I've stopped talking, full stop. I've somehow lost my voice along the way."

"It's still there, Wolf," Jude added. "That straight-talking man inside you just needs reminding what a wonderful person he is."

"Thanks, darling," Wolf replied.

"My truth's worse," Jude continued with a sigh. "I've been collecting a disability pension for the past two decades because it was easier to pretend I needed the money. But the truth is I'm as able-bodied as anyone else. I just couldn't be bothered working."

"Lucky our recycling gig would have needed your help if the world wasn't ending, eh?" Wolf said as he put his arm around Jude's shoulder. "And yours, Jack."

"Thanks, I'd have liked that if we had more time," responded Mad Jack. "My truth's pretty bloody obvious, isn't it? When threatened by bullies like Ben Flinders, I've always backed down. Always. What a pussy I've been."

"I don't see any pussies here," said Wolf. "You're a real man if I ever met one."

"Appreciate it, mate," replied Mad Jack. "Whisperer, what about you? It's hard to imagine you having any sordid truths to tell."

"Oh, but I do," whispered the Whisperer. "In fact, my truth is more sordid than the rest of yours combined. Do you want to know the real reason I show tourists the beauty of our wildlife? It's because I used to shoot kangaroos for money, and I'm still trying to get over the guilt. Every night, I used to head out into the bush to murder those beautiful, intelligent animals for a few measly bucks. Often, I'd even leave their joeys alive in their dead mothers' pouches just because I couldn't be bothered checking. Imagine dying like that inside your dead mother's body."

The group were silent. It was the hardest truth for all of us to hear.

"You're not that man anymore, I can feel it," interjected Miranda.

"You're right there," the Whisperer stated. "But I need to live with the pain and misery I caused those poor innocent creatures. That never goes away."

"We all have regrets to live with," added Miranda. "Why do you think I've been so focused on talking with dead pets all my life? When I was seventeen and had received my provisional driver's licence, I was singing at the top of my voice as I drove some of my girlfriends around. A smiley little dachshund ran across the road at exactly the wrong moment, and I was too caught up in being seventeen to react in time. I ran the poor fellow over, and I've been trying to ask him for forgiveness ever since. However, I've never been able to find him in the afterlife. Maybe he'll never forgive me." Miranda wiped a few tears away as her painful words entered the world of the living.

"You've made so many dogs' lives better since then, Miranda," I said.

"I have," agreed Miranda. "But it still hurts—every single day. How about you, Will?"

"Mine won't surprise any of you. My truth is I got on a plane to fly to Australia because I wasn't happy in Yorkshire. I blamed my need to escape on my girlfriend Heidi dumping me in the most brutal of ways. But that was bullshit. The truth was I wasn't happy on the inside. That was too hard for me to admit, so I convinced myself Australia could miraculously fill the many holes in my life," I confessed. "But, of course, that was impossible for any country to do. Now here I am. Mia's desperately sick, the holes are still there, and I'm still fighting to find my place in this world."

The group was silent for a few minutes as our truths introduced themselves to one another.

"If only we could ask Mia her truth, eh?" asked Wolf in a clumsy change of subject.

"Funny you should say that," I responded. "Mia does have a unique way of communicating. I'd ask her, but she's exhausted."

Mia opened half an eye and watched me. Her breathing was labored, and the lumps on her body were even larger and redder than earlier that day. However, she sat up and willed me to ask her.

"What do you think, Miranda?" I asked.

"Imagine yourself in Mia's position, Will," Miranda replied. "Would you like to be able to express your truth while you were running out of time in this world?"

"Guys, we need to build an alphabet right now!" I exclaimed.

The group looked around the room for available resources. The village hall was sparsely furnished, so all we had to work with were the plastic chairs lining the floor and the long desk on the stage.

"I'm on it," stated Wolf as he stood up without asking any questions. "We've got everything we need to make this work."

"Really?" I asked.

"On my count, there are one hundred and thirty chairs in the room, which means we have five chairs per letter to work with," Wolf stated without explaining when he'd had time to count the chairs. "Guys, I need twenty-six groups of five chairs spread out at equal intervals. I can do the rest."

Jude wiped a tear from her face as she charged off to gather chairs.

"We're getting the alphabet ready, Mutt Dog," I explained. "Rest easy in the meantime."

Mia lay back down and fell straight back to sleep.

The group went to work collecting chairs, and soon clusters of five chairs emerged all around the room. While that happened, Wolf focused his efforts on building the letters. I wasn't sure how he was going to create an entire alphabet from such a simple system, but it all became clear once he built the A. To create the base, he kicked the front legs off two chairs and bent their back legs backwards, before lining the backs of the two chairs up against one another. Then he picked up another chair and whacked the ground with its legs, knocking all of them off in the process. He placed the top of the chair in a triangular position on top of the base, and the letter A came to life with two chairs spare.

"You're a genius, Wolf," stated Billy Baxter as he walked past the A. "I can see why she chose you."

"I'm no better than you are, Billy. Surely you can see that," Wolf responded. "Come over here and help me with the letters."

"I'd like that," Billy said.

In short order, Wolf and Billy bent, broke, adjusted, twisted, and placed the chairs into a make-do alphabet around the room. By the time they'd finished, all the letters were decipherable.

"Wow!" Miranda exclaimed as she perused the completed alphabet. "It's almost as good as the beach."

"I must say, it felt mighty satisfying to dismantle some village association property," added Billy as he high-fived Wolf.

With the alphabet complete, the group returned to where Mia was sleeping. I stroked her gently but she didn't stir. The lumps seemed to be expanding before our eyes, even on her head where I was stroking her.

"Guys, her cancer is running rampant. Nothing we're doing is making the slightest difference. I don't think Mia has got the energy for this," I said.

As I spoke, Mia raised her head despite obvious discomfort.

"Will, she's got something she wants to say," Miranda explained as a few tears ran across her face.

"What's the right question to ask?" I asked.

The group remained silent. I closed my eyes. Images of Mia rolling on the sand during one of her beloved beach trips ran through my mind, and I knew the question she needed me to ask her. "Mutt Dog, have you found meaning in your life?"

Mia considered my question, then she tried to stand up. However, her legs wobbled and she fell back over. I picked her up off the floor and helped steady her.

"Would you like me to carry you?" I asked.

Her eyes told me no, she wanted to do this by herself. So on her wobbly, almost-useless legs, Mia stepped toward the letters before her. I struggled to watch the immense pain she was in as she tried to walk. Miranda held my hand as we both cried in silence. Billy put his arm around my shoulder, and the rest of the group followed his lead with everyone interlocking their arms. Mia eventually hobbled all the way over to the Y.

"It's OK, Mutt Dog," I called out. "We know the first word is YES. Anyone who's met you, knows that."

Mia reconsidered her next move, then she hobbled over to the B and the Y. However, as she contemplated the next letter, she collapsed. I ran over to her and helped her back onto her feet. She panted and wheezed and coughed as the cancer was doing terrible things to her insides. Despite it all, she smiled at me through her beautiful eyes and took another step forward, and another, until she eventually made it to the L. Then something inexplicable happened. Mia reacted as though someone had shot a starter's gun nearby to begin a race. She forced herself into a slow trot even though her legs wobbled in disagreement with the idea. She made it all the way to the O, then she continued to the V, the I, the N, and then the G. She paused for a moment, and the loss of momentum looked like it would force her to the ground. She coughed and wheezed so violently her body shook. I had to look away. Even though she couldn't breathe properly anymore, she sucked in some air and forced herself onward. She dragged her body all the way to the M and the Y. Then a vicious wave of wobbles erupted throughout her body forcing her off her feet. As she was falling, one of her legs miraculously kicked out to the side and somehow rebalanced her body in time to avoid the fall. She then forced in a miniscule amount of air through her constricted airways, and limped over to the L, the I, the F, and finally the E.

In silence, we all digested Mia's beautiful truth... *she'd found meaning in her life by loving her life.*

Mia stared at the letter E, then she turned around to make eye contact with me through her smiling eyes. I jumped up and sprinted across the room toward her, but she was already falling. She collapsed onto the ground without a sound. Within seconds, I was by her side. Her eyes remained wide open, but her body had stopped working. I collapsed beside her and held her tight. "Thank you, beautiful girl," I said, "for showing me what real love is, for being my best friend, for being the best dog ever." Her warm body continued to comfort me as she passed away.

Then I fell apart. Sobs of pain took control of me, and I thought I was going to die as well. Breathing through my uncontrollable tears was nigh on impossible, but I didn't care if I breathed ever again. Someone stroked my back and someone else put their arms around me. I don't know who. Another person cried beside me as I remained frozen to the spot. We stayed like that for an eternity as time stopped and would surely never start again.

The Sixth Guinea Fowl

Minutes later, someone spoke to me. "She heard you, Will." It was Miranda.

"Pardon?" I asked.

"When you thanked Mia for showing you what real love is," Miranda continued, "Your words were the last thing she heard as she passed through to the other side."

"Is she here now?" I asked.

"No," Miranda said. "She's got some settling in to do, but part of her is residing inside your heart, and always will. Once she's figured her new home out, her spirit will regain its freedom and she'll be able to visit you from the other side from time to time."

"But I want her here with me. Now. *In this life,*" I responded as another flood of tears arrived.

"I know," Miranda said. "But she's in a better place now. Believe me."

"I do," I stated. "I do."

Wolf, Billy Baxter, Mad Jack, Jude, and the Whisperer left Miranda and me to sit with Mia's body as they relocated to another part of the room. They appeared to be constructing something, but I didn't care anymore.

Sometime later, the front door opened, and Dũng marched in, alive and well.

"How's Project Nuclear Bomb progressing?" asked Jude, without the stress the question should have demanded.

"Ben Flinders made his final mistake," Dũng responded. "When he suggested Big Man wear the protective suit he'd left him to protect himself from the nuclear blast, he forgot the protective suit is for a normal-sized man, not a giant. Big Man tried to squeeze into the suit and split it open in the process. He then refused to shoot their uranium gun at the enriched uranium which would have triggered a nuclear explosion. Big Man knew that doing so would kill him too. When Ben Flinders tried to wrestle the uranium gun out of his hands while wearing his own protective suit, Big Man clobbered him so hard he knocked him out. He's in police custody now."

It was welcome news, but it didn't mean anything to me.

"What goes around comes around, eh?" said Billy Baxter.

"Indeed," responded Dũng as he walked over and placed a hand on my shoulder. "Will Watson, I'm so sorry for your loss. Let's reconvene when you've had time to grieve to make the changes we discussed at the meeting. The truth is, I pursued a career in rubbish collection to teach all those Aussies who laughed at my name that I could be the king of whatever I put my mind to. But it's time to do what's right."

Dũng walked out without another word.

Wolf, Billy Baxter, Mad Jack, Jude, and the Whisperer carried over a stretcher, which they'd constructed out of the leftover chair legs and some pieces of clothing. They placed it gently on the ground beside Mia's body.

"Shall we carry her to her final resting place, Will?" asked the Whisperer.

"Let's do that," I said as I stood up, knowing exactly where Mia wanted to be buried.

Wolf and Billy lifted Mia's body onto the stretcher where she appeared to be in a peaceful slumber. Then Wolf, Billy, Mad Jack, and the Whisperer each picked up a corner of the stretcher and placed it on their shoulders. The seven of us then walked outside where the sun shone bright in the clear blue sky. Most of Maleny's population were hanging around in the town center with the bemused expressions of people who'd been gifted a second chance without feeling like they deserved it.

"Shall we head left?" asked Billy when we reached the roundabout.

"You know where we're heading, Billy," I responded.

Billy Baxter nodded and guided the other three pallbearers to the left.

We walked into the town center where a young girl noticed Mia's body lying on the stretcher. She ran over. "It's not the smiley doggy, is it?" she asked.

I nodded but was unable to say the word "yes." The girl whispered something to a few of her friends who followed us alongside the road. In short order, a group of locals formed a line behind us, then more people followed their lead. As the road filled with people who either knew Mia or were interested by what everyone else was interested in, the crowd following Mia's body grew larger.

As a group, we turned off the road and walked through the field behind the café which connected with the Serenity Trail. Billy whispered directions to the other three pallbearers, and we were soon standing in the bushland setting where Mia had communicated with the local wildlife only a day earlier. The pallbearers laid the stretcher down in the clearing and placed Mia's body on the mossy undergrowth. Then there was silence. No one spoke a word as we all gazed at the beautiful golden retriever lying motionless on the ground. I half expected her to sit up and smile at everyone to help us through the pain—or rather, to help me through my pain. Because that's what she'd always done for me—made every day better in a million ways.

I sat down beside Mia's body on the grass. "So this is Mia," I stated to the crowd gathered around. "Some of you will know her as the golden dog who was always smiling, always happy. I knew her as my best friend, and what a best friend she was. She loved me as though I was a perfect, whole person who deserved her love and friendship more than anyone else in the world. As if that miracle wasn't enough, she also loved every person, every living creature in this world, with every ounce of her being. She made it known to all exactly how she felt."

As I spoke, a number of animals joined the crowd, intermingling with the people. First, the wallabies arrived, then the possums, the kookaburras, the platypuses, and the currawongs. Then a guinea fowl stepped forward, and it was soon followed by another, and another, and another, and another, and another. I was stumped for a moment. Six guinea fowl was one more than I was expecting after the recent car accident. I stopped talking and double-counted to confirm their numbers. There were indeed six of them. I felt an overwhelming desire to share with Mia the wonderful news that our friend had survived against the odds. I couldn't wait to see her grateful smile when she realized. However, as more animals joined the crowd, I remembered everything had changed. As another wave of pain hit me, a squadron of pelicans swooped down from above. By then, there were just as many animals as people congregated around. Neither the people nor the animals present were surprised to be standing or perching alongside one another because Mia was at the center of it all.

"Mia was an angel who visited our lives for only a short while," I continued. "I'll be forever changed by the role she played in my life, and I'll spend the rest of my life trying to be the man she believed I was."

I can't recall much of what happened next. I assume each animal and person went their separate ways after the logistics had been dealt with. All I know was I ended up at home later that day. All. By. Myself.

Breaking News Story

The first morning after Mia's passing was the worst. When I awoke, what had happened the day before didn't compute. In the early morning daze, I sat up in bed and searched for Mia by my side. When I couldn't find her, I jumped out of bed and searched the house. Then I remembered the awful truth. I sat down on the sofa and remained motionless amidst the barrenness which washed over me until I was soaked to my core. My tears wouldn't run anymore, that tap had run dry. All I had left was breathing.

A couple of days later, I was sitting at home with the television playing in the background, willing it to distract me from the pain of living. I was even watching the news, an act of desperation in itself, when a breaking story caught my interest.

"The mystery behind Brisbane's stomach bug has been solved," said the blonde-haired female newsreader. "And the truth is more shocking than anyone could have imagined. It's been revealed that one of Brisbane's principal water sources, Lake Baroon in the Sunshine Coast Hinterland, is in fact mildly radioactive. The land underneath the lake was used as a uranium mine for over a decade before the valley was flooded. Ray Byard is reporting from Lake Baroon."

"Thanks, Tina," responded Ray Byard, a young reporter with wavy brown hair who was standing beside Lake Baroon on the bright sunny day it was. "I'm at the scene of the crime with Queensland's Chief Medical Officer Sylvia Fontane and the CEO of Pristine Water Corp, Rock Smidley, who is responsible for managing Brisbane's water supply. Sylvia, let's start with you. Can you please fill us in on what's known so far?"

"Sure, Ray," Sylvia Fontane responded. "We now know that the valley underneath Lake Baroon was used for illegal uranium mining up until fifteen years ago. At that point, the perpetrators stockpiled the mined uranium at a local pub where they've continued to enrich and sell it ever since. They arranged for the valley to be flooded to cover up their crimes while profiting from supplying water to Brisbane. They were somehow able to remain hidden from the authorities despite supplying Brisbane's drinking water for the past fifteen years."

"It's hard to comprehend how such a shocking crime was possible at this scale with the whole world watching, isn't it?" asked Ray Byard.

"It is indeed," responded Sylvia Fontane. "At this stage, we know the main perpetrator, a Ben Flinders, was a highly regarded member of the community who repeatedly abused his position as the chairman of the Maleny Village Association in order to commit the horrendous crimes we're only now hearing about. We've been told he spent his entire life conducting illegal activities and making them appear legal with the help of his inner circle."

"Sylvia, a question many people have right now is why did Brisbane's population only suffer mild stomach problems in recent months considering Lake Baroon is one of the city's main water supplies? And why wasn't toxic poisoning a longer-term problem for Brisbane's residents?" asked Ray Byard.

"It's a good question, Ray," said Sylvia Fontane. "The authorities discovered the village association hired contractors to install a sophisticated filtering system at the pipe connection point which feeds the water into Brisbane to ensure all the dangerous chemical sludge remained in the lake. It allowed them to deliver relatively clean water to Brisbane, thus covering up the truth. That filter was washed away in the recent extreme rainfall event, which explains why Brisbane's residents have only been drinking polluted water for the past few months. Thankfully, their drinking water was only ever mildly polluted during that time. At over a thousand hectares and fifteen yards deep, there was an enormous volume of water in Lake Baroon to dilute the toxic effects of the remnant uranium waste from the mine. That's why the origins of the city's gastro illness was so hard to identify. You see, mild radioactive poisoning appears similar to most other gastrointestinal illnesses."

"Sylvia, while we're talking about the impacts of radiation, can you please tell us the strange story behind the nuclear bomb threat that occurred three days ago in Maleny?" continued Ray Byard.

"I can only tell you what the police have publicly disclosed, Ray," answered Sylvia Fontane. "Apparently, Ben Flinders threatened to blow up Maleny with a nuclear weapon once the community confronted him about his illegal activities. His colleague refused to detonate the bomb which in turn led to his arrest."

"What a piece of work this Ben Flinders is. How on earth did he have access to a nuclear weapon?" asked Ray Byard.

"The irony is, he didn't," stated Sylvia Fontane. "If you shoot a gun containing extremely enriched uranium at extremely enriched uranium, you've got yourself a dangerous nuclear weapon. However, Ben Flinders and his cronies were only enriching their uranium to the 3 to 5 percent needed for use in nuclear energy generation. Unbeknownst to them, uranium for nuclear weapon usage needs to be enriched to 90 percent. Luckily, Ben Flinders was ignorant of this key fact. So while he believed he was threatening to detonate a powerful nuclear bomb, in reality it would have been useless."

"I'm sure the people of Maleny are grateful this Ben Flinders is so inept," added Ray Byard.

"Maleny is surely the luckiest town in the world," replied Sylvia Fontane. "The town's residents remained safe on a day when things could have turned really ugly."

"Lucky indeed. Thanks, Sylvia," responded Ray Byard. "And now over to Rock Smidley, the CEO of Pristine Water Corp. Rock, there's no polite way to ask this... how did this happen on your watch?"

Rock Smidley shifted on his feet as he searched for the right words. "Look, Ray, mistakes have been made, that's clear. I'd like the public to know we're on top of it now, so Brisbane's residents can rest assured their tap water is 100 percent clean and healthy."

"How can you guarantee that after all that's occurred, Rock?" asked Ray Byard with gravity.

"Well, for starters, we've turned off the supply pipes from Lake Baroon to Brisbane until the water is considered safe by the health authorities," replied Rock Smidley.

"That's good to know," continued Ray Byard with one eyebrow raised. "But at a deeper level, how can the public ever trust you and the Pristine Water Corp team again? After all, you've been found to be sleeping at the wheel."

Rock Smidley searched around for an exit, but the camera was positioned to capture his every move. He gazed at the lake for a few seconds before he turned back to the camera. "Listen, Ray, I won't be spoken to like that. What's happened here at Lake Baroon is most unusual and most illegal, I'll grant you that. However, it just so happens there are some people existing in this world who are so evil they'll always find a way to mess things up for everyone else. And that's what we're talking about in this case. This Ben Flinders and his colleagues are really bad eggs."

"So it's not your fault, is that what you're saying?" asked Ray Byard.

"That's right, Ray," responded Rock Smidley. "This isn't about blaming Pristine Water Corp for what's happened here. It's about bringing these criminals to justice, and you can rest assured we'll do that. I'd be surprised if this Ben Flinders ever experiences life as a free man again."

"I suppose that's a minor comfort, Rock," added Ray Byard. "Is there anything else you'd like to say?"

"Yes, there is, Ray," said Rock Smedley as he stepped closer to the camera like a well-trained actor ready to deliver his lines. "Life is full of inexplicable ups and downs, and I'm sorry for the pain this particular down has caused members of the public. The only comfort I can offer is that the existence of evil is a necessary prerequisite for good to coexist alongside it. Let's focus on finding the good things that can grow out of this story."

"So you're saying some *good* will come from your long list of mistakes?" Ray Byard asked the camera with two raised eyebrows.

"Don't mince my words," a tense Rock Smedley replied. "All I'm saying is that one day we may be able to retell this story with some positive angles to it."

"There you have it, folks," responded a perplexed Ray Byard. "Pristine Water Corp isn't taking an iota of responsibility for their mistakes which originated at this seemingly innocent body of water. Back to you, Tina."

"Thanks, Ray," answered Tina back in the newsroom. "What an astonishing story. And we've just received footage from a Maleny resident of the main perpetrator, Ben Flinders, being taken into custody. A warning for viewers: the language used in this footage may upset some people. Children are advised to switch off now."

The video footage was initially blurry, but I recognized the back of the Hairy Lemon Pub where I'd collected the five steel bins from. As the video became clearer, Ben Flinders could be seen getting up off the ground wearing his protective suit, presumably after Big Man had clobbered him. A number of police were approaching him from multiple directions, guns held high. It was obvious he was caught, but Ben Flinders, being Ben Flinders, tried to turn the tables. "Thank god you're here!" he exclaimed to the police. "The village association meeting was overrun by classless louts in a most illegal way. If you follow me, I'll show you who needs to be arrested and who needs to be deported."

"Put your hands in the air now!" instructed a policeman with the help of a megaphone.

"I get it. You need to dot your i's and cross your t's," said Flinders as put his hands in the air. "Once we're done with this hygiene exercise, we can focus on enforcing the law, eh?"

A young policewoman ran over to Ben Flinders and grabbed one of his hands which she thrust into handcuffs, followed by the other. She then read him his rights. The camera footage focused in on Ben Flinders's face which was fighting to remain relaxed. A slight eye twitch revealed his façade was slipping. "You stupid bastards!" he exclaimed. "Don't you know who I am?"

"We know exactly who you are, Mr. Flinders," responded the policewoman. "You're under arrest for corruption, bribery, abuse of a public position, and no doubt a whole lot of other lowlife acts by the end of this investigation."

"This is tall fucking poppy syndrome at work!" shouted Flinders who was suddenly aware he was being filmed and so turned to address the camera. "Let's all take down the one and only person in Maleny who gets shit done, eh? The one and only legend responsible for the smiles that have made Maleny Australia's most welcoming town for so long. Hear me, brothers and sisters, those smiles don't come for free. I'm the only one who was brave enough to pay the full price of admission. And another thing—"

The person filming the footage could be heard saying, "We've heard enough of your bullshit, Ben *bloody* Flinders," before the video footage ended.

"That's it for now, folks," said Tina, back in the newsroom. "We'll keep you informed as this event unfolds."

A Familiar Face

Over the next few days, I didn't show up at work and I didn't text Raymond to let him know why. I didn't contact anyone for that matter. Jude and Wolf popped around a few times, no doubt to check up on me. Miranda called and texted many times for the same reason. I couldn't face anyone, so I didn't respond. I didn't even attempt to move from the sofa.

Then one morning, I heard a knock at the door accompanied by a familiar deep voice which sounded foreign on my doorstep. I opened the door, and there was Emmanuel standing there. He stepped forward with a warm smile and a suitcase in his hand. "Surprise!" he exclaimed.

"Emmanuel! What are you doing here?" I asked.

"After an eternity of lying still in that damned hospital bed, the doctors gave me the all clear," he stated. "I realized it's time I started searching for answers above the water's surface."

"Come on in," I said, before I led Emmanuel to the spare room where he deposited his suitcase.

"What's wrong, son?" Emmanuel asked once I'd served him a cup of tea on the sofa.

"Mia died a few days ago," I explained as some uninvited tears ran down my face. The words hung in the air, but the air didn't seem comfortable with them.

"Oh no!" he responded. "What happened?"

"Cancer," I said.

"I'm so sorry to hear it," he stated. "You must be in pieces."

"I feel like a gigantic hand has ground me into miniscule granules and spread me on top of bottomless quicksand," I explained. "I've never known pain like it before."

"Grief can be excruciating," Emmanuel said as he put his hand on my shoulder in a way he'd never done when I was younger. "I wish I could carry this weight for you."

"I appreciate that. How are you doing?" I asked.

"I'm alive," he replied. "That's more than I thought I'd be a couple of weeks ago. I've decided being alive is now my defining feature."

"I'm glad to hear it," I responded.

"But the real reason I've travelled all this way is to apologize to you," Emmanuel continued.

"For what?" I asked.

"For not being there for you all those times I should have been when you were growing up. For running off to Loch Ness without a thought for you when I believed my life was ending. You know, minor things like that. I got everything wrong, didn't I?" he replied.

"Join the club," I said. "I'm the guy who travelled all the way around the world to escape from my life because a woman I had nothing in common with did me a favor by breaking up with me."

"I'd say we're blood relations after all," Emmanuel replied with a grin.

"Yes," I added with a chuckle. "We've both been expert escape artists when it comes to the land of the living."

"At the very moment Terrence the Toll Collector appeared in each of our lives, we turned into Eddie the Escape Artists," Emmanuel replied.

The stuffed frogs were again rearing their heads. Who knows why, but this time it was a comfort. "Tell me about Eddie," I said.

"Every year, Eddie the Escape Artist was one of my worst sellers—no one wanted the poor fellow," Emmanuel explained. "Yet, for some unknown reason, I kept creating new improved versions of him—every goddamn year. Those hundreds of Eddie the Escape Artists all got stockpiled out the back of the shop in cardboard boxes of shame. I never knew why I had such an obsession with the little guy until now. I'm Eddie. You're Eddie."

"I *was* Eddie," I added. "But when Mia died, I was forced to stop escaping because everything caught up with me in that moment. I've officially surrendered to all the stuffed frogs I was fighting against."

"I hear you, son," Emmanuel responded. "Maybe that's also why I'm here with you rather than sitting beside Loch Ness. We can't let our demons weigh us down forever, can we?"

"That we can't," I agreed.

"I reckon we're two of the lucky ones who've stopped trying to shake off all the troublesome stuffed frogs riding on our backs," Emmanuel continued. "Only when you stop fighting them will those green freeloaders willingly disembark and walk off in their own directions."

"What a perfect description of what I've been through," I added.

"Has there been one stuffed frog in particular you've had to face up to?" Emmanuel asked.

"There have been a few, but Austin the Aussie has been particularly challenging," I replied. "That frog had a vendetta against me since the moment I landed here. He's been doing his best to eradicate me from Australia on a daily basis."

"I can just picture him as you speak," Emmanuel stated.

"I finally know who Austin is. You know, behind the stuffed frog façade. It's the same answer as for Terrence the Toll Collector, and all the other imagined stuffed frogs who've been so intent on making my life harder," I continued.

"Go on," Emmanuel said.

"They're every self-doubt about myself I've ever had," I explained. "This place has a way of teasing people which can seem mean and derogatory. However, Austin the Aussie, Terrence the Toll Collector, and all the others were just the challenges I needed to overcome to become at peace with myself—to stop doubting Will Watson. Despite their ugly green faces, they were gifts."

Emmanuel wiped some tears from his face as he gave me a fatherly hug in a way I'd always imagined fathers hugged. "I can see you passed those bastards' tests with flying colors."

Emmanuel stayed with me for another ten days. It was the best time we'd ever spent together. We asked each other questions and we both listened to the answers. I even learnt why Emmanuel had adopted me as a teenager—the real reason.

“So what inspired you to become a foster father all those years ago?” I asked as we sat together on the veranda’s top step one evening.

“Well, I’d always wanted to be a father,” he replied. “The truth is, I was a father for a brief moment when I was a younger man.”

“What happened?” I asked.

“My wife Marjorie gave birth to a beautiful baby boy called Max,” he explained. “Unfortunately, giving birth killed Marjorie, and Max only survived for a few short minutes. I lost them both that day.”

“Oh my god. Why didn’t you tell me this before now?” I asked.

“As you’ve learnt, I’ve been living as Eddie the Escape Artist. Not talking about it was my way escaping from the pain,” he replied. “I’ve been a real genius at work throughout my life.”

“I’m glad you finally told me,” I said. “And I’m belatedly sorry for your loss.”

“While we’re talking like this, do you know something else?” Emmanuel continued. “I think I’ve subconsciously blamed you in Max’s stead for his mother’s death. It’s like I’ve been viewing you as a surrogate for the world of unresolved emotions losing my wife and son deposited on my doorstep. I know that makes no sense, but I’m sorry for it all the same.”

"I get it, and I forgive you," I said. "To be honest, I think I've been doing the same with you. Without my parents around to help guide me through the emotional rollercoaster their early deaths led to, I've been directing some of my anger and frustration at you. I'm sorry too."

"All is forgiven. I like this new expressive version of you," Emmanuel stated.

"With losing Mia I've been forced to accept that life is incredibly short," I said. "So anything less than authentic is a waste of time."

"This place has been good for you, Will," Emmanuel replied. "You've lost yourself and found yourself here."

"It's certainly forced me to grow up, I'll give it that. So what's next for you?" I asked.

"I'm going to return to my true passion which I should never have thrown away so flippantly," he stated.

"The stuffed frogs?" I asked.

"The stuffed frogs," he replied. "I've agreed to buy back my old shop from the fellow who bought it for the same price he paid for it. He was grateful for my offer once he realized most of the shop's inventory were Eddie the Escape Artists."

"So why do you want to return to the stuffed frogs?" I asked.

"Because working in that shop was the only time in my life which has made any sense to me," he stated. "It's where I'm meant to be."

"I know what you mean," I stated. "More than I'd have guessed before I moved here."

"And guess what my next creation will be called," Emmanuel said.

"Tell me," I said.

"Mia the Magical," he stated. "She'll be my wisest, most beautiful creation yet."

"She'll like that," I replied.

After those ten days together, it was time for both Emmanuel and me to get on with whatever was coming next. I ordered a taxi to drive Emmanuel to the airport for his return flight.

"Take care, son," he said as he gave me a hug, the new normal thing for him to do.

"You, too. Please remember I'm just a phone call away," I said as I walked him to the awaiting taxi.

The taxi driver looked remarkably similar to the one who picked me up when I arrived at Brisbane Airport. I stepped closer to double-check. It was indeed the same fellow.

"Hello," I said to him. "Remember me?"

"Sure do," he replied. "You're the British fellow who shat on poor old Brissie from a great height when I picked you up from the airport a few months ago."

"I was joking, but I'm sorry for my poor timing. I've learnt a lot since then," I explained.

"Nah, mate. No need to apologize," he responded. "I'm also joking and with just as poor timing as you had. I'll never forget you because your attempt at a light-hearted joke highlighted to me that I'd become one of those asshole taxi drivers who talk up where they're living to mask the fact they really want to leave. You helped me realize that, and I moved to the Sunshine Coast Hinterland a few weeks later. Would you believe these days I don't feel inclined to tell everyone I meet that my home is the best place in the world?"

"Really?" I asked.

"Because I'm happy here, mate, *finally*," he said as he held out his hand and shook mine.

The taxi driver then reversed back down my driveway and drove away with my loving foster father who was waving at me from the backseat.

From Beyond

Over the next week, I continued to wallow. I knew I had a life to live, but it just didn't seem to be worth all the fuss. Then, one morning I heard three artistic knocks at the door that could only be one person. "Hi, Miranda," I said when I opened the door.

"You're alive, then?" she responded as she marched in.

"Give or take," I stated. "Can I get you a coffee?"

"Yes, please," Miranda said as she walked through to the living room.

I returned with the coffees to find Miranda whispering to herself in the living room.

"So showering hasn't been a focus of late?" she asked as she held her nose.

"Not much has, to be honest," I replied.

"That's normal, Will," Miranda responded. "It's lucky I'm here."

"Why's that?" I asked.

"Mia's settled into her new life," Miranda stated. "She's popped over to check on how you're doing."

"She's here now?" I asked.

"She is," Miranda responded.

I took a large swig of coffee and a deep breath.

"You can communicate with her?" I asked.

"Yes," Miranda responded.

"How is she?" I asked.

"She says it's like constantly rolling on the soft sand where she is, although she misses being with you in person," Miranda explained.

"Tell her I miss her too," I said.

"She says she can smell that," Miranda stated.

I laughed. "I'm in pieces, Mutt Dog."

"Mia says she needs you to get on with your life," Miranda explained. "She says she experiences joy when she sees you happy. And that's all she wants—to see you happy."

"I'll do my best, but it's easier said than done," I responded.

"She says you can do it, Will, because you're not only the world's best doggie owner, you're also a great man," said Miranda.

"Thanks, Mutt Dog," I replied as I wiped a rogue tear from my face. "It's just I always believed you were all that was great about me."

Miranda fell silent for a moment as she listened. "Mia says the two of you brought out greatness in one another because you loved each other so much. But she says the home you've been searching for was always inside your beautiful soul. She knows this because a part of her is residing there. She wants you to promise you'll start loving yourself as much as she does."

I nodded as I wiped more tears from my face. "I promise, Mutt Dog. I'm sorry for taking you on this wild goose chase. We travelled all the way around the world to find something which was inside me all the time. Thank you for guiding me home."

"She's got to pop back over to the other side now," Miranda explained. "She says she loves you."

"I love you too, Mutt Dog," I said.

Miranda and I were silent for a few minutes.

"So how are you?" I eventually asked.

"I'm moving to Maleny," Miranda stated.

"Wonderful," I responded. "Are you after a tree-change?"

"Just change," explained Miranda. "I decided to take Mia's advice about getting my own dog, and I saw a puppy advertised up here. When I arrived at the lady's house, I got chatting with her. She explained she used to work as a receptionist at the vet's surgery, and had recently resigned from her job. So I left her house with a black Labrador puppy in hand and an idea in mind."

"Well done, you got a puppy! So what was your idea?" I asked.

"Well, these past few months have taught me that dog owners can learn so much from their living dogs. So I put forward a proposal to Michelle the vet. I suggested I take on the receptionist's job while also developing a side business for her based on helping owners communicate with and train their living dogs."

"That's a fantastic idea," I said.

"Thanks," she replied. "Besides, I like some of the living humans in this part of the world. They're almost, but not quite, as nice as the dead dogs I hang out with."

I laughed. "So where will you live?"

"Well, it turns out Michelle and I get on like a house on fire," Miranda explained. "She's single like me, loves dogs like me, and is a bit mad like me. She's invited Lottie, my black Labrador puppy, and me to become her tenants in the granny flat behind her house."

"You've certainly fallen on your feet," I said.

"All because I responded to an email from the mysterious Will Watson," she stated.

"I'm glad you're glad you met that guy," I replied.

Home

Mia was right. I'd allowed her to be my one and only cheerleader for far too long. The best way for me to reunite with her forever was to join her on team Will Watson—at home on the inside. The moment I did, things started changing fast.

Upon returning to work, it was soon apparent a lot had changed during my absence. Raymond grinned when he noticed me standing in the morning training circle with the rest of the trash dashers. He threw his notepad onto the ground with even more force than usual.

"Morning, team," he said. "Today, I'm going to update you on Holy Crap Rubbish Removal's business plan."

"We already know that one, boss," replied a bored Beefy. "We collect the rubbish, we get paid, and the big boss earns the big bucks. Yada yada yada."

"No, Beefy, that was the past," Raymond stated as he drew a large circle. "From now on, everything we collect will be dropped off at Wolfhound Recycling in Maleny. You'll also receive a bonus for each additional recyclable item you pick up en route to the drop-off point."

Beefy muttered something under his breath.

"What's that, Beefy?" asked Raymond.

"Recycling is for pansies," said Beefy. "Why would we waste our time with this crap?"

"You see, Beefy, we're all a part of a circle. From now on, you're either inside that circle, or outside of it," Raymond said as he drew a few stick figures outside the circle and then crossed them out as though they were terrible mistakes.

Beefy shifted on his feet before he fell silent.

"That's what I thought," Raymond stated. "Oh, and one more thing. We've got a new head of sustainability I'd like to introduce you to."

A couple of the trash dashers rolled their eyes skyward at the idea.

"His name is Will Watson, and he's officially a full-time employee now he has a skilled migrant visa the company applied for on his behalf," Raymond continued as he put a hand on my shoulder. "He'll be working closely with Dũng to build our company and this wonderful region into a beacon for the future."

From that moment onward, my life flourished. Dũng and I did exactly what Dũng and I believed we could. We transformed the business into a sustainability leader which collects and recycles enormous quantities of rubbish. We now save more trees each year than I could have dreamt of when I arrived in Australia. Dũng is still known as the King of Trash, and these days I'm known as the King of Recycled Treasure. We even developed the in-house expertise to clean up the polluted waters of Lake Baroon, which has since become a major attraction for tourists who are fascinated by its sordid history. It's already the most photographed body of water in the Southern Hemisphere. I heard the other day that a group of locals have started watching the lake's surface at regular intervals as they believe there's something lurking beneath its impossibly dark waters apart from an abandoned uranium mine. The Whisperer told me this always happens when humans are presented with darkness they don't understand.

Wolf's recycling operation is now the largest employer in Maleny. It's known all around the country as a purveyor of unique functional art that's way ahead of its time. The other day, I popped in to see what Wolf was working on with Mad Jack and their cast of thousands. When I saw their latest piece of work, I initially thought it was a windmill from the future, but upon closer inspection I saw it was a rusty, one-armed robot on a bad hair day. "That's a serious piece of art!" I exclaimed.

"I'm happy with the way it works holistically, artistically, and functionally," explained Wolf. "All our creations need to tick all three of those boxes, you see."

"What do you call it?" I asked.

"It's working title is 'No need for a taxi,'" explained Wolf with a smile.

"Brilliant. Where's Jude?" I asked.

"She's gone shopping with the money we've been earning fair and square," Wolf explained. "And do you know the funny thing?"

"What's that?" I asked.

"The moment Wolfhound Recycling was born, my voice came back," Wolf stated. "And not just any words, but words which actually mean something."

"So are you guys going to stick around?" I asked. "Jude mentioned you were thinking of moving to New Zealand."

"You couldn't pay me to leave this life behind," Wolf replied. "The truth is we only wanted to move away to escape from what we didn't like about ourselves. But why would I want to escape this?"

"I can't think of a single reason, the pot said to the kettle," I said.

"Nah, it's just Wolf," he replied as high-fived the one-armed robot. Its arm dropped from above its head to its side where it flopped limply. "I'll fix that later."

It wasn't just Wolf who changed. Billy Baxter has become known as the Musical Cyclist and can often be found taking people on musical bicycle tours through the local bushland. He sometimes works in partnership with the Whisperer who takes visitors on wildlife tours all around the region, including to Mia's grave. The local wildlife who congregated around Mia when she was alive still regularly gather around her grave with the same enthusiasm as when she was alive. And Monty the python has taken possession of Mia's dog basket in the living room. It no doubt reminds him of his friend.

All these characters have become friends, genuine friends. Then there's my romantic life, which once again has a pulse. A few months after she moved here, Miranda Minsky and I started seeing each other. At first, I was cautious since the main connection between us was based upon our shared experience of Mia, while I was also dependent on Miranda to be able to communicate with Mia on the other side. However, after holding back for those reasons for a few months, it was obvious we just really enjoyed each other's company as fellow living humans.

"You know, Lottie approves of you as my partner," Miranda said to me the other day. "That's more important than my parents' approval for me."

"Mia also approves of you as my partner," I replied.

"How do you know?" asked Miranda.

"I just know," I answered. "*Finally*, I know everything's right in my world."

"Welcome home," Miranda replied.

"What a golden home it is," I said as I held Miranda's hand in mine.

Author's note

It won't have escaped your notice that the beating heart of the *Golden* story is Mia's voice. I've felt her energy inside me ever since I lost my real, adored golden retriever Mia a few years ago, so it was a joy to find an outlet for her voice in writing this book. Mia was my best friend and always with me. Losing her was unbearable. At the time, it was hard to imagine anything positive could come from her passing, but I've since learnt that the special people and animals in our lives leave us with so much when they pass. It's up to us to see the gifts they leave us for what they are.

There was also another inspiration for writing Golden which is at greater risk of being misinterpreted: my relationship with Australia.

By way of background, I grew up in Australia with English family, then I spent most of my adult life living in the UK and travelling Europe and the US extensively for work. As is the case with many long-term travellers, I found myself during my two decades of globetrotting. But I also lost my sense of national identity, confirming the often quoted theory that once you leave where you grew up, you never feel like you totally belong there again. So I became a global citizen who was at home everywhere, but of course not really at home anywhere.

Before leaving Australia as a bright-eyed youngster, I believed nationality meant something, even though I viewed myself as equally Australian and British. I loved my childhood experiences growing up in Australia, but I also felt a strong connection to the UK as it was where my family and ancestors came from. Even at a young age, I was also attracted by the UK's deep, sturdy sense of history and self-identity which contrasted with Australia's more ephemeral, shape-shifting self-identity. From my perspective, there was a lack of post-colonization Australian history to be proud of, and too few role models to look up to. In the absence of real inspirational stories that could be weaved into a national identity, fictional films like *Crocodile Dundee* and *The Man from Snowy River*, and songs like "Down Under," filled those glaring gaps. They were so well marketed that they arguably formed the basis of the world's stereotypical image of Australia: an exotic country full of laid-back heroes who couldn't be upset or tamed. But everyone seemed to forget that they were fictional tales.

From my faraway life in the Northern Hemisphere, I was curious how Australia had changed in all the years I'd been away. I also wondered whether I was remembering Australia with rose-colored glasses, which tends to be the way memory works. I'd encountered so many people around the world who were enamored by the stories Australia sold the world of its laid-back charms and natural riches. Even my own picture of the country was starting to be influenced by the same TV and film-driven myth-weaving that I'd recognized as misleading when I was a youngster. But from where I was sitting in Scotland's dark, inhospitable climate, part of me wanted to believe in that fictional version of Australia for the simple reason it was such a beautiful picture full of hope, sunshine, and an abundance of everything.

For those reasons and others, my wife Jess and I made the decision to return to Australia a few years ago. When we arrived with our daughter Rosie, our dog Mia, and our two cats Oscar and Heidi, I was a very different person to the boy who'd left. I'd grown more confident and I'd found my voice through all those years of exploring the world. I'll never forget the first couple of years of settling back down to life in Australia. My accent was decidedly global and un-Australian, so I was treated as a foreigner. That was challenging, but the silver lining was it allowed me to get to know the country again with the benefit of the broader perspective only outsiders are gifted.

What I experienced surprised me in both good and bad ways.

On a positive note, I'd forgotten how stunning the country's beaches, bushland, wildlife, wide open spaces, and climate are. It's hard to describe the feeling of waking up on a warm sunny morning to the contagious laughter of a kookaburra with the earthy smell of nature filling the air. After living in a cold, dark climate for so many years, I loved it.

On a more negative note, I encountered racism, close-mindedness, and an endemic lack of empathy for others that was challenging to accept. There seemed to be a lot of entitled characters like Ben Flinders who enjoyed making life hard for others, despite enjoying privileged lives themselves. This reality couldn't have been more at odds with the image of itself Australia sold to the rest of world, or the national self-identity that still seemed to resonate with so many locals. It certainly confirmed that I'd been wearing rose-colored glasses during my time overseas.

Readers may notice similar themes throughout *Golden*. The story was always intended to be born out of truth. The truth is I wrote the book as I faced up to my own Aussie-accented demons who were equally impassioned and skilled as Austin the Aussie at making life difficult for others. However, as the Golden story jumped onto the page I noticed my focus shifting. Despite their best efforts to hold my attention, I began to ignore my green-skinned tormentors in favor of rooting for all the great people, the quiet achievers, who weren't as in-your-face as the challenging characters like Ben Flinders, but who had hearts of gold—characters like Jude, Wolf, Miranda Minsky, the Platypus Whisperer, Mad Jack, and Billy Baxter. I also found myself noticing these beautiful souls more in the real world, which inspired me to empower those quieter, more community-minded characters to stand up and be counted in the novel. It was a wonderful case of reality inspiring fiction, which in turn allowed reality to be more like the life-affirming aspects of the fiction it had inspired.

Writing the novel reminded me that loving and hate-filled people coexist in all countries and communities, but it's the positive ones who are really in the driver's seat everywhere because they're the ones who care enough to take action when it's needed. The inspiring characters in Golden also reminded me that if you open your eyes to all the good in the world and let it into your life, the bad stuff loses its power over you. I certainly appreciate my wonderful home in Australia more as a result. And I no longer care about my perceived nationality or lack thereof. Being a kind-hearted person who's at peace with themselves trumps being Australian, or British, or whatever descriptive term the masses identify with.

I hope the novel similarly helps readers who are struggling to find their place in this world. Remember: the grass is always greener on the other side and you'll be exactly the same.

SS Turner

Acknowledgments

Thank you to our Golden Retriever Mia for being the best dog ever and my best friend. Mia passed away three years ago after she was diagnosed with cancer a few months prior. I've never experienced such a heartbreaking experience as witnessing her demise. However, Mia gave us so much love and left us with so many life-changing memories that I'll always be thankful for our precious time together. I'm hopeful part of her will live on within the pages of *Golden*.

Thank you to my wife Jess for your love and support despite how emotional it was for you to reconnect with Mia in the pages of *Golden*—particularly when you read the chapter "Truth or Truth." I know Mia misses you too.

Thank you to my daughter Rosie for your constant joy, and to my son Freddy for your never-ending smiles and laughter. Being a parent offers writers so many opportunities to learn and my two children are particularly active teachers.

Thank you to my publisher Lou Aronica and The Story Plant team for publishing my novels and believing in life-affirming fiction. Lou, your intensive editorial feedback on *Golden* was a game-changer and much appreciated. I look forward to watching The Story Plant thrive in its bigger and better form.

Thank you to all the lovely readers of *The Connection Game* and *Secrets of a River Swimmer* who have been so interested in and supportive of *Golden*'s launch. I'm blessed with unusually positive readers who'd rather read an uplifting novel than wallow in all that's wrong with the world. If only everyone were like you.

Thank you to Gregory Berns for your kind endorsement quote after reading the novel. Gregory's moving book *How Dogs Love Us: A Neuroscientist and His Adopted Dog Decode the Canine Brain* has become a staple source of information for readers who want to understand their dogs' cognitive abilities and emotions.

Thank you to Neil Abramson for your kind endorsement quote after reading the novel. Neil's novels *Unsaid* and *Just Life* feel like kindred spirits to *Golden* and are well worth reading if you enjoy cracking stories centred around the gifts animals bring to our lives.

Thank you to Neil Andison, the real life Platypus Whisperer who loosely inspired the fictional character by the same name in the novel, for your positive response to the book. Neil runs wonderful platypus tours (https://www.platypuswhispers.com.au) in beautiful Maleny, Queensland, and can tell the most inspiring stories about the elusive but fascinating platypus.

And thank you to all the dogs in the world for loving us humans in ways we don't deserve and often can't reciprocate. Some of us understand that you make our lives better in a million ways.

About the Author

S.S. Turner (Simon) writes surprising, irreverent, funny books about inspiration, transformation, and thriving in the modern world despite the very modern challenges faced by his characters. His characters are unique and memorable, and many of them are underdogs. They're not offended when readers refer to them as quirky, particularly Benny Basilworth in The Connection Game who considers it a great compliment. Of all his characters, Simon is most like Freddy in his first novel Secrets of a River Swimmer who walked away from a career in fund management because it didn't align with his values. Simon and Freddy also share the same love of dad jokes and laughing in unfortunate situations.

After living in London and Edinburgh for many years, these days Simon lives near the Sunshine Coast in Australia with his wife Jess, daughter Rosie, son Freddy, one playful dog, two bossy cats, and ten fluffy chickens. When he's not writing at a local café, he can often be found acting well below his age with the help of his children and his adolescent Golden Retriever Lottie. His other passions include reading, music, wildlife, the natural world, films, travel, and silliness.